TEMPTED BY FATE

A BAD THINGS NOVEL

New York Times and *USA Today* Bestselling Author

CYNTHIA EDEN

PROLOGUE
(FOR LUKE AND LEO)

The Way It All Began…Maybe…

Once upon a time, twin boys were born. One was predicted to be a bearer of light, the destined ruler who would protect all humans. He would fly through the skies and guard from above. He would be on the side of good. The righteous.

The other twin…his fate was to be much darker. No goodness was seen in his future. Witches feared him on first sight. Seers turned away, shuddering at the visions they saw.

Because he was born for darkness. Every creature that hid in the night would bow to him. He would rule them. The world would fear him.

He would do very, very bad things.

Time passed. The boys grew up. They lost their humanity and became something far, far more.

One was good…wings spread from his back. Angels bowed to him.

And his brother…

He had a really fucking good time as he did his very, very bad things.

CHAPTER ONE

The music was bad. The drinks were cheap. And none of the humans in the rundown bar had any clue that they were being served by one of the most powerful paranormal beings in the world.

Mora tucked a strand of her dark hair behind her ear as she let her gaze drift around Resurrection. The bar might not look like much, but the place was hers. All freaking *hers*. When she'd first arrived in town, she'd been a waitress at the bar. She'd bided her time, she'd taken over slowly, and now she owned the place—every creaking board there—and the people who frequented Resurrection…well, she even thought of the humans as hers, too.

Mora pushed a shot of whiskey across the bar toward the rather dangerous-looking biker who sat with his shoulders hunched. He wore a battered leather jacket, but she could see the tattoos that peaked out from his sleeves. "This one's on the house." She patted his arm. A friendly little pat.

He looked up at her. She stared into his eyes a moment and she saw…too many things.

Let it go, Mora. Let it go. Keep your mouth shut. Keep—

"They're going to find out." Oh, dammit, she needed to stop talking. She needed to stop interfering. But some habits were just hard to break. Mora leaned over the bar, and she moved her hand so that it was pressed hard to his. To outsiders, it would look as if they were flirting. But as a rule, she didn't flirt. Especially not with humans. When she touched him this time, a dozen images spun through her head, and it took her a moment to speak. *It's worse than I thought.* "You're going to die, and it will be horrible. You'll suffer for a very, very long time."

The biker—he went by the name of Dax— drained the whiskey in one gulp. "Aren't you a ray of sunshine tonight, Mora? But, luckily, I don't have any clue what you're talking about…"

She kept her hand on his, and she kept leaning over the bar. She'd gone too far to stop now. "You're pretending to be something you're not. You won't get the man you're after."

She saw the faintest tightening near Dax's dark eyes.

"He'll get you."

A muscle jerked in his jaw. "Are you threatening me?" His voice was low and lethal.

"Lady, you have no clue who you're dealing with."

No, you have no clue.

"You think because you serve me a few drinks, and we share a few laughs that you can get into my business?" His voice was still only for her ears. "Think the hell again." Dax snatched his hand from hers. He shoved to his feet and tossed some cash down on the bar. "And screw the free drink. I always pay my own way."

He didn't get it. She was trying to help—

The door to Resurrection opened. It shouldn't have been anything special. The door opened and closed all the time, as doors did. That was their whole purpose.

But as soon as the door opened *this* particular time...

Mora felt *him*. The awareness started as a slow shiver, one that worked its way all over her body. Goosebumps rose on her arms. Her breath caught. Her heart raced faster. A flood of memories filled her mind, and she wanted to turn and run.

She'd spent centuries running.

"Mora?"

She blinked. Dax was still in front of her. Only now he didn't look angry. He looked worried.

"You okay?" He squinted as he studied her. "I swear, you've gone ghost white."

That was because a ghost from her past had found her. Her head turned — very, very slowly — and she found herself looking toward the door. *He* was there. Standing in the doorway, filling up all of the available space. And sending her night straight to hell.

Leo. He was a legend in the paranormal world. Little baby paranormals whispered about him. And big, adult paranormals? If they were smart, they steered clear of him.

He was the Lord of the Light. The ruler of the so-called "good" paranormals. He was the protector. The all-powerful being who could snap his fingers and make the earth shake.

He was also — as far as Mora was concerned — the biggest bastard on earth.

"Y-you should leave," Mora whispered to Dax. Actually, everyone in that place should leave. Because what was about to happen next in her bar? *Not pretty.*

Leo was staring straight at her. His eyes seemed to be drinking her in as the temperature in Resurrection spiked.

Leo was still handsome. Damn him. His hair was dark, his eyes deep and golden, and a faint growth of stubble covered the perfect square of his jaw. The man was tall. Muscled. Sexy.

She hated him.

He smiled at her.

"The bar is closed!" Mora's voice boomed out. That boom cut across the bad music and the voices and led to absolute shocked silence. Humans gaped at her.

"But—but it's barely midnight!" A woman in a red dress cried, her make-up perfectly in place. "The party just started!"

No, it had just ended. Because Mora's jerk of an ex was in town. She opened her mouth to speak...

"You heard the lady." Leo's voice didn't boom. It just...carried. Deep and rolling and sinking beneath her skin. "The place is closed, so get the hell out." He waved his hand across the room and a swell of power swept out to cover Resurrection.

Her eyes narrowed. *He* got to play with humans, but other paranormals were supposed to keep their hands off them? Not exactly fair.

"What's happening?" Dax asked her.

The others in the bar were grumbling, but they were leaving. Probably because Leo had put a compulsion in his words. Now the humans were helpless and had to do his bidding. Controlling a mortal was particularly easy for Leo when a human's inhibitions were already lowered, and drinking at Resurrection was a guaranteed way to lower inhibitions.

Everyone was following Leo's command. *Almost* everyone. Dax wasn't leaving.

Her head cocked and her gaze slid back to him. Wasn't that interesting? He was still standing in the exact same spot.

"You're afraid." Dax rolled back his shoulders. "Should I go kick the ass of the joker who just walked in?"

Her lips parted. "Ah, no, trust me, that's not a battle you want." *Or one that you can win.* "And you've already got more than enough trouble coming your way. You don't want to add my baggage to your list."

A furrow appeared between his brows.

"I meant my warning," she whispered to him. Because she couldn't change what was coming. Unfortunately. That power wasn't hers. People had to change. People had choices. There was only so much she could do in the grand scheme of things. "You need to watch your ass."

The furrow deepened. "But—"

A hand slapped down on Dax's shoulder. "I don't know you," Leo drawled. "But it's time for you to hit the road. *Now.*"

Dax glanced back at Leo. Back...and up. Because while Dax might slip past six foot, Leo was even bigger. His shoulders were broader. *He* was more powerful.

He was also the toughest bastard she'd ever met.

"You'd better not be a new lover," Leo said suddenly, and his face hardened even more than normal. "You'd—"

Mora sighed. "Leo, I know it's second nature to you, but seriously, try *not* to be an asshole for five whole minutes, okay?" Mora gave him a wonderfully fake smile and tried not to choke on her hate. Because hate was what she felt for him. Had to be. Nothing more. Nothing less. "Dax is a customer, and he's leaving."

Everyone else had already slipped out— because that was what Leo did. He cleared a room.

Leo dropped his hand.

And still, Dax hesitated.

"Get out," Leo snapped. He jerked his thumb toward the door. "Mora and I need to talk."

Dax glanced at Mora. "Are you okay with him?"

"Uh…" No, *okay* was the last thing she'd ever be with—

"I would *never* hurt her," Leo said, nearly growling the words and actually sounding as if he meant them.

Her back teeth ground together. He was such a liar. He'd hurt her more than any other man ever could. Why else had she avoided him all these centuries? Some guys just could not take a hint.

Leo was definitely one of those guys. No, he was probably the leader of those guys.

"It's fine, Dax. I can handle him." Now she was the liar. But at least her words got Dax to leave. She followed him to the door, skirting around the tables and chairs, and making sure to lock up once Dax was gone. She didn't want any unlucky humans stumbling in on the little catch-up scene that was about to play out.

Her fingers were trembling a bit as she turned the lock. She didn't look back to face Leo, not yet. She needed to regain her composure first.

"I've…missed you."

Her eyes squeezed shut. He had *not* just said that to her. He had not let his voice dip and go all tender as if the years hadn't passed in a horrible, terrible, *painful* blur. As if he hadn't taken her heart and ripped it right out of her chest.

He cleared his throat. "You're a hard woman to find."

"That's because I didn't *want* to be found." She opened her eyes and schooled her expression. Breathing slowly, Mora straightened her shoulders. Then she turned to confront him. "Well, you sure can still clear a room. Nice to see that winning personality of yours hasn't changed."

She expected anger in the face of her taunt, but…he didn't look angry. Didn't even look mildly annoyed. If it had been *anyone* else, Mora

would have sworn that he looked *happy* as he
stared at her. His gaze slid slowly from the top of
her head all the way down to the tips of her heels.

"Fate," he breathed, "you are even more
beautiful—"

"Mora." The name blasted from her. "That's
my name. Picked it out all by myself because I
liked the sound of it. Fate is just some dumb title
that I was saddled with a long time ago. If you're
going to talk to me, use my name, got it?" She
stalked forward. Her heels clicked on the wooden
floor. "And you'd better talk fast. I'm giving you
five minutes—just five—and then I want your ass
out of here."

He leaned back against the bar, crossed his
arms over his chest, and just stared at her.

Could he hear just how fast her heart was
beating? Could he smell her fear? His senses were
all super amped up, she knew it—he probably
had the best senses of any paranormal beast.
There was a reason he was at the top of the
paranormal badass ladder.

She kept her chin up, and she didn't let her
pace slow. So what if he smelled her fear? She
was more than just fear. "Shouldn't you be out
saving angels or something?" Mora muttered.
"Do you really need to be here, messing up my
life?"

"You hid from me."

Why, *why* did she still find his voice sexy? "Guilty." She gave him a smile. One that she knew would not reach her eyes. "Ever so very guilty. I hid and I would have stayed hidden, but you just burst up into my place. Without an invitation." She stopped about a foot away from him. Close enough to touch. Not that she planned to make that epically bad move. *No, thank you.* Mora tilted her head as she stared up at him. "How did you find me?" The clench in her gut told Mora the answer, and she *hated* this new betrayal. *I was not ready for him yet.*

There was only one person who knew where she was. Her cousin. A muse with unfortunate taste in men.

Like I'm one to judge.

"Sabrina sent me."

And there it was—another knife to her heart. Her cousin *had* sold her out.

"She made a deal," he added, his voice rumbling right over her. "She was desperate, and you were the only thing I wanted."

You were the only thing I wanted. If *only* those words were true.

No, no, she didn't care if he wanted her. Not now. But back in the past, it would have been nice if his feelings for her had actually been genuine.

"So Sabrina told me where I could find you," he continued, seeming to carefully choose his words, "and in exchange, I helped her."

"Yeah, I'm sure you helped her plenty. I know how the deals you and your brother work play out—you and Luke are the only ones who really seem to benefit."

He didn't deny her charge. Probably because she was dead-on right.

"Have you thought about me?" Leo asked her.

She blinked. "What?"

"Because you've been in my head. Every single damn day." He gave a grim laugh. "Though I have to say, the nights were the worst. The worst…" He paused. "And the best. Because the things that happened in my dreams—"

"Do *not* say another word." And suddenly, she was standing toe-to-toe with him. "How dare you?" Mora demanded. "*How fucking dare you* come back into my life this way? You're going to stand there and spout out some bull about dreams? *You* threw me away. You used me. You lied to me. You betrayed me." *You ripped out my heart. Stomped on it. Then stomped on it some more.*

"I'm not the same man."

Now she had to laugh. Bitterly. "No, I suspect you're even worse." Her gaze held his. "Lord of the Light." Her voice was mocking.

"Should I bow or something? You know, since I'm in the presence of such greatness."

His jaw was rock hard.

She spun from him. "Your five minutes is tick, ticking on down—"

He grabbed her wrist. "You don't bow to me. You don't bow to anyone. You're Fate. You hold the world..." Now he looked down at her hand—the one he'd trapped. "You hold the world in your hand."

His touch seemed to burn her. She hadn't wanted to touch him. When she touched him, Mora felt too much. Her breath was already panting out. The desire she felt for him—it surged inside of her. She *hated* him, but she still wanted him. That was the way it was between them. No sense, no reason at all, just a savage need.

The first time they'd met...it had been so very, very long ago. Savagery had ruled the land back then, and the wild desire she'd felt for Leo as they stood at the foot of a volcano? It hadn't seemed so strange. In fact, she'd thought it was rather perfect.

She'd been wrong. About many things.

But the desire hadn't died. After everything that had happened—every terrible thing—it was still there. Their skin touched, and her body primed. His touch charged her, and every inch of her body seemed to yearn.

"Let. Me. Go." Her words were ice cold even though she was burning red hot. She might want him—her body was betraying her that way—but she was more than just a body. She was a mind and a broken heart.

No, it's not broken. I'm over him. Have been for centuries.

His thumb smoothed along her inner wrist. "Your pulse is racing."

"Because you make me angry."

His thumb caressed her again. "Just anger?"

"*Lots* of anger." She licked her lips. Her whole mouth felt desert dry. "I figure you have about three minutes left. So tell me why you're here, why you made a deal with Sabrina." *You are totally paying for that one, cousin!* "And don't waste any more time talking about dreams." She snatched her wrist from him and took several reassuring steps away from Leo. "Because I don't want to hear about those."

His lips thinned. "Do you want me to say I'm sorry?"

Did she want—Her jaw dropped. *I don't want you to say that you're sorry. I want you to scream it. I want you to bleed sorry, I want—*

"Because I am," Leo rasped. "I lost you, and I fucking hate that. You know how humans have all those trite expressions they love so much? Like how you don't really know what you've got—"

"Until it's gone." The words slipped from her and she wanted to throw her hand over her own mouth.

He nodded. "I didn't know how much I wanted you until I couldn't find you." His hands fisted at his sides. "You cloaked yourself from me. I've searched this whole earth—again and again—and there was no trace of you. Not a scent, not a whisper. *Nothing.* It was as if you'd never been here at all." Now there was anger in his voice, slipping through the cracks of his control. And he'd always prized that precious control of his.

Do not weaken. "Yes, and right after the next two minutes are over, I'll be doing my cloaking routine again." She marched behind the bar. She needed a drink so she helped herself to a little bit of scotch and then slammed the empty glass onto the countertop. "Because, you know, I'm avoiding you for a reason."

"I need your help."

Mora rolled her eyes. Same old story. "Everyone wants Fate's help." She should have another drink. Or five.

"I'm not everyone."

Her hand was gripping the glass. She was afraid it might shatter soon. "No." She forced herself to stare at him. "You're just the man who sent me to hell."

His hands flattened on the bar. "No one was supposed to hurt you." His voice was hoarse. "I had claimed you, I had —"

Now she laughed. "You're the Lord of the Light. You can't claim someone from the dark."

"You aren't dark. You *aren't* evil."

She smiled at him. "I am now."

Surprise flashed on his face. Real shock. Nice to know she could still stun him. She waved her hand, and a little burst of electricity shot from her fingers — and right into his chest. She didn't hurt him — Mora had total control — but the power burst pushed him back a few feet. "Your time is up, Leo. So get your ass out of my bar."

But he…shook his head.

Her eyes narrowed so much that she was sure they had become slits.

"I need you," he said.

Those were *almost* the words she'd fantasized about so long ago. *I'm sorry. I need you. You are the only woman I could ever love* —

Nope. Not happening. She slammed the door shut on that long-forgotten fantasy. He wasn't really sorry. He could just lie very, very well. An unbecoming trait in someone who was supposed to be so good.

He's not nearly as good as he wants the world to believe. She knew that secret better than most.

"I don't need you." Her voice was flat and her spine was ramrod straight. "And I don't want you anywhere near me. So, for the last time, get out." She felt the hum of her power beneath her skin. "I won't tell you again." She'd just hit him with every bit of magic that she possessed.

"Mora—" But he broke off and his gaze jerked toward the front door. She saw his eyes widen. For an instant—one crazy instant—she could have sworn fear appeared in Leo's gaze. But that was absolute madness. He feared nothing.

No one.

She shook her head, disgusted. "We are done—"

"*Never.*" He flew toward her. His wings were out. Big, giant, scary wings. *A dragon's wings.* He grabbed her in his arms and held her tight even as she roared her fury at him. Even as—

Fire erupted. There was a deafening boom, and Resurrection shook all around her. Mora felt the rush of flames lance over her skin. Terror clawed at her.

But his arms wrapped around her. Leo bounded into the air, holding her tight as he flew straight toward the ceiling. She looked up, terrified, because flames were up there, too, rolling across the ceiling. The fire was unnatural. No way should it have spread so fast. No way should those flames be so big. No—

"I'll keep you safe."

Like she was supposed to believe his guttural promise. Mora ducked her head and held him even tighter as they flew right through those flames. She held him tight, and she braced herself to feel the fire on her flesh.

Unfortunately, it wouldn't be the first time she'd burned for him.

And I'm afraid it won't be the last.

CHAPTER TWO

"Let me go!"

She was angry. Probably closer to *enraged.*
But Leo still didn't want to let her go. He wanted
to keep right on holding her. She felt good
against his body. She *fit* him, and it had been far
too long since he'd been able to touch Fate.
Correction…*Mora.*

"My clothes are smoking. I think I'm on fire.
Let. Me. Go."

His arms opened.

She scrambled away from him, slapping at
her shirt and that super sexy short skirt that she
was wearing. Sure enough, she was smoking.

She is damn hot.

"You could help, you know, instead of just
gaping at me." She slapped her skirt again.

He rolled his shoulders, feeling the burns and
blisters on his back and his arms. He'd covered
her when they'd gotten out of that bar, but the
flames had certainly enjoyed attacking his flesh.
He'd heal, though. He generally always did. And
if Mora wanted him to help her…

Leo stalked toward her. He pressed his hands to her slightly smoking skirt. There was no fire on her, no burns, so he took his time pressing down and loving the way her hips felt beneath his touch.

"You are not helping." She glared at him from the most incredible pair of eyes that he'd ever seen. Bright blue, but with flecks of gold buried inside. The gold gleamed when her power was amped.

Or when she was aroused.

"You're *not* helping," Mora snapped again. "You're *groping*."

Guilty as charged.

She shoved at his arms. "Just, stop, okay, just—" Shock flashed across her beautiful face. *Still just as beautiful, all of these centuries later.* "You're hurt." Her fingers fluttered over his arms. Over the blisters and burns. "Oh, Leo." Her lower lip trembled. It was a full, sexy lower lip. Once upon a time, he'd loved to lick that lip. Loved to nip her. Loved to—

She spun him around and gasped when she saw his back. "Leo! You should have said something!" Her fingers fluttered lightly over his skin. "How long will it take you to heal?"

Leo glanced over his shoulder and, beneath the bright moonlight, he just had to drink her in. Her hair was shorter now than it had been so long ago. The heavy, jet black locks skimmed over her shoulders, framing her heart-shaped face. Her eyes were big and utterly spell binding. And her lips promised every sin imaginable.

He could imagine plenty.

She was petite, but curved in all the right places. He'd always enjoyed picking her up, holding her tight while she wrapped her silken legs around him, and then plunging so deep into—

Mora snapped her fingers in front of his eyes. "You're already healing, so I'm going to stop worrying about you."

"You...worried for me?" If she worried, then that meant she still cared. He could work with caring.

But Mora turned away. "I worry about everything and everyone. It's kind of my deal, you know." Her face was directed toward the blaze in the distance. He'd flown them fast and far, but it was still easy to see the burning remnants of Resurrection in the darkness. "Dammit, look what you did."

Now he stiffened. "*I* didn't start that fire." Did she seriously think he had? That he would have burned that place around her? "I heard someone shuffling around outside, I felt the stir of magic in the air—you know that wasn't a normal fire. Paranormal powers were at work." He edged closer to her. "I'm the one who saved you. I got you out of there, with only a bit of smoking clothing to show the danger you'd been in."

"Oh, thank you." Her voice was breathy. Damn, but he loved it when she got breathy. But her hands had clenched into fists. Not the best sign. "Whatever would I have done if you hadn't tracked me down, hunted me like prey, and found me here?" Now she spared him a withering glance. "Wait, I know. I would have continued with my life. Totally normal." Her right fist lifted and opened — and she pointed at him. "You think it's coincidence that you arrive and five minutes later, my bar gets torched? With *you* inside?"

He tried not to wince.

"That fire wasn't meant for me. No one around here knew who I was! That fire — *you* brought danger to me. You didn't save me. Your sorry ass is the one who put me in jeopardy!" Her breath heaved out. "So do me a favor? Stay away from me. Because like I said before, I don't want you close." Then she started marching away.

They were in the middle of nowhere. On an old, dirt road in Nevada. And she was just walking angrily at a fast clip. Leaving him to stand there and, well, leaving him to hate what was to come. Leo could feel the pull of his skin as his flesh healed. He'd always healed so fast. But Mora hadn't been so fortunate.

She didn't call herself Mora when I knew her before.

He braced his legs and stared after her. "Fate!"

She kept walking.

"Fate!"

She threw up her hand and flipped him the bird.

His eyes narrowed. In the next breath, he was in front of her, and she barreled right into him. His hands flew up and grabbed her shoulders.

"Don't do *that*!" She glared at him. "I hate that super-fast move thing you do. It sucks!" She tried to break from his hold.

Leo just tightened his hands. "I'm trying to be courteous. You aren't giving me many options."

If looks could kill, Leo figured he'd be a dead man right then.

"I am *so* sorry," she announced dramatically, her body stiff in his hold. "Here I am, disrupting *your* life and —"

"I'm not letting you go." Enough games. "I won't ever let you go again."

Her eyelids flickered. "Leo?"

"You hid from me for centuries. I tore this world apart looking for you." He shook his head. "But you weren't there. The whole planet went dark, and I nearly lost my sanity...*because you weren't there.*"

She paled. "I meant nothing to you, remember? Just insignificant little Fate."

"There is nothing insignificant about Fate." He knew that all too well. "You will not leave again. You will not vanish, not even if I have to chain you to my side."

Her slightly pointed chin shot into the air. "Don't even think it."

If she only knew…"Love, I've fantasized about it."

He saw the surprise on her face.

"But I am trying to give you a choice," he continued doggedly. "I want you with me willingly."

She laughed, and it was a mocking sound. Once, he'd heard her real laughter. It had sounded like music. Sweet bells. Now her laughter held the ring of bitterness. "Bull," Mora told him. "You don't give choices. You take them away. You order your light paranormals about and you try to control the world." She leaned closer to him, absolutely shocking Leo. "But I've got a newsflash for you. You don't control me. And neither does your brother. I'm not a pawn in your war."

She'd always been more than a pawn.

"You think you can use me." Her mouth was inches from him. "Use me up and then walk away again? It's not going to happen."

No, it wasn't. Because he didn't plan to walk away. Not this time. Never again. "The dark is closing in on me."

She blinked.

"I'm being hunted. The past is catching up to me. The end will come, and when it does, do you want to just stand there and watch as the world is destroyed around you?"

But she shook her head. "It's...it's not time yet."

Excitement burned inside of him. Mora had always known what the end would be. How could she not know? She was Fate. Only...

He knew that she kept secrets. He knew that she could change the fates of humans and paranormals. For the right price, she would alter lives.

"You need to look into the future again," he told her grimly. "You need to look into *my* future. Because that big battle? The one *you* told everyone would come?"

She shivered. "I told everyone...what I saw. You will fight your brother to the death. Light and Dark will battle, and only one will survive. Then the earth will fall to chaos."

"Right. Yes. Thanks for that bit of sunshine news." His fingers were still wrapped around her shoulders. "My time is up. Unless you help me, *everyone's* time is up."

"It can't be. Not yet." Then she bit her lower lip. Sweet, sweet hell. He wanted to be the one biting.

"You aren't sure about what's happening now. That means you need to scry to see for certain." Witches could scry to see the future. They stared into a dark mirror and saw glimpses of the past and the future. But when Fate looked into that stone...*she can see everything.* "Scry for me."

Her gaze cut away from him. "I want you to take your hands off me. I don't like it when...when you touch me."

Those words stabbed right in his heart. "You used to love my touch. You'd beg for it, remember?"

She didn't glance back at him, but her delicate jaw hardened. "That is *such* an asshole thing to say. Especially when you are trying to get me to do a huge favor for your jerk self. You know, all the other paranormals talk about you. They have a nickname for you. Want to hear it?"

"No."

"It's bastard. They call you bastard. Cold-hearted bastard. Ice-cold bastard. Bloody bastard or—"

"I get it," he gritted out from between clenched teeth. "But you don't need to be popular in order to have power in the paranormal world."

She finally looked at him again. "We both know you've never cared too much about making friends."

No, he hadn't. Friendships created weaknesses. Any emotional connection was a weakness. He couldn't afford to be weak.

"You're still touching me."

He was. "I want you to change my fate."

"Isn't that what everyone wants?"

His hold on her tightened. "I've seen you do it. I know you *can*. You've done it before, just with whispered words in a mortal's ear. A small change that leads to a different ending. Hell, according to a story I heard, you once stopped the complete decimation of a city in the Old West just by moving a damn wagon ten feet."

She frowned. "I remember…the horses were going to break free. They would have run wild through town and the blaze that erupted from the ensuing chaos would have taken too many lives."

He nodded. "That's what I'm talking about. You saw the fire coming. You changed what would be. You did it for those humans, and you can do it for me."

"You don't quite understand how it works."

"Then you can tell me. Everything."

"Because you aren't letting me go?" Her voice was soft and sad and if he'd possessed a soul, it would have made him ache.

Leo didn't waver. "Because I'm not letting you escape me again."

She swallowed. He saw the small, delicate movement of her throat. "Then I guess I don't have a choice." Her lashes swept over her eyes.

"No, there isn't a choice." His gaze fell to her mouth. That sweet, delectable mouth.

Her tongue slipped across her lower lip. A nervous gesture, but one that made every muscle in his body tighten. "Mora..." Leo decided that he liked the new name she was using.

No, he just liked her.

Her lashes lifted. The gold in her eyes was brighter. He knew exactly what that brightness meant. *Arousal.* She felt the same forbidden attraction that he did.

Fate wasn't supposed to take a side in the war between light and dark. But Fate...she'd always been swayed by him.

His mouth took hers. The kiss was deep and hungry because he'd been hungry for her—he'd been desperate for so very, very long. Her lips parted and his tongue thrust inside. Just like that—*just like that*—an avalanche of need hit him. Desire poured through his body. His cock jerked eagerly for her. His heart thundered in his chest and—

She kneed him in the groin.

Leo staggered back.

"Yeah, asshole, I have a choice — and it's not to be used by the jerk who left me with a broken heart centuries ago." She'd ripped herself out of his hands. And he realized — too late — that the gold in her eyes was deepening not because she wanted him, but because Mora had called up her power. Her hair whipped around her face as she raised her arms. He could see the spark of magic near her fingertips and —

Four winged men appeared from the night. One moment, Leo and Mora were alone on that old road. And in the next, the strangers were there. They grabbed Mora, holding her tight even as she screamed at them. Leo surged forward, ready to fight those bastards but when he swept out with his hands —

One of the men shot him. A hit straight in the heart. Normal bullets would have no effect on Leo. He'd been shot plenty of times by human weapons. But this gun…

He stared down at the blood gushing from his chest. A dull ringing filled his ears, and he tried to figure out just what in the hell was happening even as more bullets ripped into him.

"Fate can't help you now," one of the men snarled. "She's ours."

"Leo!" Mora screamed.

His head whipped up. The winged men were flying fast through the sky. Their wings were huge and white. They looked like…shit, they looked like they were freaking angels.

Impossible. I control the angels.

His knees gave way. Some of the bullets had passed through his body, but others were lodged in him. *One is in my damn heart.* And the bullets were draining him of power with every moment that passed.

"Leo!" Mora's cry was weaker now. She was farther away. *"Help me!"*

His fingertips became claws as he began to cut into his chest. He'd get those bullets out. And he'd get Mora back.

He hadn't been lying when he said that she wouldn't escape him again. He'd searched too long for Mora. And no one— *no one* — would take her from him again.

CHAPTER THREE

"I thought she would be more impressive." The guy to her right gave a grim nod as he studied her. "Are we really to believe that this woman is the all-powerful Fate?"

All-powerful was a huge stretch.

Mora had been chained up — *chained like a beast!* — in some low-rent, cobweb-filled basement. The men who'd taken her had flown hell-fast and even though she'd tried to fight them, her magic had yielded zero impact.

She tested the chains that held her. They were old and strong, and things were not looking good for her. "Am I supposed to believe…" Mora demanded as she gazed at her captors. "That angels kidnapped me?" Their wings looked like angel wings, that was true, but she wasn't buying this act. Angels would have no reason to abduct her.

The man to her right — tall, with red hair and green eyes — gave a quick laugh. It wasn't a reassuring sound. "We're hardly angelic." And with a snap of his fingers, the wings vanished.

There were three other men with him. One was a thin blond, one sported a dark tan and even darker eyes, and the third guy...oh, hell, he was currently transforming.

Into what?

"Aidan, go patrol the perimeter. Let's see if he comes after her."

Aidan was the one doing the shift. As she watched, his hands hit the floor. He tossed back his head and a moment later, bones were snapping and breaking. Fur exploded all along his skin. His face contorted—

"Oh, shit," Mora whispered. The guy had just transformed into a panther.

An angel one moment...a panther in the next breath?

She yanked on the chains. "What is going on here? Who are you? And why did you take me?"

The redhead laughed. "It's so funny. You make demands like you have power." He waved his hand and the other men filed out—even the panther left. *Off to patrol the perimeter?* And she was alone with the guy who was seriously creeping her out. He stalked toward her, and he put his hands on either side of her head.

"You're in my space," Mora snapped at him.

"And you are in my *way.*" The guy glared at her. "Fate. Fucking Fate. I thought you were long gone from this world until Leo high-tailed it across the country to find you."

The chains were made out of silver—pure silver. Had to be. That was why she couldn't muster up enough power to break free.

She had a wee bit of a silver allergy. And the jerks who'd taken her had known that. They'd barely gotten airborne before silver handcuffs had been slapped around her wrists. Then when they'd gotten to this hole-in-the-wall place, the cuffs had been replaced with chains. The guys had moved with the supernatural speed that she hated, and Mora hadn't been able to break free.

"I've got to know…" His fingers curled around her chin. "Are the stories true? Did the Lord of the Light really fuck Fate?"

Her stomach clenched. She didn't like the way the guy was looking at her. She didn't like the way he was touching her. And she didn't like the way he was talking to her. "No," she snarled right back. "Fate fucked him."

Her captor blinked.

"Who are you?" Mora asked him, her voice cold and flat. But there was something about him that nagged at her. An odd familiarity. *I've seen him before…* The problem was that when you lived for thousands of years, you tended to forget a few faces.

Her captor just laughed. "You're Fate. Shouldn't you know everything?"

She didn't answer him.

"Let me tell you what I know," he murmured. "I know that Leo will follow you. Hasn't he already followed you to the ends of the earth? And beyond?"

She'd certainly run to the ends of the earth to escape him.

"He'll come for you, and when he does…we'll have him. It's time for a change, you see. The status quo? Not working for me and those like me. We want the battle. We want the end. And we know it's going to be spectacular."

"I'm bait?" That news was hardly reassuring.

But her captor nodded. His eyes gleamed. *I've seen those soulless eyes before.* "What will happen when Leo learns that light paranormals killed you? His precious Fate? I mean, he saw with his own eyes that angels took you."

His touch was making her skin crawl. "You aren't an angel. We established that."

He finally let go of her chin. He put his index finger in front of his lips as if to silence her, and he said, "Shh. Let's keep that part secret for now." Then he stepped back. "Leo has to break, you see. He has to lose every anchor he has. We've waited, we've stayed to the shadows, but a price must be paid. You're that price."

This was not her night. *What will happen when Leo learns that light paranormals killed you?* "I hate to break it to you," Mora snapped, "but I'm not exactly easy to kill." Technically, though, she was. It was the *staying* dead part that was a sticking point for her. "So if you think you're just going to stab me or shoot me, think again." *Been there, done that.*

His eyelids flickered. "I have a few tricks to try…And you know the old saying, if at first you don't succeed…try, try again."

Oh, hell.

"And I will be sure to try all night—"

The ceiling exploded. No other word for it. Chunks of ceiling and plaster rained down on Mora and the redheaded jerk. When the dust cleared, she saw that Leo was there. Leo with his dark, menacing wings spread so wide behind him. His head was up and his eyes were locked on the redhead who'd abducted Mora. The mysterious ring leader.

"You're dead," Leo said simply. Then he launched across the room. He grabbed the redhead and threw him—threw him so hard that the guy flew right through the wall. Then Leo turned to go after the jerk…and probably pound him some more.

"Wait!" Mora cried out. "Get me out of the chains first!"

Leo swung toward her. His eyes—they were different. They were…red. Glowing with fury. *Not normal.* Not a Leo kind of thing.

For a moment, she forgot to breathe. "Leo?"

He stalked closer to her. "Did they hurt you?"

"Uh, no. And if you get me out of the chains, they won't. You can use those awesome wings of yours and fly us both far away from this place."

He grabbed at the chain that bound her right wrist and with one yank, he pulled that chain right from the wall.

Footsteps thundered on the stairs. Mora's head turned. The guys who'd abducted her were rushing down those stairs. Yes, it would have been hard to ignore the crash of Leo's arrival so their frantic return was only expected. "We need to work on your stealth," she whispered.

He took her left wrist and yanked that chain from the wall, too.

Silver still encircled her, but at least she could run now. "They aren't angels, Leo," she said, her words tumbling out fast. "They want you to think they are but—"

Gunfire exploded. The men who'd burst down the stairs were firing at them. Mora screamed, expecting to feel the bullets rip into her flesh but...

Leo.

His arms were around her. His wings were protecting her. He was shielding her.

"I've got you." His voice seemed to vibrate around her. Her head tilted back and she stared into his eyes. Still that scary red—and she missed the burnished gold of his gaze. She'd loved that unforgettable gold.

His body jerked against her, and she knew the bullets were sinking into his flesh. "Let's get out of here," Mora said. "Now."

But he shook his head. "They…pay."

"Okay, let them pay *later*. There are at least four of them…and one's a panther." She could hear his growl. "I do *not* want to tangle with a shifter." Her hands slid over his chest and…

Blood.

A lot of blood.

"Leo?"

He staggered. "Not…ordinary…bullets…"

His knees buckled, and he fell on top of her, sending them both crashing to the floor. The panther's growls got louder and the thud of footsteps closed in.

"How many bullets hit him?" That was the redhead's voice.

"At least a damn dozen." The response was a hard growl.

Mora tried to shove Leo off her. He didn't move, but he did groan.

"We have got to get out of here," Mora whispered. "So push past the pain, lock those arms around me, and fly."

"Did any of the bullets hit her?" Again, it was the redhead. The ring leader.

"Can't tell." A grunt came from another man. "He's covering her."

"That's because he cares too much about fucking Fate." Footsteps came closer and then—

"Fly, dammit," Mora ordered Leo as her hands clenched around his shoulders. "Save us both."

He rose into the air—a short, jerky lift—and her breath choked from her. Mora kept a death grip on him even as her captors started shouting. Shouting—and firing. One of the bullets burned over the side of her arm. "Fly faster!" *A lot faster.* "And higher. They have wings, too, remember?"

And he erupted. Leo blasted through the basement ceiling—going up, up—breaking through another ceiling and then a wall and finally surging into the night. He didn't stop. He flew fast even as shouts echoed behind them. The wind whipped against Mora's face, and she tried to look beyond his massive wings to see if her abductors were following them.

She tried to see—

"S-sorry…"Leo muttered.

"What? What are you sorry for? You got us out. You—"

They were falling. Dropping straight down to the ground. *Oh, no.* "Leo! I don't have wings!" And an impact with the earth wasn't going to be pretty. Her eyes squeezed shut as the ground rushed up to meet them. This would hurt, a lot.

But he twisted his body. His arms curled carefully around her and then —

They hit the ground. He hit first, obviously trying to cushion the fall for her, but Mora slammed into him and the impact — falling from so high in the air — knocked her out.

***

"We should go after them!"

Reever shoved his hand against the chest of his friend Banyon. "No," Reever said quietly. "Not now." He stared at the gaping hole above him.

"But we wounded him! You saw the blood!" Banyon gestured around the basement. Then he raked a hand through his blond hair. "Hell, his blood is everywhere! Those magic bullets fucking worked. If we can hurt him, we can kill him. If we — "

Reever smiled at him. "He came for her. The stories are true."

The other men closed in around him. Reever spared them all a quick glance. "I told you, she's the weapon we need in this fight."

"She's *gone.*" Those growled words came from Aidan. No longer in the body of a panther, he stood with his shoulders hunched and glared at Reever. "We can't use a weapon that we don't possess."

They didn't understand the particular end game that Reever wanted. Soon enough, they would.

"We should have followed them." This snarl erupted from Benjamin. He rammed his hand into the wall. A small dent immediately appeared. Benjamin always had the hardest time controlling his rage. His dark eyes reflected his fury. "We could have ended this—"

"We will end things." Reever wasn't about to lose this particular battle. "But we have to be smart. We started a chain reaction tonight. The Lord of the Light will unravel for us. We know his weakness. We know how to break that precious control of his. We will shatter him, one piece at a time, and soon there will be nothing left."

"The bullets worked!" Benjamin pounded the wall again. "We could have fired those bullets into his brain and killed him!"

"No." Reever was getting tired of explaining himself. "We filled his body with a dozen bullets and even with their magic in him, Leo was still able to fly away. We aren't the ones that can end him. You *know* the prophecy. You all know it. The only way for Leo to die…it's by his brother's hand."

The Lord of the Light must battle his twin brother. It would be a battle to the death.

"We have to push them toward that final fight," Reever murmured. He smiled. "And then when Leo falls, we'll get the power we deserve." The power they had been promised.

After all, a deal…was a deal.

***

Mora sucked in a deep gulp of air. She *hurt*. And she was also sprawled all over Leo. Seriously sprawled. Her breasts were smashed against his chest. Her legs straddled his hips, and his arms were still locked tightly around her waist.

"Uh, Leo?" She lifted her body up a few inches. "You can let go now."

But his eyes were closed. His face was slack. He barely seemed to breathe.

She tried to slip from his arms.

His hold didn't loosen. Even unconscious, he was holding her tight.

Her jaw clenched, and she moved her hands, pressing to his chest. Mora shoved down so that she could push herself up more—and her hands immediately were soaked in blood. His blood.

"Leo?" Worry slithered through her.

He didn't stir. She grabbed for his hands and pried them away from her, and then Mora rolled off him. She started to sprint away—

He's hurt.

Mora froze. She looked back at his prone form. So much blood. Hesitating, Mora bit her lower lip. He was a fast healer, she knew that. He probably should have woken up before she did.

But he hadn't.

And he still seemed to be bleeding from the wounds he'd gotten.

Her eyes widened. *The bullets are still in him.* And considering the way he was being so slow to heal, she figured those had to be bullets that packed some kind of paranormal bonus punch. She edged back toward him. The chains rattled as they trailed her. The damn things were still bound around her wrists. "Tell me that you're going to heal on your own," she ordered, aware that her voice was gruff. "Tell me that I don't have to save you."

But he couldn't tell her anything.

Slowly, Mora lowered to her knees beside him. Her abductors could show up at any moment. And if they did, he wouldn't be able to fight back in this condition. "I'm going to help you," she said, her breath hitching a bit. "But then we are done, got it?" Her fingers were already covered in his blood. They inched toward his chest, but the minute she touched him—

"*Mora…*" The rasp slipped from him even as his eyes stayed closed.

"Yep, it's Mora. Doing the dirty work. About to dig bullets out of you when I should just leave you here—"

"*Missed…you.*"

Her heart was beating too fast. "Leo?"

His lashes were still closed. And he wasn't talking any longer. Maybe that had just been some delirious nonsense that burst from him. Maybe the words had meant absolutely nothing.

But…the sad truth was…*I missed you, too.*

Her shoulders stiffened, and she got to work on those bullets.

CHAPTER FOUR

Leo opened his eyes. A bright, blue sky stared back at him. He blinked, trying to figure out where in the hell he was and—

Mora.

He sat upright, adrenaline burning through his body. He didn't see Mora. Had she been taken from him again? Oh, hell, *no.* He leapt to his feet. His body ached, but the wounds were closed. He vaguely remembered being shot—again and again. Some of the bullets had gone through him, but the others...hadn't they been lodged inside of him?

His hands slapped at his clothing. Holes were there—where the bullets had torn through the fabric—and his shirt was stained with blood, but his wounds had healed.

"I dug out the bullets."

His head whipped to the right. Mora was standing beneath the small shade of a nearby tree. Her arms were crossed over her chest and her hair blew lightly in the breeze. She sighed as she stared at him, and then she rolled back her shoulders in a shrug. "I figured I owed you, since you flew in and got me away from those creeps."

He hurried toward her.

Mora lifted her hand. "Stop."

Leo immediately stilled.

"Don't go thinking this is some kind of — of a *thing*, all right?"

Her saving him wasn't a thing? It seemed like a thing to him.

"I didn't dig those bullets out because I still have feelings for you or anything emotional like that. It was simply a repayment act. You saved me. I saved you. Now we're even. Done."

He wasn't sure they'd ever be even. As far as being done? *Not while I'm still alive.* "How long was I out?"

"Long enough for the night to end and the sun to rise." A faint smile curled her lips, but that smile never reached her eyes. "I kept thinking those jerks would swoop in after us, but they never showed. Odd, isn't it? That they didn't give chase?"

His jaw locked as his gaze swept over her. Then he stalked forward. She stiffened at his approach, and he hated that. Once, she'd smiled when he drew near her. She'd smiled and her body had seemed to soften. She'd lit with a special glow that told him how happy she was just because he was near.

She wasn't happy any longer.

His hand flew out and locked around her arm. The silver chains were still around her wrists.

"I should have mentioned my no touching rule first," she muttered, frowning at him.

He stared at her arm. "You were hurt." The wound hadn't healed, not completely, not yet. He could see the red slash that went across her lower arm. A slash that had come when a bullet grazed her tender skin.

"It's not a big deal. I just don't heal as fast as you do. We both know I'll be fine."

She'd be fine and those who took her would be *dead*.

He noticed then that her hand was clenched — her fingers were fisted around something. He turned her hand over and her palm opened.

"Thought you might want these," she said. Blood-covered bullets were in her hand. "They're not normal bullets. Normal bullets wouldn't do much to you, right?"

"No, they wouldn't." He took the bullets from her. They were heavy and oddly warm to the touch. Leo tightened his fist around the bullets and he squeezed, crushing the bullets until only dust remained. Then he lifted his hand toward his nose and inhaled... "Angel feathers."

"What?"

"The bullets are made from angel feathers." An angel's feathers were rich with power, and those jerks had used that power...*to attack me.* He opened his hand, and the dust flew away in the breeze.

"Those weren't angels," she announced with a firm nod. "I saw one of them transform into the shape of a panther. Angels can't shift like that. Their wings looked like angel wings, though." A faint line appeared between her delicate brows. "And they were using me as *bait.* They wanted to lure you to that place. They wanted to kill you."

He gave a bitter laugh. "Good thing I'm so hard to kill." Leo didn't think his enemies had been angels, either, but they'd *taken* feathers from an angel in order to make their weapons. Another sin against them.

"You're hard to kill, yes, but you *can* die." She pulled her hand away from him. "We both know that."

"We both know that the only way I die is at my brother's hand." He wanted to touch her again. Wanted it so badly. He ached just staring at her. She didn't understand what all the long centuries had been like for him.

And what if she *had* disappeared while he'd been unconscious on the ground? What the hell would he have done then? "You...didn't leave me." He edged closer.

She stiffened. "It's not what you think."

"You dug the bullets out. Trust me, I'm grateful. But then you stayed." A slow smile curved his lips. "You stayed for me."

Spots of red color flared on her cheeks. "You were unconscious on the ground. For all I knew, those winged jerks were going to swoop in and grab you."

"You stayed to protect me."

She gave a rough laugh. "We both know my magic isn't the most helpful in terms of physical confrontations." She lifted her wrists and the broken chains dangled and clinked. "I couldn't even get out of these."

His fingers curled around the chain on her right wrist. With one pull, he shattered that silver.

She swallowed. "I am *not* impressed by your strength."

He took her left wrist. A hard jerk had the chain breaking apart.

"I do *not* think it's sexy," she added.

A rumble of laughter came out of him. "I have so fucking missed you."

Fear flashed on her face. Instantly, his laughter vanished. He swung around, putting his body in front of hers while he searched for danger. But no one was there. They were alone — in the middle of pretty much nowhere. He'd flown as far as he could during the dark, and then he'd dropped from the sky when he'd lost too much blood.

"You said that before," she whispered from behind him. "But I thought you were just delusional."

He looked back at her.

She gave another nod. "I still think you're delusional. You didn't miss me, not really. I think...I think it just pissed you off that I'd gotten away. That I vanished."

He turned to fully face her. He didn't like being out in the open, and he was about to get them the hell away from that place, but first... "Pissed doesn't begin to cover the way I felt when I couldn't find you."

She slipped back, but a tree was behind her, so there was no room for her to retreat too far.

His hands closed around her shoulders. "I nearly tore this world apart for you."

"Ego." She shook her head. "You couldn't stand that I—"

"*You mattered.*"

Her lower lip trembled. "Liar."

Not to her. He'd vowed *never* to lie to her again.

"Look, I have no clue where I am, okay? Just take me to my bar. Or rather...take me back to whatever the hell is left of Resurrection. Then we can go our separate ways."

His gaze was on her lower lip. The trembling lip. "You still care."

"I care about a lot of things. I care about little kids and puppy dogs and moody teens. I care about too *many* things. I'm Fate, remember? Caring is part of the massive load I carry on a daily basis."

"No. You *care* about me. That's why you dug the bullets out. That's why you stayed to protect me."

She didn't speak.

And he realized that all wasn't lost. Not yet. There was still hope.

Because there was…Fate.

His head lowered toward her.

Mora's hands immediately flew up and pressed to his chest. "What are you doing?"

"Kissing you." Technically, he wasn't, not yet, but he *would* be kissing her, soon.

"No. Absolutely not. Take me to Resurrection, *now*."

Fear quivered in her words. He hated that she feared him. Everyone else feared him. Mora had once been different.

"They wanted to use me as bait. The redhead—he was the ring leader. And whoever that jerk was—didn't exactly catch his name—he was planning to torture me. No, I didn't look into his future to figure that shit out. The guy just *told me*. Not like I could use my power on him,

anyway, not with him using silver to bind me.
The SOB was using the old, let's-hurt-the-girl
routine to get at the guy. I *hate* that routine, and I
am not going to be part of your war." She
exhaled. "Take me back to Resurrection."

"I'll have to fly you back."

"Whatever. Just do it."

"You'll have to put your arms around me."

Jaw tight, she inched closer to him. Her
breasts brushed against his chest as her hands
rose to circle his shoulders. Arousal flooded
through his body. He'd had more lovers than he
could count in his very long life, but when he
closed his eyes at night...

Her face was the only one he ever
remembered. Her body was the only one he
craved.

She didn't get just how fully she'd marked
him so long ago.

Mostly because she seemed to only
remember his betrayal.

"I'll need to carry you." His voice had
deepened. That happened when he got aroused.
The slant of her eyes told him she knew that fact.
She *remembered.* Leo cleared his throat. "It's easier
to fly that way."

"Carry me. Just...do it, okay? But don't enjoy
it."

Impossible. Carefully, he lifted her into his
arms. And Leo finally eased out a full breath. His

heart wasn't racing. Tension wasn't gripping him. Peace — as close as he ever came to the feeling, anyway — swept through him. Mora did that. She'd always calmed the beast he worked so hard to keep chained inside.

Most didn't know about his beast. They thought his brother, Luke, was the one who held the terrible monster inside of himself. When Luke let his control go, his brother fully transformed. Not into a wolf or a panther or any of the typical shifted beasts.

Luke became a dragon.

And since Leo and Luke were twins...*I become the same thing*. His beast was just as powerful as Luke's and just as dangerous. Usually, Leo had to fight that beast, almost every single moment. But not when Mora was near.

He swept high into the air, and Leo let his wings break from his back. He could control his shift, and he didn't have to transform fully. He could just use the dragon's wings to fly without the rest of his body changing. The wings beat against the air around him and took him higher and higher.

"Humans have to see you," Mora murmured. Her arms were still looped around his neck. "I mean, you're flying in broad daylight. Don't they ever just look up and *see* you?"

"I cloak myself from their eyes." Occasionally, he'd get sloppy and forget to use that magic, but humans were such interesting creatures. If they saw something that didn't coincide with their versions of reality, then they tended to ignore the object—or creature—right before their eyes. They were very helpful to him that way.

"Are you cloaking *me* from their eyes? Or does it just look as if a woman is flying through the air?"

He stared down at her. "I will protect you from them. I will protect you from everything."

Her hold tightened a bit on him. "I get the feeling you aren't talking just about humans, are you? It's those guys from last night. You think they'll come after me again."

He did. He also thought… "I'll kill them."

Her gaze searched his. "Since when does the Lord of the Light speak so easily about killing?"

"Since they threatened you."

She looked away and didn't speak again, not until he lowered them to the ground, right outside of the charred remains that had once been Resurrection. Very little was left of the place—the flames had obviously burned hell-hot. He saw two blackened walls that were still standing…and plenty of ash. So much ash, drifting in the wind.

"It's gone." She'd pulled away from him the minute her feet touched the ground. Now Mora hugged herself as she stared at what had once been her bar. "In one night, the whole life I'd built for myself is just...gone."

I can build it again for you. I can give you anything you want. His hand rose and curled around her shoulder. "Mora—"

She knocked his hand aside as she spun toward him. "You did this."

Leo blinked.

"You brought your danger to me. The men who took me last night—they must be the same ones who set Resurrection on fire. You led them to my door and this..." Her hand gestured behind him. "This is what's left. *Bait.* That's what I am. Something to hurt you." Then she laughed. "A crazy idea, of course, as if you'd care what happened to me."

I care more than you think. "There is nothing here for you." His voice was flat and cold, and he knew he was saying the wrong words, but Leo couldn't help himself. With Mora, everything always came out wrong. "I showed you this place, now we should leave. You can scry for me, and see if my fate has changed."

She swiped at her cheek.

Instantly, the wind seemed to quiet. The sun seemed to dim. His heart slowed.

Mora...was crying?

"If I scry for you, will you leave me alone?" Her words were so soft.

No. But since he didn't want to lie, Leo kept his mouth closed.

Voice still low, she said, "I don't want to be in your war."

He understood that but…His hand lifted and his fingers carefully brushed over her cheek — catching the tear drop there. "It's too late for that. The fools who hurt you will pay."

"I don't care about vengeance. You know Fate isn't supposed to take sides." Her lips twisted. "Fate isn't supposed to feel at all. When you feel, when you realize just how much you are truly responsible for in this world, the weight of it all can crush you."

He stared at her. Leo wished he could take this burden from her.

She took a step back from him. His hand fell to his side. Mora gazed at him and said, "You hunted me so that you could see if your future had changed."

"*You* change things, I've seen it happen. You alter —"

"You've seen, but you don't understand."

"Then *make* me understand." Frustration boiled through him.

"Fine. This is how it works. I save one person. Wonderful. Great. Fabulous. But by saving that one individual, I alter the lives of a dozen more. For every action, there is a *reaction* — often a deadly one. I think I'm helping one child, but then I end up hurting a dozen other humans in his place. There is always a price for the things I do. And when I change what is supposed to be…" Her breath heaved out. "That price is brutal."

"Mora…"

"I saved a woman last week." Another tear trickled down her cheek. "I…I shouldn't have. But she was at my bar. She was having a drink and she seemed so sad. I touched her hand —" Now Mora looked at her own fingers. "With humans, it's easy. I can touch them, and I can see what's coming. I can do that with most paranormals, too." Now her gaze slid to him. "Just not with you. You were a mystery that I could only unlock when I scried."

"What happened to the woman?" He should have let that go, Leo knew that but —

"I told her that the man she was with would kill her. I didn't need to see the bruises hidden under her make-up to know that she was in an abusive relationship. I *saw* her fate, clear as day. He was going to attack her. A jealous rage was going to overtake him, and he was going to hit her again and again until she was gone." A sob slipped from her. "I warned her. I *told* her to run…and she did. She tried to hide from him by going to her sister's house."

That story sounded like it had a happy ending but…

"When her lover couldn't find her, he lost control. His rage erupted and he attacked two of his coworkers. They are in the hospital right now, fighting to survive."

Shit. "What about the lover? Where is that bastard?"

"In jail, where he killed a guard who wasn't aware of just how dangerous Jeremy Gallows truly was."

Leo stepped toward her. "That isn't your fault—"

She laughed, and the sound tore at his heart. "Of course, it is. I'm Fate. I'm the reason everything happens, or haven't you heard?"

"I've heard that humans and paranormals have choices." He'd clung to that truth for his whole life. "Fate is what *can* be, but in the end, we're the ones who decide what actually happens. The human you warned, she had the choice to go to the cops. She could have alerted them. A different outcome could have come from your warning to her. *People* make the choices. You don't control us all."

Her lashes fell. "You think I can scry for you, and you'll be able to change what's waiting."

"I know I can change it."

"So confident. Or maybe you're just arrogant." She still wasn't looking at him. "And the men after you...you think you can stop them all? Kill them, and just keep right on going with your life?"

"I've killed before, Mora, and I'll do it again."

Her gaze rose to his. "No…remorse?" Her expression flickered, fear coming and going on her beautiful face.

"It's been a very long time." His jaw clenched. "You don't know me any longer."

She gave a bitter laugh. "I'm not sure I ever did."

Once, he would have sworn that she knew him better than any other.

"You're keeping secrets from me."

The charge was true, so Leo didn't deny it.

"The same way you did before. When I put my soul bare before you, but you kept your secrets so close." She glanced away from him. "You know who those men were, don't you?"

"I will deal with them." That was all he could say.

"The sins from the past. They always come back, like ghosts, desperate to get their revenge." Her breath expelled in a soft sigh. "I'll scry for you, Leo. I'll see what's waiting. But then, I want my peace."

He forced his hands to unclench. "I would give you the world…"

She shivered. "Leo…"

He couldn't hold back, not any longer. Not with her. Not with her standing right in front of him and tears gleaming in her gorgeous eyes. Not with her lips trembling, not with her body shaking. Not with the one woman he wanted more than anything so close.

Leo bounded forward. He caught her in his arms and pulled her against his body. "You know I would give you anything, if you just give yourself to me again."

Her eyes had widened. "L-Leo?"

"I have hungered for you. I have longed for you. You haunt me, do you realize that?" His voice was a rasp. His heart thundered in his chest. "I wake up at night, reaching for you. But you're not there. You're *never* there."

"You turned me away. You left. You're the one who betrayed *me*." Anger sparked beneath the tears in her eyes. "And you *dare* come back to me now—"

"Give yourself to me," he said again. Did she know how strong his need for her had become? A desire that twisted and enthralled. One that left him desperate for her. Only her. Always. "And I will give you *everything*."

A motorcycle's growl rumbled in the distance. Mora's eyelids flickered. She stared at him for a moment, as if she were staring at a stranger. "You're not the same."

"That's what I've been telling you."

The growl of the motorcycle grew louder. Company was coming their way. He glanced toward the sound, wondering if it was time for another battle, but he only saw a lone rider heading in their direction. Not one of the men who'd abducted Mora but...

Leo's eyes narrowed. *I know that man.* Because the dumbass wasn't wearing a helmet, Leo recognized the human who'd been at Resurrection when Leo first arrived. The dark-haired male who'd seemed too comfortable with Mora.

"I'll scry for you," she said, and her voice drew his gaze back to her. "Because I want to see what the hell is going on with you." Then she reached out and touched him.

Her power is in touch. He knew that—or at least, her power usually was in her touch. When Mora put her hands on her prey, she could see the individual's fate. What twists and turns waited. Humans were always easy for her to read. She'd told him once that paranormals took more effort.

And she'd said that she couldn't read me through touch at all. She'd enjoyed that about him. She'd liked not knowing what would come or so she'd said. The only way Mora had ever been able to see his future was to scry with his blood. He'd pushed her to see, so long ago. But he hadn't liked the fate that she'd described for him.

So I've been trying to change it. But time is running out. And if I can't come up with a new plan, I'll be killing my own brother.

Her hand was pressed right over his heart. He could feel her touch, sinking into him. The hunger he felt for her grew, coiling inside of him like a snake ready to strike. It had been too long…

"I see nothing but darkness when I touch you, just like before." Her smile almost broke him. "Do you know what a relief it was, to finally have a lover I could touch…and only see the two of us? Not his past, not his future. Just the moment. I could let myself go with you."

"*Mora…*" She was about to push him too far. *Need her. Want her.* He'd thought that he'd be able to hold his desire for her in check. He'd thought he could play the right role with her this time.

He'd been wrong.

"But since I didn't see the danger coming, there was no way to protect myself." Her hand slid from his chest. "Will I see it coming this time?"

The motorcycle braked near them. The human jumped off the bike. "Mora!" He ran toward her. "Mora, what in the hell happened here? This place *ignited* and cops were all over this scene until dawn!"

The cops weren't there now. Some crime scene tape was up, flapping in the wind, but no other sign of human authorities remained.

The guy locked his hand around Mora's shoulder. "I thought you'd burned." His voice was gruff and the concern on his face was all too real.

A problem. This human is a problem.

Before Mora could speak, Leo caught the human's hand and removed it from Mora's person. "Touching is an issue for her. So don't do it, okay?"

She'd paled at the human's touch. But Mora rallied and said, "Leo, it's — it's okay. I know Dax. He's a regular at Resurrection." Mora winced as her gaze cut back to the charred remains of her bar. "Or he *was* a regular."

Dax had stiffened at Leo's touch. "Who the hell is this guy, Mora? Are you safe with him?"

Leo swept a disdainful glance over the human. Like this fellow with his tats was supposed to be some white knight —

"I mean, this weird jerk appears, and five minutes later, your bar is in flames. That tells me the man is bad news." Dax glowered at Leo.

He's lucky I'm supposed to watch over the humans. "It's time for you to leave, buddy. Mora isn't your concern." Leo waved his hand as if he were shooing away a pesky bug. "Go, you're done here."

"Oh, jeez, Leo," Mora muttered. "*Tact.* Have some of it."

Dax's eyes narrowed. "Who the fuck are you?"

"I'm Leo. And you're in our way." Hmmm…the human should have been leaving by that point. Normally, it took only the smallest amount of power for Leo to influence mortals. But this guy's glare was just getting worse with every moment that passed. A sliver of alarm sliced through Leo.

"I don't care if I'm in your way!" Dax blustered back. "I'm here for Mora."

Oh, no, you're not. Leo's shoulders immediately stiffened.

"Here we go." Mora's voice was disgusted.

Leo's gaze shot from her to the one called Dax. "Are you sleeping with Mora?" *Answer wisely, bastard. The wrong answer will get you killed.*

Dax opened his mouth to reply—

Mora jumped in front of him. She put her body between Dax and Leo, and her white-hot stare should have burned Leo. It would have burned him, if he'd been a lesser paranormal. "Stop this." Her words snapped at him. "You don't get to ask questions like that. I told you I'd scry, and you just need to be *grateful.* You don't need to be—"

"Are you sleeping with him?" Jealousy was there, spreading like a virus in his body. Rage grew. *Mora is mine. Always mine.* And if that smirking bastard had taken her body—

Mora's index finger jabbed into his chest. "Stop it. Right now. I don't know what this new red glowing eye thing is about, but I don't like it."

Red glowing eye thing?

"You don't get to ask about my sexual partners. I'm not asking about yours, am I? Our relationship is ancient history—literally. So stop playing the jealous lover. It's not a role that suits you." She glowered at him a moment longer, then Mora turned to Dax. "You need to leave. I appreciate you coming back to check on me, but…this isn't a safe place for you."

Dax nodded once. "I see." He gave a ragged sigh. "I'd hoped to do things the easy way."

What in the hell was the fool talking about?

"But I guess that can't happen," Dax added darkly. Then he reached into his jacket, and he pulled out a gun. A gun he aimed at Mora.

What. The. Actual. Fuck?

"What are you doing?" Mora's voice broke. "Dax?"

A muscle jerked in Dax's jaw. "I need you to come with me, Mora. Right now."

He didn't give her a chance to respond. He reached out and yanked her forward, putting the gun under her chin and holding her tightly. "You and I—we're going for a little ride."

Leo didn't move a muscle. He just stared at the dead man.

"Dax…" Mora's voice was husky. "Look, I have a *lot* going on right now. You don't want to do this. You're a good person…"

"How the hell would you know that? Everyone else thinks I'm one of the worst criminals out there." He pulled her even closer against him. "But you peer at me with your big eyes, looking at me like I need some kind of help." He was backing her toward the motorcycle and keeping the gun beneath her chin every step of the way. "And you warn me…you come fucking right out and say you know I'm not who I'm pretending to be."

The fool thought he was going to get on that motorcycle. That Leo was just going to let him ride away with Mora.

You won't ride away. You won't walk away. But you will die.

"You tell me that I'm going to die." Dax's voice was rough. "And then hours later, Sammy sends two of his top enforcers after me. Shit, I know it's not coincidence."

Leo didn't know who Sammy was. And he didn't care. He took a step forward.

"*Stop!*" Dax's voice cracked. "Don't take another step. You do *not* want to be the hero here."

Leo didn't take another step. "Move the gun away from Mora."

Dax shook his head. "She's coming with me. I need to know who tipped her off. I need to know if she's in bed with Sammy..."

Maybe I do need to know who this Sammy is...

"I'm not in bed with him." Mora's response was quiet and flat. "Sammy Long is the leader of a drug cartel. I have nothing to do with him. I've never met him, and I hope our paths don't ever cross."

But Dax gave a ragged laugh. "Don't know that I believe you, Mora." They were right beside the motorcycle now. "So you're coming with me. Maybe you thought the fire was a cover. That you could vanish and I wouldn't know how deeply involved you were. *Think again.*" He slid onto the motorcycle, then pulled her down right in front of him.

The guy wouldn't be able to drive the bike, not with that gun still pointed at Mora. He'd have to put the weapon up. What did he think, that Mora was just going to sit quietly in front of him during the drive that the fool had planned?

Leo exhaled and stalked forward.

"Stop!" Dax yelled. "Stop right the hell now!" And suddenly, the gun wasn't under Mora's chin. It was pointing at Leo.

Much better. But he didn't stop walking, not until he was right in front of that motorcycle. To get out of there, Dax would have to literally get past Leo. And that just wasn't going to happen. "Mora and I...we've had a really bad night."

"Two of Sammy's enforcers tried to cut out my damn tongue!" Dax yelled back. "My *tongue!* Do you know how twisted that shit is?"

Mora winced.

"I almost died!" Dax added, his voice close to a snarl. "So don't talk to me about bad!"

"If you don't let Mora go, right now, I'll do more than cut out your tongue." This was twice — *twice* – in the last twenty-four hours that a bastard had tried to take Mora. How many other dangers had she faced over the years, dangers that Leo had never known about? How many times had she needed him, and Leo hadn't been there?

"Leo, just calm down." Mora's voice was quiet.

And had she seriously just said for him to calm down? His jaw ached because he was clenching it so fiercely.

"I can handle Dax," Mora added.

Behind her, Dax laughed again.

"He's a cop," Mora called out. "He's not going to hurt me."

Dax stopped laughing. "Shit, shit, *shit!* Don't just yell out that stuff! You don't know who's listening!"

"Cops don't pull guns on innocent women." Leo kept his hands loose at his sides. He could feel his nails lengthening—becoming claws. The better to attack his prey. "So try again…"

Mora gave a little laugh. "I bet the gun isn't loaded." She turned her head, looking back at Dax. "Is it?"

"Who *are* you people?" Dax demanded. "This isn't a game!" His gaze locked on Mora's face. "This is—"

Leo attacked. He'd been waiting for Dax's attention to shift, and it had. While Dax gazed at Mora, Leo leapt at him. His hand locked around Dax's throat, and he yanked the guy right off the motorcycle. He shoved Dax to the ground even as he ripped the gun from Dax's hand. In the next moment, Leo had the gun aimed at Dax's head. *Much better.*

"*Leo!*" Mora yelled. "Stop!"

"Let's see if it's loaded, shall we?" And Leo pulled the trigger.

CHAPTER FIVE

"Leo!" Mora jumped off the motorcycle and grabbed his arm. "What in the hell were you thinking? The gun *could* have been loaded!"

But it hadn't been. When Leo had pulled the trigger, no bullets had exploded from the gun. And now Dax was sprawled on the ground, glaring up at Leo.

"He's lucky it wasn't loaded." Leo tossed the gun aside. Then he put his claws — *claws* — to Dax's throat. Immediately, blood began to trickle from the other man's neck.

Not that Dax realized claws were cutting into him. Leo had moved fast, so Mora figured the guy had to think a knife was at his throat. *Right. Keep thinking that.*

"He's a cop," Mora said as she kept her grip on Leo. "I figured out that he was undercover a while back, but I warned him last night that others were onto him, too. I was trying to help him." Even though her attempts to help often went horribly wrong. But the bloody ending she'd seen for Dax...the torture, the pain, the fire—*I had to try.*

"How'd you figure it out, Mora? Who tipped you off?" Dax demanded. His body was taut, and she knew he was just waiting for the right moment to spring into action. *That moment won't come. Stay down.*

Mora huffed out a breath. "No one tipped me off." The implication was rather insulting.

"You're working for Sammy, aren't you? You were jerking me around and—"

"I should let Leo hurt you a bit more," she muttered. "Because you are pissing me off." She sighed. *Be patient. Do the right thing, Mora.* "But you're a cop, and I think you might be *mostly* human, so I'm going to help you, again." She pulled on Leo's arm. "Let him go. He's got his problems. We have ours. You and I need to get the hell out of here."

Leo's claws lifted from Dax's throat. Good. Very good. Mora turned away. Her gaze scanned the area. Where was her car? Had it been *towed?* Dammit! "We're gonna need your motorcycle, Dax." Because, sure, they could fly off courtesy of Leo's wings, but once Leo left her...she'd be without transportation. And she didn't feel like hunting down her ride, not when a motorcycle was conveniently available for her. "Consider it payback for pulling a gun on me." She straddled the bike. The keys were already in the ignition. Nice.

"Mora, you aren't leaving!" Dax's voice boomed. He scrambled to his feet and charged toward her.

But Leo punched him. One punch to the jaw—and down Dax went.

She winced. A hit from Leo had to be on par with running straight into a brick wall. "Was that necessary?" Mora revved the engine.

"He pulled a gun on you. I think it's *necessary* for me to rip his head off."

And again, a chill skated over her at his words. Mora turned her head to find Leo towering over Dax's groaning form. When Leo looked up at her, his eyes had a reddish tint. *I need to scry. Right away.* Because something had changed with Leo. "You're supposed to protect humans."

"Like you said, he's *mostly* human. I think that makes him fair game."

Her fingers tightened around the handle bars. "He's DEA. He's been working undercover for a very long time, and that cover of his has been blown. He's trying to help in this world. I thought you were supposed to stand up for people like him."

"I don't stand up for anyone who pulls a gun on you." He glared at her. "And *you* should be angrier at him, too."

She smiled. "I'm stealing his ride. It's payback." She motioned toward Leo. "Now will you come on? We have more important matters waiting." He shouldn't need that reminder.

Leo moved toward her, but Dax threw out his hand. Dax's fingers wrapped around Leo's ankle. "Wait..." Dax's gasp. "Have to know...who she's...with..."

Leo bent down, resting his hands on his knees. His claws were right in front of Dax's face. "Me," Leo said flatly. "Mora is with me."

"Leo!" Mora yelled. *Dammit! You just had to let him see the claws.*

Dax scrambled back. His face had gone stark white—well, white everywhere but on his rapidly bruising jawline. Darkness covered his jaw. "What are you?"

"I'm the man who can be your worst nightmare. If you ever come at Mora with a gun again—loaded or not—it will be the end for you." He pulled away from Dax. "But I'm trying to remember I'm supposed to watch out for humans...and those who are *mostly* human."

Dax just shook his head. "What is...happening?"

Mora figured the poor guy's mind was probably about to explode. "Your cover is blown. Sammy's gang is gunning for you, and you just found out that the world is very much *not* what you expected it to be. You need to get yourself off the ground, get out of here, and call in to your superiors at the DEA. You also need to stay away from me." She revved the motorcycle again. "Because like I said before, I really have enough shit going on now." She inclined her head toward Leo. "Let's go."

He smiled at her. "My pleasure." Then Leo was climbing onto the bike, sliding on behind her and she'd *thought* using the motorcycle would make things a whole lot less intimate than the flights she took in his arms. She'd been wrong. He slid behind her and his cock—*oh, my.* He was aroused. He was seriously turned on, and she could feel the press of his erect cock against her ass. His arms slid alongside hers, and his hands reached out to curl around hers on the handlebars. He completely surrounded her.

And she'd forgotten to breathe.

Because it's happening again. The need…the desire that shouldn't be there.

"What are we waiting for?" Leo's rasp was right at her ear. Mora shivered because she was pretty sure she'd just felt his tongue lick along the shell of her ear.

Her nipples were tight. Her body aching.

His scent teased her.

Scry for him. Then run.

She would not fall back into the trap of wanting Leo. It was far too dangerous. Because *he* was far too dangerous. She couldn't let him distract her.

The motorcycle shot forward even as Dax screamed her name. But she didn't look back. After all, she was pretty pissed at him, too. She'd tried to help the guy out, and he'd repaid her by pulling a gun.

Story of her life.

***

"Mora!" Dax bellowed.

But she was long gone. Long gone on *his* bike. Dax glowered after her as ash and dust blew in his face. He rubbed his jaw. Damn. For a moment there, he'd thought that bruiser had *broken* his jaw.

The bruiser with the claws and the eyes that seemed to reflect the very fires of hell.

He wasn't human. No way had that guy — Leo? — been human. Freaking claws had sprung from the fellow's fingertips. And he'd had a punch that packed the power of a sledge hammer.

He moved too fast. Like a blur, coming at me. There was no time to get away from him.

Dax picked up the gun that had been tossed aside. The gun was bent and twisted. *Leo did that. With his bare hand, he twisted the metal.*

Shit.

And Mora still didn't tell me how she found out the truth about me. Was she some kind of psychic or something? Or just some woman on Sammy Long's payroll? Either way, he couldn't just let her go.

He hunched his shoulders and started walking. His life was on the line. He'd spent the last three years pretending to be a stone-cold criminal. A killer. And after you pretended something for so long…

Maybe you stop pretending.

Mora wasn't going to vanish, not until he got his answers. And the freak with the claws? *Next time, I'll be ready for his attack.*

Dax's gun wouldn't be empty next time.

***

Mora was nervous. She was fidgeting, moving too quickly, and casting far too many worried glances over her shoulder as she pulled her scrying mirror from the wooden trunk that rested at the foot of her bed.

"You're afraid of me." Leo stood in the middle of Mora's bedroom, his hands loose at his sides. Sunlight spilled through the large window on the right, and the room seemed to be filled with Mora's sweet scent. Her bed was to the left. A big enough bed for two, barely. Given the chance, he could wreck that bed. He could—

"You should have just waited in the den." She clutched the mirror to her chest. "I was coming back."

"Considering the night *and* the morning we've had, I didn't want to let you out of my sight." Truth be told, he'd also just wanted to get inside her bedroom.

Mora swallowed. "You know all this trouble only happened to me *after* you came to my bar. I was perfectly fine, leading a perfectly *normal* life, until you appeared."

That news grated. He paced toward her, stopping when barely a breath separated their bodies. "You weren't meant for normal. You're a *goddess*, for shit's sake."

"Says who? The people who tried to *burn* me alive in ancient Greece?" Her laughter was mocking. "I'm just a woman who can see things...the worst things that tend to be out there."

She was so much more than that, and they both knew the truth.

"You live in a one bedroom house, on the edge of town, in the middle of *nowhere*." Anger growled in his voice. "You should be in a palace, surrounded by every luxury imaginable, with guards at your service to—"

"Been there, done that. And again—the ending wasn't so pretty." She gave him a brittle smile. "I'm one woman, living alone, so why would I need more than a one bedroom house? I *love* this house. I painted all the walls. I picked out all the furniture. I watch the sunrise from my bed—" She gestured to the bed. "And I stare at the moonlight as I fall asleep. This place is perfect. It's *my* home." Her lips tightened. "As far as the guards are concerned, I didn't need them, not until you swooped back into my life." She clutched the mirror to her chest and skirted around him as she headed for the bedroom door. "Don't think I won't be paying Sabrina back for this particular favor."

He followed her, slowly, casting one last glance around the bedroom. He could easily imagine Mora spread out in that bed, her hair on the pillow, as she slept beneath the moonlight.

When he slept, he often dreamed of her. Some of the dreams were sensual, visions of her body twined with his. In those dreams, he could see pleasure on her face and hear it in her voice as she called out to him.

Some of the dreams were dark. Visions of her crying, begging him to help her. Visions of her in pain. Lost.

"Are you coming?"

His head snapped toward the door. She stood in that doorway, her hands curled around what appeared to be nothing more than a pane of glass—absolutely black glass.

"Or did you change your mind?" Mora's head tipped to the side as she studied him. "Afraid to find out what I'll see?"

He rolled back his shoulders and strode toward her. Mora didn't retreat at his approach. That was one of the things he'd always enjoyed about her. "You know I don't fear much."

Her gaze searched his, then she gave a slow nod. Without another word, she turned and headed to her small kitchen. Mora carefully sat the glass down on her tidy dining table.

Leo reached for a knife in her knife block. He lifted it up, and the sharp blade glinted in the light. *Yes, that should do the trick.*

He sliced the blade right across his hand.

"Leo!" Her voice was startled, her eyes wide.

He walked toward her and only stopped when he was at the edge of the table. He opened his palm and let the blood drops fall onto the glass. "I remember how this works."

"You didn't have to make such a big cut." Her gaze was on his hand.

"Worried, love?" The endearment slipped from him. "And here I thought you'd stopped caring."

Her gaze flew to his. "You should have made the cut bigger."

His lips twitched. He put the knife down on the table and then offered his uncut hand to her.

Mora's fingers closed around his. "Fine. Let's see what waits. The good, the bad, and everything in between."

His fingers tightened on hers. This was the moment. This was what he'd risked so much to learn. Leo stared down at the mirror. He just saw blood and darkness.

Mora pulled in a shuddering breath. His gaze jerked to her. Mora's beautiful eyes changed in the next second. The color receded, becoming as black as the mirror. Power crackled in the air around him, and her fingers seemed to burn against his.

He ignored the burn, and he just held her tighter.

The way he should have held her long ago.

"What do you see for my future?"

***

"What do you see for my future?"

They were standing on a beach. Her hand was in Leo's. The sun was setting and waves were tickling her feet. Fate looked down, shocked to find herself in this place again.

She'd been scrying for Leo, but her intent had been to see his future.

Not his past.

But I'm in the past. It's all around me.

"You scried for me today." His hand lifted, and his fingers brushed her hair behind her ear. His touch was so gentle, but his eyes were hard. She'd never noticed — not back then — how hard and cold his gaze could be. "Why won't you tell me what you saw?"

Fate swallowed. "Because what I saw scares me."

"Scares you?" His fingers slid across her cheek and curled under her chin. "You know I wouldn't hurt you."

He was a tender lover. Always so concerned with her pleasure. Always holding his power in check. And she felt safe with him.

"Besides..." He nodded toward her. "We can change what you see, can't we?"

"S-sometimes..."

"Then tell me, and let's change what waits."

She drew in a shuddering breath. She needed this future to change. "I saw your twin, standing over your dead body. The final battle comes, but you don't win. Luke does."

A muscle jerked in his jaw. *"You saw the wrong fucking thing."*

***

Mora gave a quick gasp as the past vanished. Her breath heaved in and out as her heart thundered in her chest.

"Mora?" His grip tightened on her wrist. "What did you see?"

Her gaze jerked around the room—her home. Her kitchen table. Her chairs. Her slightly wilting flowers that she'd picked up from the market two days before. She wasn't on a beach. Wasn't dressed in some gauzy white dress. The past was over.

"What's going to happen?" Leo demanded.

She gave a slow shake of her head. "I saw the past. Not the future."

He swore.

"We were on the beach. It was the first time I scried for you." He'd been using her back then, and he was using her now. The only difference? This time, Mora knew she was being used. She wasn't a blind fool in love, not anymore. "And I told you that your brother Luke would kill you."

His gaze immediately became hooded. "It's not the past I'm interested in."

"It's not like I wanted a walk down memory lane, either," she muttered. But actually, for her to go into the past...*My words were a lie. That was exactly what I wanted.* Her emotions sometimes got in the way of her visions. She'd intended to look forward, but some part of her—some part was still tied to the past.

"Liar," he called her bluff.

Mora felt heat stain her cheeks.

"You want to see the past, don't you? To see just how I betrayed you? You want to know every dark moment?" His hand pulled from hers. "We don't have time for that. We have to go forward."

We have time for whatever I want. The angry retort burned through her mind. "I don't want to know about the betrayal." And this was her shame. "I think I wanted to see if any of it was real."

He flinched.

Bitterness coiled within her. He had no idea — *none* — about how brutal her life had been because of him. Maybe it was time for him to take a walk down memory lane. Maybe it was time for him to see that there was a price paid for everything.

And everyone.

She grabbed for the knife. Just as he'd done, she took that knife and sliced the blade across her palm.

"Mora!" Leo snatched the blade from her and threw it across the room.

She just gave a bitter laugh. "Don't worry, Leo. I heal. It may be a slow healing, but I can still recover. From just about anything." She watched her blood spatter onto the mirror. "You're in for a treat. I don't normally share my visions with anyone. But this time, I think you're due."

Payback.

Then her bloody hand grabbed his. She held him tight. "Let's give you a nice, up-close view of the past." Her gaze shot to the mirror as she channeled her power. It pulsed through her, rising up, up, and then it surged straight into Leo.

I hope you choke on the past.

CHAPTER SIX

Mora was on the bed.

She was naked, her bare back turned toward him, and her long, black hair slid over her shoulders.

Leo blinked. "What in the hell is happening here?" He'd been standing in Mora's kitchen just a moment ago. She'd grabbed his hand. Then a dark shadow had seemed to sweep over him.

Now I'm here? Why the hell am I here? The scene wasn't in Mora's house. The walls weren't made of wood. They were carved from stone. Silks hung everywhere.

Wait. I know this place and this time. A time that had been very, very long ago.

The door beside him creaked open. A man slipped inside—a man who had a long hood covering his face. The guy was heading toward the bed. Toward Mora.

Leo jumped in front of him. "Who are—"

The guy just walked right through him.

Leo's breath shuddered out. *I'm in Mora's vision.* Shit, shit. She'd cut herself with that knife.

Her blood had been dripping onto the mirror and then she'd grabbed him. She was showing him the past.

But he didn't want to see it.

"Stop it, Mora!" Leo snarled. "I asked for the future, not the past. That was the deal!" And no one broke a deal with the Lord of the Light. No one. Not even her. Not even...

The bastard in the hood was near the bed. Mora was still sleeping. She was alone.

I know this scene. I know this room. I know that bed. I made love with Mora in that bed.

But he wasn't in that bed with her right then. Because...*I'd left the night before. I slipped away without telling her.*

The man in the hood lifted his hands, and Leo saw the silver chains the bastard held in his grasp. Immediately, Leo lurched forward. "No! No! Get those away from her!" He grabbed for the bastard, but his hands just slipped right through the air.

Because that guy isn't really here. Nothing is here. This is all just a memory. No, not a memory. A vision.

The past.

The bastard locked the chains around Mora's wrists, and she woke, screaming.

Only...until that moment, Leo hadn't realized...

She woke screaming my name.

"Leo!" Terror flashed on Mora's face. "What's happening? *Leo?*"

"She's contained!" The man in the hood shouted. "Come in, now!"

And others stormed inside. To Leo, they were indistinct, shadowy.

Mora grabbed for the bed covers, yanking them up to cover herself.

"We know your weakness, *Fate*," the man in the hood spat. Something about his voice was oddly familiar to Leo.

I've heard his voice before...

"Your lover told us, right before he gave orders that he was done with you." Laughter came from the man in the hood. Silence from the others who'd joined him.

Mora huddled on the bed. Beautiful, terrified. She'd wrapped the covers around her nakedness, and now she was fighting desperately to get the chains off her wrists.

"Magic," the hooded man said, sounding far too satisfied. "Leo made sure those wouldn't open easily once they were wrapped around your wrists."

No, no, shit, this was wrong. "Mora, I—I wasn't going to use those on you!" Leo yelled.

But, *fuck me, I did have them made to chain her. Only I didn't give them to that bastard!*

He'd made them, yet that had been before…before he'd known her. Before he'd tasted her lips. Before he'd—

"Get away from me!" Mora screamed.

Leo flinched and took a step back. *No, she's not talking to me. She's talking to the men surrounding her.*

"You dare to come into my chambers?" Her chin lifted. "Don't you know who I am?" Her lips trembled. "*What* I am?"

"You're a false prophet," the hooded man told her, and again, something about his voice nagged at Leo. Something about the figure…*He's trying so hard to hide himself.* "You lie about your visions. About what you see."

"Get out of here!" Her breath heaved even as her gaze flew around the room. "Leo?"

She's still calling for me. Leo put a hand to his chest. It fucking *hurt.*

"He's done with you," the hooded man announced.

Mora shook her head.

"He left you in the night, and he told us to finish you off."

Once more, Leo surged forward. "The hell I did!" But…

He *had* left. He'd slipped away from her, having gotten the glimpse into his future that he'd been so desperate to have. He'd left her, knowing that he wouldn't return.

"Leo loves me." Her soft voice was desperate.

"You're a false prophet," the hooded man said again. Those around him...they were lighting torches.

Oh, the fuck, no. "Mora!" Her name boomed from Leo. "Mora, get the hell out of here!"

She crawled from the bed, edging toward the window that looked out over the countryside below.

The hooded man followed her.

Behind him, the others touched their torches to the bedding, to the clothes on the floor, and to the furniture.

Leo shook his head. *Please, no. I need this vision to stop.*

"You lied about the future you saw for Leo. He told us that you deceived him."

No! I didn't tell this asshole anything.

Her lips were trembling. The growing fire was reflected in her eyes. "I wanted to see something different. *Luke* wins. The dark *wins.*"

The other men had filed out. The flames were raging everywhere. Crackling and growing.

"If you jump, they'll be waiting for you." The man laughed. *The leader.* "My men are rushing downstairs. They'll be there when your broken body hits the ground, and then we'll still make sure the fire gets you."

She climbed onto the window ledge. "I'll take my chances." Then she glanced into the night. "*Leo!*"

More laughter erupted. "You think he's going to help you? He *left* you."

Fuck me, I did.

"You were a means to an end for him. He's done. All those pretty promises he made you? They're worthless."

"H-he never made me pretty promises." Her hands pressed to the stone surrounding the window. "Leo!" She shouted again into the night.

The hooded man lunged for her, but Mora jumped.

And then a few seconds later, Leo heard the thudding impact when she hit the earth.

"*Mora!*" Leo roared her name.

***

"Of course, the fall didn't kill me."

Leo blinked. He was back in Mora's home, his hand clenched tightly around hers. Sweat covered his body. And he was pretty sure his heart had been cut out of his chest.

"I think I broke most of my bones, but I didn't die. Though that asshole in the robe kept his promise, his men were there waiting for me."

Leo slowly turned his head to look at her. His breath sawed in and out of his lungs. Fury filled him. Pain twisted in his gut.

"His men were there," she said again, giving a slow nod. "And they had their torches ready. I screamed for you a lot that night, but you were gone." She let his hand go. "I can't tell you how long I've wanted you to see that particular scene." Her smile was cold. Cruel. "For so long, I've wanted to give you just a taste of my pain." She released his hand.

Immediately, his hand shoved against his chest. The pain was so strong—*not just a taste*. His whole world was erupting. He started clawing at his chest, wanting that pain to stop. "I didn't...send them." Each word was guttural. Brutal. "They weren't my men."

"You left me unprotected. *You* spread the word that my visions were fake. I learned that...*after*. I was broken and burned, barely surviving. I needed help, but all the humans there had turned on me."

She stared at him with such fury. *Justified. So fucking justified.* No wonder she'd run from him. No wonder she'd hidden.

Her gaze held his—showing him all of her pain and her fury.

"You left me, and you told everyone you encountered that my visions were fake."

His teeth ground together. "Mora..."

"You kissed me. You made love to me. Then you left me to be tortured—"

He grabbed her arms and yanked her closer. "I swear, *I didn't send those men.*" But he would find them. He would hunt them down. "I will find them. I will break their bones. I will burn them, I will—"

"That's not the way the Lord of the Light should talk."

His hold tightened on her. His claws were out, his teeth sharpening as his beast pushed to the surface, and Leo could feel his wings bursting from his back. He needed to pull back, to get his control.

But…

She called for me when she was afraid. "I was never as good as you thought."

Mora was pale. Too pale. And her eyes had gone nearly golden with her power. "Who said I ever thought you were good?"

His breath sawed from his lungs. "I left you because I *had* to do it. But I'd put my claim on you. I'd *taken* you. Everyone there knew you were mine. No one should have touched you. When I found out that you'd been hurt, I came back. *I came back!*"

"Big fucking deal."

He blinked.

She smiled and that smile hurt him as much as the vision had. "Did you think I wanted you then? When I needed you most, you weren't there. So I decided that I wouldn't be there, either. I wouldn't be there to scry for you." Her gaze shot to the table and the mirror that waited. She gave a rough laugh. "But here we are. Maybe I was just lying to myself. Maybe all along, I wanted to scry so you would have to see just what you'd done to me."

But she hadn't shown him everything. She hadn't shown him the fall or the fire. She... "You tricked me."

Her smile stretched.

"You never intended to scry and see the future." His wings stretched behind him. "You wanted payback against me."

Mora stepped closer to him. "Actually, I *was* trying to see the future. But my emotions got the better of me." Her head tipped back. "Besides, how is my pain possibly payback? How could it hurt you?"

It does. More than anything else could. He cleared his throat. "That was why you left, too. Why you hid all these years—to hurt me. To punish me."

"You think I don't know of all the things you've done over the centuries, Leo? You don't care who gets caught in your wake of destruction, you don't care—"

He dropped to his knees before her.

Silence.

His eyes squeezed shut. "Show me the rest."

"Wh-what?"

"Show me and give me the pain."

He kept his head bowed before her.

Mora didn't speak.

"I want to feel everything that you felt, every single damn moment of pain—*give it to me*."

Mora's fingers fluttered over his shoulders. "What are you doing?"

His head tilted back so that he could stare up at her. "Give me the payback. Give me a way to take the pain from you. *Give it all to me*. We both know I fucking deserve it. And I'll take it."

Confusion showed on her face. "Why?"

"Because you mattered. You mattered then, and you matter now. I want to take every second of pain away. I want to change—"

"Fate?" She finished, and a sad laugh scraped from her. "Still playing the same old song, huh? Trying to trick me again? You want out because you can't—"

"I used you." A brutal truth. He was on his fucking knees before her, her scream still echoing in his ears, and he could give her nothing but the truth. *I will never let her hurt again. No matter what I must do. Never again.* "I wanted to change the end I'd always been told would come. The final fight between me and my twin brother? I needed a way out. I needed—"

"You didn't want to die."

"*I didn't want to kill my brother!*" His words were a rasp. "What do you think I've fought against so long? I've never wanted to kill him—because I've always known that when it comes down to the final battle...*I can't kill him.* He's the only family I have. I knew, *I knew* that you'd see a future where he killed me, because I know I won't be able to lift my hand against him."

Her eyes had gone wide. His darkest secret, finally revealed for everyone. He'd been a fucking bastard for centuries *because I needed to save my brother!* "And if Luke kills me, despite the appearances to the contrary, I know it will wreck him. I needed a different ending. I was trying to find that ending." Her hands were still on his shoulders. "But I never, fucking *never* wanted to sacrifice you to get that ending. I never wanted you to be in pain."

Her gaze searched his. Fury was there, in the depths of her gaze. Betrayal. So much sadness. "Collateral damage?" Mora whispered. "Isn't that what they call it? From what I've seen in my mirror, you've left plenty of collateral damage on this earth."

He stiffened. "You've watched me?"

"I'm Fate. I can see anything or anyone I want. Sometimes, I needed to see you—to show myself that you were still truly the bastard I remembered."

"I'm the bastard who is on his knees before you. I'm the one who is telling you I will *never* let you be hurt again. I will find those who tortured you. They will die. They will—"

"Get out of my home, Leo."

His lips parted.

"Out of my home and out of my life. I think, given all that I've endured for you so far…you owe me that, don't you?" She pulled her hands from his and stepped back. "And I don't want you on your knees for me. I never wanted that." She turned her back on him.

Slowly, he rose. "I need to make this better." Each word was torn from him.

She didn't look back at him. "There are some things that can't be changed. There are some things that just are. *Fate.*" She stood near the table and her hand trailed over the mirror. "I can never see my own destiny. Did you know that? It's a little quirk. I can't see what's coming for me. Because if I could have seen it…" Her shoulders sagged a bit. "I would have run the minute our paths crossed."

"You're saying it was your fate to suffer because of me?"

She was staring into the mirror. "I'm saying it was my fate to fall in love with you…and the pain that came after was the price for trying to claim something that I should never have."

Fall in love with you. A dull ringing filled his ears as Leo lurched forward. He lifted his hands toward her.

"*Don't.* Don't touch me right now. I'm at my limit." She exhaled a shuddering breath. "And I'm breaking my word. I'm not scrying for your future. I did that before. I saw what will come." She finally looked up at him. Her eyes appeared to be made of glass. No emotion was in her stare at all. "You're going to die, Leo. At your brother's hand. The dark wins."

"Mora, give me a chance, let me change—"

"It's so strange. Looking at your brother—at his life and yours—I would have thought Luke was the good one."

His beast was roaring inside of him. "I want to make this right—"

But she shook her head. "You won't see me again after this day. I'll vanish and it will be the end." Her eyes still held no emotion.

But a tear slid down her cheek.

"Good-bye, Leo," Mora whispered. Another tear followed the path of the first.

And in the face of her tears, he was helpless. Leo turned and walked away.

***

Mora waited until Leo was gone. Only then did she grab the table's edge for support. Her knees were shaking so hard that if she hadn't grabbed the table, she would have fallen.

Over.

In the midst of her fury, she'd planned to show him those visions, to force him to face their past—she'd planned to show him every single moment of her pain. She'd planned for him to relive it all but...

I couldn't.

Because something had happened once he saw their shared past. She'd felt the trembles that shook him. Heard his breathing turn guttural. Seen the shock and pain that had crossed his face.

He hadn't known at all. She'd thought he'd sent those men after her. But his shock had been real.

Revulsion and fury had darkened his face. His reaction had been so visceral that his beast had sprang to the surface. She'd never seen him change fully, but Mora knew Leo had come very close during those dangerous moments. Scales had appeared just beneath his skin, she'd all but felt them. His eyes had turned blood red. Dark wings had stretched from his back. His teeth had sharpened and his nails had become black claws.

She'd stared at him, and a rage-filled monster had stared back at her...

Only to kneel at her feet.

Her eyes closed.

Leo kneels to no one. That was what the paranormals always said. That he bowed to no man.

He bowed to me.

Her hands flew out, and she shoved her mirror to the floor. It shattered, breaking into a dozen pieces. Her revenge. For so long, she'd wanted him to hurt. She'd wanted payback. She just…

I don't feel any better. The hole in her chest just seemed to have gotten worse. Mora shuffled away from the table, and her foot pressed on a shard of glass.

Yes, she knew what waited in Leo's future. She'd seen his future before, and it had broken her heart.

Death. A death I can't stop. She never planned to look at his future again. Despite everything, she couldn't stand to see him dying.

Not Leo.

Because maybe part of her still cared for him.

CHAPTER SEVEN

Leo hunted. He rushed back to the basement of that shit-forsaken house — the house that Mora had been imprisoned inside of by the redheaded bastard. He didn't try to approach quietly. He flew right inside, bursting through the ceiling and the walls, but he quickly realized that the prey he sought wasn't there.

He let power swell inside of him, a power that seemed fueled fully by his rage. It burst out of him in great surges of fire, consuming that house. Leo stared, watching until it burned to the ground around him. Until only ash was left.

Just the way Mora's bar burned.

Mora…

He caught the scent of the fools who'd taken her. Their scents lingered in the air, like a taint on the day. He followed that scent, snaking over deserted roads, staying away from the city, and going toward the woods. A cabin waited out there, a building that was little more than a slanting shack. He stared at that cabin a moment. The men he sought were in there — he knew it with certainty. He'd followed their scent trail, and it had led straight to that location.

The fools. Had they not expected him to follow?

Did they think that because he was the Lord of the Light, he would show mercy?

Not to them. Not to any who hurt her.

He sent the fire out first, letting it lick against the walls of the cabin. He wouldn't bother going inside. The prey he sought would come to him.

And they did. A panther burst from a window, running toward him with great, heaving strides. The beast's mouth was wide open, saliva dripping from its teeth. It surged toward Leo—

He caught the beast around the neck. Held it easily. "You're out of your league," Leo said simply. "And you were a fool to ever touch her."

He tossed the beast aside—and then he let his flames out. The panther didn't charge again.

Two more soon-to-be-dead bastards came from the cabin next. They flew out, bursting from the ramshackle roof. Their wings were fully extended. Did they think they'd get to escape by air?

Leo lifted his arms. Power swirled around him, and the clear sky darkened. A storm—*his* storm—swept through the area in a blink. Wind howled. Lightning crackled. And the two winged bastards were hit by those giant bolts of lightning. They fell back to the ground, their bodies twitching. Jerking.

Leo walked toward them. They were still alive. For the moment. He lifted his hands and he smiled as—

"It feels good, doesn't it?" A mocking voice called from just a few feet away.

I know that voice.

Leo shook his head, even as his gaze cut toward the speaker—the redheaded bastard who'd actually put his hands on Mora. The one who'd wanted to hurt her. The one...

"Killing gives its own rush, doesn't it?" The redhead smiled at him. "I've always thought that the only other thing to compare, well, that's a really good fuck." He took a step toward Leo. "Know what I'm talking about? Oh, wait, you've fucked Fate, you *have* to know—"

Leo was on the guy before he could say another word. Leo drove his claws right into the other man's chest. But the redhead...

Just laughed.

"Feels...good...doesn't it?" His blood pumped out. "Letting...rage loose...killing..."

The world stilled. *His voice.* "It was you."

The man smiled. "R-Reever...name is..."

"Do I look like I fucking care what your name is?" Leo snarled. He jerked his hand up, his claws tearing deeper into the man's chest. "You were the one who hurt her so long ago. The bastard in the hood who snuck into her chambers. I know your voice. I heard it...in her vision."

Reever had blood dripping from his mouth. "W-waited...long time...for this."

The storm raged around them. Lightning plummeted into the earth, again and again, shaking the land. The scent of sulphur filled the air. Leo could feel the bastard's heart beneath his fingers. "You hurt her."

"She was in...your way." Reever didn't look afraid. He looked — *satisfied.* Happy, even as he stared at death. "Lying...always lying...didn't want you to see...what we...knew."

Leo leaned closer to him. "The only thing you know...is death." *She screamed for me.* "You will never threaten her again."

But Reever gave a broken laugh. "You...are...only threat...to her...now."

Fucking bastard. Leo's beast surged forth as his claws ripped into Reever's heart. The change couldn't be stopped. Scales exploded over his body, and bones snapped as Leo transformed. The wind howled around him.

"L-Lord...of...th-the..." Reever's eyes were closing.

The sun was gone. Clouds covered the sky.

Leo dropped Reever's body.

"Dark..." Reever's final gasp.

Leo stumbled back. Then he was hitting the ground, falling onto all fours as the body of a man became a beast. And in moments, a roar filled the air, a roar of stark fury and deep *hate*. A roar that shook the ground as the dragon rose.

And then the beast opened his mouth. He swept fire over the bodies of his enemies. The enemies who'd dared to hurt what was his.

No one will ever threaten her again.

No one.

***

Mora slid out of the shower. She reached for the nearby towel, drying off quickly and raking the towel over her hair. She'd needed the shower because she hadn't been able to stop feeling Leo's hands on her. His touch had seemed to brand her skin. She'd wanted to erase him but…

I still feel him.

She wrapped the towel around her body and crept toward the sink. The mirror above the sink was fogged, cloudy, and her hand lifted. Her palm — still bearing the cut because she'd sliced herself too deeply and she healed too slowly — slid across the smooth surface of that mirror, clearing a space so that she could see —

Leo.

Surrounded by darkness. Surrounded by death. Fire raging.

Her breath caught as she stared at the image before her.

Blood was around him. And the man he'd been...he was a beast, a dragon, with eyes that glowed with red fire.

A tremble shook her body.

Then the image changed.

She lowered her hand.

Twins. One born for the light. One born for the dark.

One day...they would battle.

"Hello, Fate." The deep, drawling voice came from right behind her. As in...*right in that bathroom*. She spun around. A man stood behind her—a man who happened to look *exactly* like Leo. Only she could feel the difference. Her body didn't react to him the same way...

Fear filled her as she stared at his man. Fear, not desire.

"My name's Luke Thorne, and I figured it was time we met, face to face." He smiled at her, and she stared at the face that was the exact same...*Leo's face. Leo's twin.* His gaze raked her. "You've probably heard of me," he added. "I'm the Lord of the Dark."

He was as tall as Leo. His shoulders as broad. But Luke was before her wearing a fancy suit—*in my bathroom!* Leo never wore a suit. He was casual, understated. Like Leo, though, Luke's eyes were gold, deep and gleaming, and a faint stubble of dark beard growth covered his hard jaw.

"Didn't know where you were." Luke inclined his head toward her. "Until my brother rushed out here like he'd just found a pot of gold."

She swallowed. Her hand rose to clutch the towel tighter to her body.

"And, of course," Luke noted darkly. "I knew right away that *you* were that pot of gold."

He was in her house. The paranormal who was supposed to be the baddest threat out there. *Right in front of me.* Steam drifted lazily around them, a left-over by-product of her shower.

"Where *is* my brother?" Luke asked when she just gaped at him. "To be honest, I expected to find him glued to your side."

Mora licked her lips. "I think he's killing right now."

Luke blinked. And then he lunged forward. She backed up, fast, and her hips slammed into the sink. His hands came down on either side of her, curving tightly around the sink's edge, but never touching her.

"And just *who* is my sainted brother killing?" Luke's face had gone cold and hard. She could feel his power vibrating in the air around her.

It was so strange, to stare into his eyes. To stare into eyes exactly like Leo's and see a different man gazing back at her. With Leo, she'd always felt the pull of their attraction. A physical response that had always drawn her to him.

She felt no attraction to Luke. She just felt like...*I'm in serious trouble.*

"You don't want me for an enemy," Luke drawled. "I'm trying to be a nice guy here. But I need to find my brother. Time's up for him."

"No, it's not," she said. Her chin lifted. "And I already have your brother for an enemy, so why not add you to the list, too?"

His eyes became slits. "I don't think that's what you are to Leo. Enemy isn't the word I'd use."

He was too close. She needed him *gone.* "What word would you choose?"

His hand lifted. His fingers hovered over her cheek.

"Lover," he said, nodding slightly.

Not in a very long time.

"Obsession," Luke decided, seeming to consider things. His fingers weren't touching her cheek, not yet, but he was close. "Weakness—"

A growl broke the air.

And then a strong, tanned hand was grabbing Luke's wrist. "*Mora doesn't like to be touched.*"

Leo. Leo's snarling voice. Leo...*standing in the bathroom doorway.*

Was the place just wide open to everyone?

Luke gave a rumbling laugh. "Ah, see, I was right. *Obsession.* I figured you had to be close. Not like you'd just wander away after having lost her for so many years."

Mora turned her head and her gaze slid over Leo's face.

Something is different.

A wild edge seemed to cover him. His smile was a little cruel. His eyes glinted with a power that seemed dangerous. His hair was tousled. He didn't even have on a shirt, just a pair of jeans that clung low on his hips. His arms bulged with muscles, his chest appeared bigger than before and —

"I can't believe Fate lied to me." Luke's face reflected mock shock. "She stared me right in the eyes and said that you were out killing. Like I was supposed to buy —"

Leo shoved his brother aside. "She doesn't have on clothes."

"No, she doesn't." Luke nodded. "Very astute of you to notice."

Leo growled. Then he waved his hand toward Mora. Instantly, she was dressed. Covered in a soft t-shirt and jeans. Her wet hair slid over her shoulders. Leo caught her hand and pulled her from the bathroom. He didn't speak, just double-timed it down the narrow hallway and into her kitchen. The shattered pieces of the mirror were still on the floor.

Luke appeared in front of them. Just—bam. He was there. "You had your turn with Fate." He smirked at Leo. "Now I want a go at her."

What the hell? Like she was some toy to be passed between them? "You're as insane as Leo is!"

Luke blinked.

Mora jerked her hand from Leo's grasp. "You both need to get something straight. I'm not in this war. I don't have a side. And you two—you *won't* use me."

Leo turned toward her. His breath came in rough pants.

Something is way wrong. Her shoulders stiffened. "Leo?"

"They're dead." His voice was different. Rougher. More guttural. "They'll never hurt you again."

Luke inhaled. "Is that blood I smell?" He edged closer to his twin. "Blood on your hands?" He tsked. "Didn't think you liked to get your hands dirty, much less bloody—"

Leo's hands flew out and fisted in Luke's shirt. "You don't know me."

Luke just laughed as Mora glanced worriedly between the two men. "Of course, I know you," Luke announced with a dramatic sigh. "I know you better than you know yourself. I'm your mirror, remember? The broken one."

But as she stared at them, Mora couldn't help but think that Leo was the one who appeared to be broken.

Goosebumps rose on her arms and she pushed her way past those men. She needed to get away from them. They were dominating the space of her home.

"Speaking of broken mirrors…" Luke's voice followed her. It was hard to say exactly how she knew it was his voice. He did sound so very much like Leo, only *Leo's voice sinks beneath my skin. My body reacts when he talks. It's primal.*

Luke's voice was deep and dark and rumbling, but…*I know he's not Leo.* Just as she'd known, with one glance in the bathroom, that she was staring at Leo's twin, and not him.

"Did you scry for my brother?" Luke asked.

Mora stilled. She glanced over her shoulder and saw that he'd picked up a chunk of broken glass.

"I've got a witch who's pretty good at scrying." Luke rubbed the mirror piece with his fingertips. "Cordelia can see all kinds of things. For example, she swore that she saw my dear brother going on a rampage. *For you.*"

Her head jerked in an instinctive denial, but Mora's gaze flew to Leo. He stood there, with his hands clenched and his eyes wild, and she could almost see the shadow of wings behind him. "I saw…" Mora whispered.

Leo stared at her.

"You," she finished softly, her voice little more than a rasp. When she'd put her hand to the mirror in her bathroom...*Oh, damn, it was real. I still had the cut on my hand and when I put our hands together earlier to show him the past, our blood mixed...*

Leo flinched. Then he lunged toward her. Once more, Leo grabbed her. "It was the same fucking bastard. That redhead? He called himself Reever. He was the one who chained you in his basement—"

"My, you two have been busy," Luke said, his voice amused.

"*Fuck off,*" Leo snarled without glancing at him. His eyes were on Mora. His hands locked around her wrists. "He was the same hooded freak from your past. The one you showed me? It was him. I recognized his voice, and he *confessed* to me. He was taunting me with what he'd done." Leo's breath heaved out. "How could I let him live? After what he'd done to you? He'd come after you *twice*. He'd hurt you." Leo shook his head, hard. "No one can do that. I won't let *anyone* ever hurt you again. No matter what I have to do."

The drumming of her heartbeat filled her ears. The man in the hood...the man whose identity had always been hidden from her, no matter how hard she tried to see him…he was dead?

"They're all dead," Leo told her. He wasn't holding her too tightly any longer. His fingers had begun to carefully stroke the inside of her wrists. "You have nothing to fear."

"Wouldn't be too sure about that," Luke muttered. "I think she has plenty to fear."

And she saw a change sweep over Leo's face. It was slow…a stiffening. A hardening of his eyes. A chill that swept into his gaze. Steely determination.

A wisp of sadness darkened his stare, but that emotion vanished as he blinked. Then Leo inclined his head toward her. "Stay behind me, Mora."

What?

He turned to face his brother. "You think you'll hurt Mora?"

"I *think* she needs to be afraid. She's Fate, right? She knows what's coming…why else has she hidden all this time? Trying to avoid the inevitable." Luke gave a rough laugh. "But you can't hide forever. And I want my turn to see what the future holds." He advanced.

But Leo's hand flew out and flattened on Luke's chest. "You don't touch Mora."

"*Fate.*" Luke growled that title. "She's Fate. And I want to know what she's been holding back. Hardly fair that you've had the advantage with her. But then, you fucked your way into her good graces, didn't you? Such a bad thing…for the *good* twin to do."

Mora backed up a step. She didn't want to be in their war. The temperature in the room was heating up. Those two were about to erupt. She knew what beasts lurked in their hearts.

Dragons. Twin dragons.

If they shifted in her house, they'd destroy everything around them. *Maybe even me.*

She risked another step back. While they were focused on each other, she could rush out the front door. She could jump on the motorcycle that still waited outside and slip away.

Leo will come after me.

Maybe. But not if he was dead, not if he was killed in the battle that had been promised so long ago.

"You fucked her," Luke continued and it was as if he were deliberately baiting Leo, trying to push him to the edge, "and then you left her. You—"

Leo's hand flew out as he drove his fist into Luke's jaw. The blow was so powerful that Luke flew into the air and slammed into her wall. He left a giant, gaping hole there on impact.

"No!" Mora screamed. "You're going to wreck my house."

Leo's head snapped toward her.

Shit. Should have kept my mouth shut and ran when I had the chance.

"I wasn't using you," Leo said. The words sounded like a promise.

Her lips parted.

But Luke's laughter filled her home. He brushed chunks of plaster off his shoulders and rose to his feet. "Of course, he was. You think the Lord of the Light has some undying love for you, *Fate?* He wanted you to change the future." He rolled back his shoulders and flames began to dance above his hands. "He wanted to save his ass because he knew this battle was coming. He knew we'd be fighting to the death. He wanted to see the best way to defeat me."

Leo stormed toward him. "You will not hurt her!"

"I'm going to do anything I want with her," Luke threw back. *He's definitely taunting Leo. Trying to push him over the edge.* "Just like you did. Only maybe I won't leave her as broken as you did. Oh, yes, I heard the stories. You think the tales didn't reach me? How her bones were twisted, how the fire consumed her—"

Leo let out a roar. He grabbed for his brother.

"Stop!" Mora shouted. Then she was racing toward Leo. She didn't wait for him to respond to her. She grabbed his shoulders. "Stop *now!*"

He looked at her. "Mora…it's not safe. Get back!"

Instead, she got right between them. Her breath heaved from her as she put one hand on Leo's chest and one hand on Luke's chest. "You will *not* fight here."

Power rushed through her, seeming to come from each brother. She had her hands over their hearts and —

Oh, no. No! Mora screamed because visions were hitting her, tumbling through her mind, one right after the other. Visions of life and death. Of pain and hope. Visions of two brothers.

Visions that showed her just how wrong she'd been.

The world went dark. So very, very dark.

CHAPTER EIGHT

Mora's eyes had gone absolutely black. Her hand seemed to burn a brand into Leo's chest and her whole body was bow tight.

"Lord of the Light, Lord of the Dark." Her voice was low, husky, and oddly distant. As if she were speaking through a tunnel when she was right there. *"Lord of the Light, Lord of the Dark…"*

"So is this shit normal?" Luke asked, voice gruff. "Does your girlfriend do this often?"

Mora's head tipped back as she screamed — over and over again. Her body jerked as if she were getting shocked, charged up with electricity or —

Power. "She's a fucking conduit!"

"What?" Luke snapped.

Leo didn't explain. Mora was touching him *and* his brother, and power was pulsing through her body, again and again. He locked his arms around her, yanking Mora away from Luke, and the minute she stopped touching his brother, her body stilled. Her screams stopped.

She sagged in Leo's arms, unconscious.

"What in the hell was that?" Luke demanded.

Leo held Mora carefully, his worried gaze on her face. She was still breathing. But…

"That happen a lot to Fate?" Luke pushed, his voice curt.

"Mora," he gritted out as he stalked toward the couch. Very carefully, he put her on the sofa, then he crouched at her side. "She has a name that she uses. She's not a thing. She doesn't like to be called Fate. She's Mora."

"Right. Mental note." Luke stood on the other side of the sofa, and his glare was on Leo. "We're not done, you and I."

Leo's hand was on Mora's wrist as he checked her pulse. *Too fast.* "I don't have time for you right now. She matters more."

Silence.

It took a moment for Leo's words to register in his own mind. *She matters more.* When they did register, he looked at up his twin.

Luke stared at him as if he'd never seen Leo before in his very long life. "You were fighting me…" Luke spoke haltingly. "Because of her?"

They needed to be clear on this. Leo smoothed back Mora's hair and then he rose. "I just killed for her." His gaze held Luke's. "No one hurts her. No one uses her."

Luke's chin notched up. "Not even *you*, brother?"

Leo took that hit. "Not even me." He wouldn't be asking her to scry again for him. He wouldn't be asking her for anything. She'd already paid far too much for him.

So it's time for me to pay her back. Time for me to make up for all that she has lost.

"We both know the end is coming." Leo gave his brother a cold smile. "You can only put off the inevitable for so long." He went right back to holding Mora's wrist. His fingers pressed to her pulse. He just…he needed to feel her. She soothed the beast within him. The one who'd been moments away from erupting and attacking Luke. "But our battle will not be here. And she will *not* be caught in the middle."

Luke's gaze fell to Mora. A muscle jerked in his jaw. "Fate can be cruel."

"You *won't* touch her. Or I will destroy everything that you value."

Immediately, Luke's head snapped up. His eyes had gone cold and dark. "Tread carefully, *brother*. You don't want to threaten what I hold dear."

"Then you don't fucking threaten what matters to me. You don't attack her. You don't get anywhere near her." His touch was still light on Mora's wrist. Her pulse was steadying. He glared at his brother. "You fell in love. The big, bad, Lord of the Dark. You fell for one of *my* paranormal creatures. A creature of the light. And I let you keep her."

Luke growled at him. *"Let…?"*

"What I gave…" Leo's eyes narrowed. "I can take."

This time, Luke was the one to grab him. "You *dare* to threaten my mate?"

"And you *dare…*" Leo tossed right back. "To threaten mine?"

Luke's mouth parted in surprise.

"We'll have our battle," Leo promised him. "But it won't be here."

"L-Leo…?" Mora called, her voice slurred.

"I'm right here, love." He turned his back on his brother. *Because the choice has been made.* He'd spent so long trying to figure out how to stop the coming battle with Luke, how to save his twin, but…

Mora will not be the price I pay for Luke's life. She'd suffered enough. There would be no more pain for her. He brought Mora's hand to his mouth and pressed a kiss to her knuckles. "You're okay. You're safe."

He would do everything within his power to always keep her safe.

He felt the rush of wind behind him, and then Mora's front door slammed shut. He glanced over his shoulder. Luke was gone.

For now.

But Leo knew his brother would be back. Their time was almost up. There was no way out, not for either of them.

Mora's eyes fluttered open. Confusion clouded her stare as she looked at him. Then...she smiled. "There you are."

His heart jerked in his chest. The way Mora was looking at him...

It's the way she stared at me so long ago.

"I knew you'd be here when I woke up." Her eyes were filled with so much...*love?* No, no, couldn't be. But she stared at him as if he were the most important person in her world, and her face had gone soft and tender. "Isn't it funny...but I think I even missed you while I was dreaming."

It wasn't funny at all. He swallowed. "I...missed you." More truthful words had probably never been spoken by him. Every single day without her had been like acid eating away at his insides.

She's confused. I freaking charged her up with my power — and she got hit with Luke's. She doesn't understand what happened. I need to back away.

He needed to do the right thing with her. "You should relax a few moments." He rose to his feet and his hand slid away from her. "You got hit with too much power—"

Her hand grabbed his. "Don't leave me."

Fuck. So this is hell. Always wondered what it was like.

"I dreamed that you left me. And I was cold and I hurt, and I just wanted you back."

Move. Away. He cleared his throat. "You…you took the brunt of some powerful magic a few minutes ago. Just…do you want me to put you in your bed? So you can rest?"

"Yes." Her voice was husky and sexy and it slid right over his body. "Put me in bed."

He swallowed. Twice. Then he bent and picked her up in his arms. For a moment, he just inhaled her sweet scent. She smelled good and fresh. Like flowers. She'd always smelled that way. Her body was soft and warm, and she just seemed to fit perfectly against him.

One of her arms wound around his neck.

He started walking toward her bedroom.

Mora pressed a kiss to his throat.

Shit.

"I've always loved the way you taste," she whispered, and Leo felt the lick of her tongue on his skin. "Do you like the way I taste?"

He was at the door of her bedroom. "Baby, I *love* the way you taste."

She gave a soft laugh. Then she lightly nipped his neck. His cock jerked as arousal flooded through him.

He hurried into her room. He lowered her onto the bed and started to step back, but her arm was still around his neck.

"Aren't you going to kiss me?" Mora asked him.

He wanted her mouth more than he wanted a breath. Through clenched teeth, he gritted out, "Do you know where you are?"

She licked his lower lip. "Of course, I'm with you."

Every muscle in his body tensed. The things she could do with her little pink tongue...*Focus.* "Baby, do you know *when* you are?"

She eased back a little, staring up at him with a furrow between her eyes. He wanted to put his hands on her. *All* over her. But instead, he grabbed the wooden headboard behind her. Leo caged her between the bed and his body as he waited, knowing that his time was running out.

She's going to stop looking at me as if I'm the only man she's ever wanted.

Maybe he should kiss her. Get one last taste. A memory to see him through the darkness that was coming.

She deserves more. He'd wronged her enough.

And he could see it happen. The memories came flooding back to her. The cloud of confusion left as her eyes widened. Her lips parted, and she seemed to pale.

"I know..." Her voice was a rasp. "*When.*"

She knew him. She knew all he'd done. Leo could see it in her eyes. So he gave a grim nod. "Luke is gone. You don't have to worry about him. I'll take care of my brother." His hands lifted from the headboard. "Good-bye, Mora." He turned away.

But she pulled him right back with one word. "*No.*"

He glanced at her.

Mora's eyes were blazing. The tender emotion from before was long gone. And in its place, was that desperation? Fear?

I can't let her be afraid. I won't.

He cupped her delicate jaw. "You'll be protected, I swear it. The Lord of the Dark will never touch you."

Her lips trembled. Her eyes swam with— *dammit, with tears.* "You are wrong," she told him with a twisted smile. "So wrong."

Alarm knifed through him. "Mora?"

"Kiss me."

Those were the last words he'd expected. He thought she'd want to throw his ass out. He thought—

"Maybe it won't be the same. Maybe you're different." There seemed to be a stark hope in her voice.

Did she think that she wouldn't desire him any longer? That the wild need that had always burned so hot and fiercely between them would be gone now? That they'd be free of the primal connection?

Leo knew the truth...*I'll never be free.* The woman before him had haunted his dreams for centuries. He'd reached for her, time and time again, only to find an empty bed. And if she wanted him to kiss her, if she was asking for his mouth...

She sure as hell didn't need to ask twice.

But he didn't take like the starving man he was. Instead of falling on her in desperation, his head slowly lowered toward hers. He was giving Mora the chance to turn away. Giving her the option to refuse him.

She didn't. She leaned toward him. She parted her lips.

His mouth pressed to hers. Softly. Carefully. He wanted to seduce. He wanted to tempt. He wanted her back. His tongue slid over her full lower lip, and then he lightly nipped that lip, before sucking it gently with his mouth.

Her gasp filled his ears, and her hands curled around his shoulders.

His tongue thrust into her mouth. So sweet. He'd always felt as if he got a little drunk off Mora's kiss. He'd come to crave her taste. She was his wine. The kiss became rougher as the lust he'd held in check pushed past his control.

Mora.
Mine.

His hand slid to curve around her hip. He eased onto the bed, closing in on her. He was fighting to stay gentle, because he *needed* her to want him. He needed her desire. This wasn't a dream. Mora was real. She was beneath his hands. She was—

Kissing him back.

Her tongue moved lightly against his, driving up the fever of his arousal. Her lips parted even more, and she gave that sexy little moan that he remembered so well. Her moan stroked right over him, cracking his control.

He wanted to strip her. He could have her clothes gone in a blink. He could have his jeans off with a wave of his hand. Then he'd be on the bed with her. He'd push apart her thighs and drive deep inside of her. Her nails would rake over his back. He'd plunge into her, again and again, not stopping until she *knew* that she belonged only to him. Mora would cry out her pleasure. She'd buck up against him and ask for more. Always, more. He'd never get his fill of her. He'd make sure she was as addicted as he was. She wouldn't ever get away again. He wouldn't lose her, he—

No.

Leo pulled away from Mora. He stood at the side of the bed, his hands clenched into fists, his breath heaving. Her eyelashes slowly lifted and she stared up at him, not speaking, but her breath was rasping out in the same rough rhythm that his was. She lifted a hand and touched trembling fingertips to her lips. Her lips were red and wet from his kiss, slightly swollen. Her cheeks were flushed, and he could see the desire in her eyes.

He knew she had to see the savage need stamped on his face.

"Leo?"

He forced his teeth to unclench. "I'm going to make everything better for you."

Her head cocked.

"I can make it right. I *can* do something good." He forced himself to smile at her. "After all, I'm the Lord of the Light. I swear, I've done more than just wreck the world. I know it doesn't look that way, but just give me a chance. I can prove myself to you." He needed that chance with her.

Her hand slid away from her lips. "I didn't ask you to stop."

He had to take a quick step away from the bed. It was either step away — or grab her again. "I need to take care of some things." His control was about to shatter. He had to get away from Mora before that happened. His need had been denied too long. He had to tread carefully — *very* carefully with her.

"You're leaving." She didn't move from her position on the bed.

"You should rest. Not many paranormals could recover from that kind of power blast."

"I'm not like the others."

No, she'd always been different. Not light or dark, not good or bad. She'd always just been...*the one I wanted most.* "I wish I could change the past." He hadn't meant to let those words slip out, but they were the truth. Brutal and savage. "I'd give my life to take away your pain."

Her eyes widened and she leapt from the bed. Mora grabbed his arms and held tight. "*Don't* say that."

Why not? It was the truth.

"Never offer a life, not when you're standing in front of Fate." She licked her lips. He wondered if she could still taste him. He could still taste her. "You don't...you don't fully understand how my power works." Her words came fast. "There are some things that I can't control. Some things that just happen."

His hand lifted and curled under her chin. On this, he wanted to be clear, and he didn't need any warning. "I would give my life to take away your pain."

She stared at him as if he were a stranger. As if she wasn't the lover who knew him better than any other. "Leo?"

He wanted to kiss her again. Because he wanted it so badly, he stepped back. "Let me into your life again."

"I-I don't understand."

"For the time we have, let me in. Let me have the chance to show you that I'm not the monster you think."

She caught her lower lip between her teeth. He had the feeling she was trying to stop herself from speaking.

Maybe that meant…she was going to give him a chance? *I have to work harder. I have to show her that she can count on me.*

"I'll be back soon," Leo promised her.

Her lashes lowered. "Where are you going?"

Once again, he told her, "There are some— some things I need to take care of." *My brother being the main damn thing.* He knew Luke had to be lurking close by. But there was more that Leo needed to do, for Mora. He'd already taken so much from her. It was time he gave back. He turned away, before he gave into the need that pulsed just beneath his skin. Did she understand how badly he wanted her?

No, if she did, she wouldn't let me so close.

He was nearly at her bedroom door.

"I saw what you did."

Her words stopped him.

"I-I didn't mean to scry. I wasn't trying to see you, I swear." Her words were low. "But our blood had mixed, and I touched a mirror, not even thinking. The image came to me, and I saw what you did to those men."

His hand rose and gripped the door frame. "They had it coming."

"Leo?"

He looked back at her. She stood next to the bed. "When they hurt you, they signed their own death warrants. If I'd known the truth sooner…" And the fact that it had been *hidden* from him for so long infuriated him. Rage grew inside of Leo, but he held it back. There was only one being who could have shielded those bastards for all those centuries. *Only one.* "They would have received their retribution sooner."

She wrapped her arms around her stomach. "Punishment."

Exactly.

"But you were supposed to be the one who protected."

"And I will protect you. *Always.* I will never let you down again." His words were a vow. Did she understand that? He would never put another before her again. In the time that Leo had left in the world, Mora would know that she mattered.

That she'd always mattered.

She didn't call out to him again, and he walked out of her house.

***

Mora didn't move, not until she heard the soft *snick* of her front door closing. Then she rocked forward onto her feet.

This is bad.

A shiver slid over her body. She could still feel Leo against her skin. Against her mouth.

So very bad.

Mora rushed out of her bedroom. She hurried down the narrow hallway and then burst into her den. She flipped the lock on her door, wanting that small bit of security in a world gone absolutely, positively mad.

What was she supposed to do? How was she supposed to stop the train wreck that was coming her way?

And—the question that had her insides shredding—*how* could she save Leo?

I can't. He's already gone too far.

CHAPTER NINE

Luke Thorne never had a hard time finding trouble. Usually, trouble found him. So when the sun set—because he preferred the dark—it wasn't hard to find his way to the dive with the unexciting name of Sammy's Place. Music blared from the old speakers, drinks poured freely, and plenty of gruff voices filled the air.

Luke sidled up to the bar. The bartender glanced his way, raising a brow. "What you need?"

"Tell me that you have some decent whiskey in this place." Luke's fingers drummed on the bar top.

The bartender shook his head. "Not even close."

Figured. "Then give me whatever crap you've got." He sat on the stool, then turned his back on the bar, the better to study the humans around him. A few were clustered around a door marked PRIVATE, and those few had the big, bruising look of hired muscle. They glared whenever anyone got too close.

They glared and one even flashed fang.

Interesting. Luke slanted a quick glance back at the bartender.

The bartender grunted as he pushed a drink toward Luke. "Here's your poison."

"You have no idea," Luke murmured. He downed the drink in one gulp and slammed down his glass. *You didn't savor cheap whiskey. You knocked it back.* "You were right. It was shit."

The bartender grunted.

Luke tossed him some money. Curious now, because he wondered just what — or who — the fanged thug was guarding, Luke sauntered toward the fellow. With every step that he took, the guards in front of that PRIVATE door seemed to tense more.

You should tense. I've had a bad day, and I'm about to take out my pound of flesh on the nearest fools I can find.

From behind the door, he heard a faint, pain-filled moan. Then a thud. Another thud… Sounded like a fist connecting with someone's face.

"You need to keep walking, buddy." One of the bruisers stepped into Luke's path. "This ain't your business."

Luke swept his gaze over the fellow. About six feet, with tree-trunk-like arms. Obviously, someone liked to work out. "You'd be surprised at the things that are my business."

Another faint moan reached his ears.

Too interesting to pass up. He was getting into that room. Luke narrowed his eyes on the human before him. "Get out of my way."

The human's eyes seemed to glaze. "Yes, sir." He immediately stepped to the side.

But the guy with the fangs — the guy who didn't even seem a little hesitant to be flashing his too sharp teeth with humans all around — immediately got in Luke's way. "You don't want me to hurt you." The guy's words were a growl.

Luke's gaze swept over him. This fellow had to be around six foot three, and he was built along thick, stocky lines. His shaggy hair and his eyes were brown. Three scars slid across his upper right cheek — the guard must have received those scars when he was very young. *Because I know this fellow's a shifter, and shifters usually heal better than that.* Conspiratorially, Luke leaned toward the guy. "Bear." He smiled. "You have to be a bear, right? I'm usually great at calling these things."

The bear shifter's muddy eyes spat fury at him.

"Run along." Luke motioned vaguely with his hand. "You're in my way."

The bear shouted back, "Fuck you, bastard!" Then the fool had the absolute audacity to put his hands on Luke.

Your mistake.

Luke caught the guy and sent him hurtling in the air. The bear shifter crashed into the bar, and the music just kept right on playing. Luke rolled his shoulders. "I'm feeling a little better now." He kicked in the door. Nothing was PRIVATE when he was near. And, as soon as that door was out of Luke's way...

He saw that his suspicions had been dead on. Sure enough, someone was getting the shit beat out of himself in there. A man with dark hair and a swollen, bloody face was tied to a chair in the middle of the room. Luke rolled back his shoulders and called, "What fun do we have here?"

The man who'd been beating the poor bastard in the chair spun toward him. His hand was bruised all along his knuckles—yeah, that happened when you used your fist as a battering ram. The guy's head was completely shaved, and a gold hoop hung in his ear lobe. "Who the fuck are you?"

"I'm someone who was bored and in the mood for a fight." Serious understatement. "May I ask, why are you beating the hell out of that fellow?"

"Angus! Braun!" Veins bulged as the fellow shouted for his crew. "Eliminate this joker!"

No one rushed in at the guy's command. Luke gave a little laugh. "Sorry, I think I've already *eliminated* your guards. They won't be running to the rescue." Luke sauntered forward.

"This is *my* place!" Spittle flew from the screaming man's mouth. "You can't just—"

"Oh, so you're Sammy?" Luke nodded and tapped his chin with one finger. "Got to tell you, your whiskey selection sucks. If you expect me to keep visiting, you must do better."

Sammy swung at him. The guy's fist thudded into Luke's jaw. Luke didn't move. But Sammy sure did start screaming.

"My hand! You broke my fucking hand!"

"That's what happens when you hit steel." Luke shrugged, unconcerned. "Oh, yeah, and it's my turn." He drew back his fist and drove it straight into Sammy's face. He cold-cocked the guy with one punch. Too easy. "Had to be a human," Luke said as he studied the fallen man. "I wanted more of a fight." Oh, well. He turned for the door. The fight had ended far too soon. He'd have to find another battle.

The battle with my twin is waiting. Our time is up.

"W-wait...L-Leo..."

Luke's shoulders stiffened. "What in the hell did you just call me?" He spun to glare at the bound man.

The fellow's lips were busted and bloody. "L-Leo...I know...y-you're Mora's f-friend."

Luke's head cocked. "Is that what I am to Mora?"

"N-need…help…"

"Yes, you quite obviously do." Luke motioned to the unconscious man in the room. "Sammy will wake eventually and probably start beating you again. But getting involved in human affairs isn't typically my thing." Still, he found himself stalking closer to the injured man. Luke's nostrils flared as he scented all of the blood soaking the guy. "Interesting." Now he was even more curious. His curiosity had always been a weakness. "Your blood…it's not *fully* human. What exactly are you?"

"DEA," the injured man gasped.

Luke frowned. "That's not a type of paranormal."

"D-Drug Enforcement…A-A—"

"Oh, right. That has nothing to do with me. And I still don't get why you think Leo—um, why you think *I*—would help you."

"Y-you took my m-motor…cycle. Y-you…owe me."

"Not likely." He should walk away, but something about the fellow was nagging at him. "How well do you know Mora? Are you her *friend?*" Perhaps he could use this DEA person.

"Th-thought so…" He strained, trying to break out of his ropes, but he just bled more. "Sh-

she tried to...w-warn me...sh-should have trusted...her."

Now Luke hurried toward the man who'd just become the most interesting human ever. *Semi-human?* Luke crouched down so he could be on eye level with the bleeder. "Mora told you—she *told* you about your future? She told you what was coming?"

"Yes...she was w-waring me...s-see that now...trying to ch-change things..."

That interfering little trickster. If Mora had intervened with a human's life—or semi-human's life—then what would she do for a powerhouse paranormal? Especially one she'd been fucking?

Oh, Leo. The game is hardly fair between us. Not when you've been stacking the odds in your favor.

"Tell you what..." Luke grabbed the ropes and ripped them apart with one tug. "I'll save your bloody self, and then you can owe *me*. Got it? I'll be your new boss, not the DEA."

He waited for the fellow to nod. Instead, the guy just slid out of his chair and hit the floor. Typical. Sighing, Luke bent and scooped him up. He threw his "friend" over his shoulder and sauntered out. The humans were still dancing and drinking. They barely even glanced his way, and a few moments later, he was outside, free and clear. He glanced around the lot, trying to decide which vehicle he'd steal. He settled on a pick-up truck. Luke dumped his new protégé in the back and headed for the driver's side. He—

"You wanted Mora dead."

Right on time. He'd just started to have fun, so it only stood to reason that Leo would be appearing now. And, sure enough, that was his twin storming around the front of the truck and marching up to Luke. Luke wrenched open the door—

"What the fuck are you doing?" Leo slammed the door shut in the next breath. "You have freaking wings! Since when do you drive a pick-up truck?"

Since he hadn't wanted to scare the human—semi-human—shitless by having the guy wake mid-flight. But Luke didn't bother to explain himself. He never did…well, not unless he was talking to his mate, Mina.

So instead of answering Leo, Luke swept his gaze over his brother. "Shouldn't you be seducing Fate again? Trying to convince her that you're her one true love?"

Leo grabbed him and shoved Luke up against the side of the truck. "I *killed* them."

"You'll need to be more specific. I'm sure you've killed a lot of people." Luke smiled. "And how does that work out for you? I mean, you're supposed to be so *good*. Yet death follows you like a shadow."

Leo growled.

Luke just kept smiling. He knew his smile always infuriated his brother. So strange, once upon a very long time ago, they'd been the closest confidants. Best friends. And then a prophecy had torn everything apart.

One brother will kill another.
And the world will fall.

"You sent those bastards after Mora," Leo accused furiously. "They were *dark*. Just like you. Did you think I wouldn't ever find them? Did you think I wouldn't find out the truth?"

"I think I have no idea what you're rambling about. So why don't you try explaining yourself, *clearly.*" *Before I lose my patience and let my claws fly.*

Leo lifted his hand — and then he drove his fist into the side of the truck. Again and again and again. A deep dent appeared beneath his blows.

Luke watched him, frowning. This was...unlike Leo. A wild tension gripped his brother, something that Luke had never seen. "Leo?"

Leo's fist stilled. "They hurt her. I-I didn't know...I swear, I didn't. I would have gone back to her immediately. But they hurt her. Tossed her from the window. Broke her bones. Put *fire* to her skin. And they said I'd sent them." His eyes burned bright red.

Okay, what in the hell is up with that? Since when did Leo's eyes turn red?

"She ran from me. Ran and stayed hidden because she thought I'd done that to her...but it was you." Leo stared at Luke with hate stamped on his face. "You sent those bastards after her again, didn't you? Last night? But I was there. I'd found her, and I stopped them."

"Leo..." Luke began carefully. "I'm really not sure what you're talking about."

"*The dead paranormals that I left near the shack! The dark ones!*" He grabbed Luke's shoulders and shook him. "I know you sent them! You hurt her! Dammit, I didn't want the end to be this way! I was trying — all these fucking years *trying* — to find a way out for us! I didn't want to kill you. I didn't want to ever attack my own brother!"

Luke couldn't speak. For once, someone had caught him truly by surprise.

"But you went after her." Leo's teeth had become fangs. "You hurt *her.* And now I don't have a choice." Leo's claws dug into Luke's shoulders. "I'm going to kill you."

He'd always known this moment would come. But... "I swear to you, I didn't send anyone after Fate. I have *never* sent anyone after her."

Leo's gaze just burned brighter. "The paranormals who hurt her weren't mine. They were *dark. They were yours.*"

"Then they weren't acting under my orders. Even you know we don't get total power over every being that's supposed to bow down to us." A jeep careened into the lot. Luke ignored it—and the humans around him. "Take me to these paranormals. I'll question them myself. I'll get answers."

Leo's laughter was mocking. "Told you, I killed them. Nothing left but ash because *they hurt her.*"

"Show me," Luke demanded. Something wasn't adding up for him. Something just felt *off.* "Show me where you killed them. Take me there now." The human in the back of the truck would just have to wait.

He had more important matters to deal with right then. End-of-the-world matters.

Leo nodded grimly, but his eyes still blazed blood-red.

***

Mora's hands were tight around the motorcycle's handle bars. She eased into the lot, and the bike spat gravel from beneath the tires.

Sammy's Place. When darkness had fallen and there had been no sign of Leo's return, she'd realized that she couldn't just sit and twiddle her thumbs forever.

She was Fate. And she had work to do.

She'd tried to deny who she was for so long. She'd been so afraid of using her powers and getting more pain or heartache as a result but...

Maybe things can be different. Maybe.

So she'd come to Sammy's Place because...she had a bike to return. And a man to save.

She braked the motorcycle near the back of the bar, and yeah, she felt a flare of envy as she stared at the building. Sammy Long was a criminal to his core, a killer, a drug dealer. And *he* got to keep his bar while her place burned?

Fate...

She slid off the bike. If her visions had been right—and they were, she knew it—tonight was the end for Dax. He'd die in that bar. Get beaten to death. Then Sammy's goons would dismember him. In her vision, she'd seen a guy with claws tearing Dax limb from limb. *Sammy has a shifter in his stable of guards.* She'd tried to warn Dax. That hadn't worked so well.

So now she'd come to save his hide.

I have to do something. I'm tired of the world just passing by. I want to change the end for Dax.

Because if she could change Dax's fate, if she could give him a different ending, then maybe, just maybe, there was hope that Leo could have a different ending, too.

She headed briskly for the front door. She wouldn't look like much of a threat. A pretty face would fool the idiots in her way. She'd get inside, find Dax and then—

A groan reached her ears. A very pain-filled groan. She stopped and turned around, her gaze sweeping over the lot.

The groan came again. Her head jerked at the sound.

"*H-help…*"

She bounded toward the plea. The whisper had come from the back of a battered pick-up truck. Like, seriously, it looked as if something had pounded the hell out of the side of that truck. A deep dent was on the driver's side. The whispered plea had been so faint that she knew humans hadn't heard it. But her paranormal hearing had picked up on the cry.

She grabbed the side of the truck and peered into the bed. Her jaw dropped. "Dax?"

"M-Mora…help…"

He was bleeding like a stuck pig. She heaved herself into the back of the truck and put her hands on his wounds, trying to stop the flow of blood. He'd been beaten—that was clear in his broken and twisted nose and in all the bruises that covered his face. But he'd been stabbed, too. Or…

Were those claw marks on him? Did Sammy let his shifter get started early with his cuts?

"L-Leo…saved…me…"

What? Her eyes widened. But then she shook her head. "You aren't safe yet. You're lying in a pool of your own blood, and if we don't get you help soon, you *will* die." She had zero healing powers, so she couldn't miraculously save him with a wave of her hand. Angels could heal — they kind of excelled at that thing, but she couldn't summon one down to her. That was more Leo's thing.

Maybe that's where he is. Maybe he went to get an angel.

But…

Dax started jerking beneath her touch.

"I'm getting you to a hospital!" Mora cried out. "Just — don't die yet, okay? I really, really need you to live." Then she jumped out of that truck bed. She wrenched open the driver's side door and fumbled around inside, searching for keys.

No helpful driver had left keys behind.

So she hot-wired the truck. After all, she owned — or *had* owned — a bar. And she'd met her share of interesting clientele over the years. One woman in particular had spent some time teaching Mora some handy tricks, like hot-wiring. And money laundering and…

The truck revved to life. Mora shifted to reverse, and the truck flew backward with a heaving groan. Then she shifted hard into drive. They raced out of the graveled parking lot, careening a bit too much as they headed for the highway. Mora rolled down her window as she kept one hand on the wheel. "Stay alive back there!" she yelled at Dax. "You have to stay alive!"

Because if he lived...if he made it through the night...

Fate can change.

CHAPTER TEN

"Nothing's here." Luke paced toward the small cabin — one that bore the black marks of flames on its wood. "Where are the bodies?"

The scent of ash still lingered in the air. "I burned them."

Luke glanced back at him with raised brows.

"I shifted fully." He rarely did that. Leo didn't like it when the beast took over so completely. When that happened, things got...bad.

For everyone.

Leo cleared his throat. "You know how hot the fire burns when it comes straight from the dragon."

Luke looked worried. A very unusual occurrence. Also, probably something the guy was just faking. But Luke strode toward him with narrowed eyes and a heaving chest. His hands were clenched at his sides. "You don't let your beast out — and you *never* let him burn your enemies until they're only ash."

Leo gave a bitter laugh. "I *saw* what they did to her." Not everything, but enough to push him over the edge. "And they tried to take her from me again a second time. I wasn't going to let them just walk away to threaten her again. I made sure they weren't a threat."

Luke glanced around. "Yeah, but now there's no clue for me here. I mean, I thought there'd be *something…*" He whirled and strode toward the cabin. "Maybe something was left inside."

Leo had searched earlier and found nothing. He didn't follow his brother. "How long are you going to continue this game?" He figured this place was as good as any other for a final battle spot. At least there were no humans around. No one who would get caught in the cross-fire.

I didn't bring Luke out here so he could prove himself to me.

I brought him out here so I could kill him.

Luke was on the cabin's sagging porch. "I do like games." He grabbed the wooden railing. "Only this time, I'm not playing." Then he kicked in the door and strode inside.

Leo's beast stretched inside of him.

This was it. He'd tried to find another ending, but it hadn't been in the cards, not for him. Not for his brother.

And as soon as I learned what you tried to do to her, brother, I knew your end had come. Once, he'd planned to not fight Luke. To not raise his hand against his brother. He'd wanted to let Luke live.

But if you sent those men after her...you're dead, too.

***

"I need help! Now!" Mora burst into the hospital's emergency room. Her breath was coming in gasps as she glanced frantically around. A security guard rose from his post near the check-in desk, a cup of coffee half-way toward his mouth. A blonde nurse sat behind the desk, and she just waved toward Mora vaguely. "Fill in our patient form and—"

"No!" Did she *look* like she had time to fill in a patient form? Dax's blood was all over her. Mora spied a gurney and grabbed it. "I've got a man dying in the back of a truck—I need help *now!*"

That snapped the nurse to attention, but Mora didn't wait to see if the lady actually sprang into action. She was too busy shoving that gurney out of the sliding glass doors at the ER and rushing her way back to the truck. She yanked down the tail-gate and grabbed Dax's feet.

He let out a ragged groan. The pain-filled sound was good. It meant he was still alive.

"Keep living," she urged him. "Don't you dare give up." She yanked—using her paranormal strength—and he landed on the gurney. She ran back toward the emergency room and nearly collided with the blonde nurse and the security guard. As soon as they saw the condition of the guy on the gurney, they got to work helping her get him inside.

The nurse yelled for a doctor—lots of them.

"L-Leo…"

Mora glanced down at Dax's form. Oh, jeez, but that was a *lot* of blood. If he'd been fully human, she was sure he never would have made it to the hospital. Whatever his paranormal side was…well, that *other* half was keeping him in the land of the living. For the moment. "Forget about Leo right now," she told him curtly. "Focus on surviving."

"S-saved me…"

She still was stunned by that news. It made her heart feel funny. Made her whole body feel warmer.

"I-I…owe h-him…"

Doctors were running toward them.

"Don't worry about your debt," she assured him. "I'll take care of it. But for us to have an even exchange, you have to live, got it?"

The doctors were taking him away.

"Live!" Mora yelled after him.

***

Leo breathed slowly. He stared down at his hands and saw the black claws where his fingertips should have been. Claws — the better for ripping and tearing in battle. Soon his body would be covered in scales. Soon he'd be breathing fire.

Soon he'd be killing his brother…

Or he'll be killing me.

Wasn't that the fate that Mora had seen for him so long ago? His body broken and bloody, surrounded by darkness? When she'd first told him that terrible truth, tears had made her voice break. Tears had tracked down her beautiful cheeks.

He'd wondered — as he stared at her pain — just why she cared so much. Fate had to see hundreds of people die. Thousands. Millions.

But she'd cried for him.

And then…then he'd wondered…*how does she know I'm the one in that vision? Luke and I look the same.* The exact same on the outside, but so different beneath the skin.

"Leo!" Luke was roaring his name.

Leo glanced up at his brother's shout. Luke was back on the porch, his body tense. Leo swallowed what tasted like ash and said, "I asked her how she could tell the difference between us…when she saw the vision of our final battle and she saw which brother won…I asked Mora how she knew who was victorious. I mean, we have the same face, right? How could she tell the difference?"

"Leo, you need to get your ass in here — and stop waving those claws at me!"

"She said…she said…she'd always know me. That she could be blind, and she'd know me. That she could feel my very soul." He laughed. "Bullshit, right? That was what I thought. I thought I'd fooled Fate. That I'd gotten her to fall for me." His laughter faded away. "I left her, still thinking I was the fucking shit —"

"This sharing session was not on today's to-do list," Luke snapped at him. He waved his hand toward the cabin. "Will you get your ass in here?"

He took a lumbering step forward. "But then I…missed her."

"You are such a mess." Luke shook his head.

"I went back for her, but she wasn't there." He took another step forward. Hating this. Hating that he was going to kill his brother. But Fate wasn't wrong. She was never wrong. "I…I wanted her back." His hands lifted and he clawed at his chest, barely feeling the skin tear. "I hurt…here. And no matter what I did, the pain wouldn't stop. She was gone."

Luke stared at him.

Leo bounded onto the porch and stood toe-to-toe with his brother. "I didn't think I'd ever feel pain like that again."

"We all feel pain," Luke said softly. His face was a tight mask. "And it's a bitch."

"But then…then I learned that *you* were the one behind her torture. *You* were the one who hurt Mora, and the pain was just as bad as before." Leo grabbed his brother's head. Their foreheads touched. "I would have fought anyone and anything to keep you alive. I was doing that, don't you see? I wanted a chance. For both of us. But then you hurt *her.*"

"Leo…"

His left hand rose, and his claws pressed right over Luke's heart. "Only one of us will leave today."

Luke's whole body was tense. "You need to fucking look in the cabin."

"I already did. Nothing was there. And I'm done with your lies." Leo braced himself. His brother's blood would be on his hands. "Guess you can't change fate. No matter how hard you try."

***

Mora's eyes were locked on the giant clock that hung on the waiting room wall. One minute until midnight. One minute and it would be a new day.

I saw Dax's fate. He was supposed to die. But if he can make it past midnight…

Then he would be living a future that she hadn't seen. He would have changed his fate.

Or maybe I changed it. Or Leo did – but, it would be changed!

A throat cleared, a rough, nervous sound. Her head jerked to the right and she expected to see Barbara. The blonde nurse had tried to get Mora to fill out a police report about Dax— Barbara had asked a million questions, but Mora had just ignored the other woman.

Until the questions stopped.

But Barbara wasn't there. A man in blue scrubs stood looking at her. Deep lines bracketed his green eyes.

Was this the doctor who'd operated on Dax?

Mora jumped to her feet. "Is he okay?"

The doctor ran a shaking hand over his face.

Mora hurried to him. "Is Dax all right?"

"He…" The doctor paused, swallowed, and the click of his Adam's apple was too loud in that tomb-quiet waiting room. "He…he died on the table."

Mora's knees gave way. She just…fell. Hit the tiled floor that smelled heavily of antiseptic.

I couldn't change his fate. I can't change anyone's.

I can't…change Leo's. Despite all my effort and my hope and —

The doctor's hand landed heavily on her shoulder and he squeezed. "He died." His voice was a rasp. "He was gone...for *fifteen* minutes."

She'd failed. Again.

"But then he came back."

Her head whipped up.

The doctor stared at her in shock. "I didn't do anything to make him come back." His voice was low and ragged. "I'd...I'd given up. Too much blood loss. But then, he took a breath. He just took a breath and opened his eyes, and the guy was *fine*." He shook his head, as if he still didn't understand. "That man came back."

She jumped right back to her feet and glared at him. "You lead with that shit—you don't start by telling a stressed out woman that her friend *died*." She tried to push past him so that she could go back and see Dax.

But the doc grabbed her arm. "He *came* back! Against science. Against everything I know, that man started breathing again. His wounds healed." He shook his head, again and again. "What happened?"

She had a suspicion, but she'd need to see Dax to be sure. "Take me to him."

Swallowing again, his whole body shaking, the doctor nodded.

***

"Don't commit an act you'll regret." Luke's voice was calm even though his body was tight with battle-ready tension. He wasn't fighting Leo. He was just standing there. Waiting. "Because there's a line...one that neither of us has ever crossed."

No. Luke had crossed all lines when he hurt Mora.

"Come into the cabin, brother," Luke told him quietly. "Because you missed something before. Something pretty damn big."

Leo blinked. He wanted to believe his brother. "You lie so well. I'm not even sure your closest friends can tell your truths from your lies." He'd stopped being able to tell the difference long ago.

Luke just gave him a twisted half-smile. "You're one to talk. All this time, I thought you were the biggest asshole on earth, and you were trying to find a way to stop us from killing each other?"

"Not each other," he said quietly. "Only one dies, remember?"

The smile slipped away from Luke's face. "Get in the cabin. Just *look* at what I found."

And, because killing his brother was always the last thing he'd wanted, Leo gave him one more chance. He slipped into the cabin.

Fire immediately appeared above Luke's hand.

Leo tensed, wondering if his brother had tricked him—

"Relax," Luke drawled. "I know we both can see fucking fantastically in the dark, but you missed this before, and I didn't want you to miss it again." He waved the fire toward the floor. A big, woven rug had been kicked aside, revealing markings on the floor. Markings that had been made—

"That's blood," Luke said, inhaling heavily. "And I might be a bit rusty because that is a language that I haven't seen in a *very* long time, but I'm pretty sure we're staring at a spell."

Leo's entire body locked down. "What kind of spell?" He'd never seen markings like those. Didn't recognize the language. His brother could be bullshitting him but...

When Luke looked up, there was worry in his eyes. "It's a spell to bring back the dead."

Impossible. And Leo called his brother on that fact. "Bullshit. We both know it takes a whole lot more to bring back—"

"Not if you're dealing with a hellhound."

"With a what?" Now he was lost.

Luke licked his lips. "Hellhounds die, and they go back to the fire. They stay there, until they're called again. This...this is a summoning spell. It raises them from the fire."

"Hellhounds…" Leo couldn't remember the last time he'd even heard of them. "They're *yours.*"

"They aren't of this earth, not really, so they've never answered to me." Luke's eyes gleamed. "These men you say that you killed…Tell me what they looked like. *Exactly* what they looked like."

"I thought they were angels at first. They had wings that stretched behind them—"

Luke's eyes closed. "Hellhounds can manifest wings anytime they want. They can also transform into the body of any beast that they want."

He remembered the panther that he'd seen in that godforsaken basement. "Like a black panther?"

Luke's eyes opened. "Yes, and they can take the guise of men. But they're not really men. At their core, they're something else."

Leo's temples were throbbing. "You say you've seen this spell before…*when?*"

"Centuries ago." Luke's voice was halting. "Right after you lost your Fate. Didn't think it was connected, not then."

Fucking hell. "*You* swear you don't control them?" Leo wanted to believe Luke but…

"I swear on my life, I don't control them. I haven't sent them after you. Or after Mora. I'd hoped they were long gone from this world. They don't just attack humans or the good paranormals…" He raked a hand through his hair. "They come after the dark, too. They feed on chaos and bloodshed. Pain gives them strength. Fear makes them nearly invulnerable."

Not good. "When was the last time you saw them, *exactly*?"

Luke tilted his head as he seemed to consider the question. Then he gave a bitter laugh. "*Exactly?* When Atlantis fell. They sank with the city."

Atlantis…Shit, that had been right after he left Mora. He bent down to study the markings on the floor. "Who summoned them back? If they were in the fire, who brought them back to this world?"

Luke didn't answer.

Leo surged to his feet. "*Who?*"

"I don't know, but I'll damn well be finding out."

Another enemy. Someone who'd been hiding in the shadows all of this time? "Maybe it was one of them," Leo muttered as he tried to think past his rage. "There were four of them. The leader was some guy named Reever. Maybe the others died long ago—maybe Reever lived and brought them all back?"

"Maybe." Luke didn't look convinced. "But this spell is fresh. Someone cast it recently. Someone *knew* you were coming to attack, and that person wanted to be sure that the hellhounds rose again after you were gone."

Shit. "How long until they rise?"

Luke looked back at the markings. "I need my witch. Cordelia would be able to—"

"*How long?*"

"I don't fucking know! I can't read all of this. As I said, *I need my witch.* I'll get Cordelia out here. She'll be able to tell us what's happening. Maybe even give us an idea as to who cast the spell." He inclined his head toward Leo. "Of course, you could also just get Fate out to this cabin. She can scry from right in the middle of this mess and see exactly what happened—and what's going to happen. She can tell us everything we need to know."

Fate. His heart jerked in his chest. "They targeted her before."

"Yeah, all the more reason to get her here. She's involved, she's—"

"They could already be back." The drumming of his heartbeat filled his ears. "They could already be going after her." And he'd left her alone. He'd thought she was safe.

Oh, *shit.*

His wings burst from his back. In the next breath, he was hurtling straight through the cabin's sagging ceiling and up into the night.

"Leo!" Luke bellowed after him.

But Leo didn't stop. He had to get back to Mora. He had to make sure she was safe.

I can't let them hurt her again.

***

"No, no, it's okay!" Luke shouted after his asshole of a brother. "I don't want to come with you. Really, I'm fine. I'll just go get my witch and figure out this mess on my own." He glowered after his brother.

Leo had flown fast and far…Fear would do that to a man, though. Twist him up. Blind him. Make him weak.

Luke glanced back down at the markings. He'd lied…a bit. That was part of who he was.

The hellhounds weren't back, at least not yet. But he'd needed Leo to return and get close to Mora. *Because we will need her.*

If Luke was reading the spell right—and he was about sixty percent sure that he was—then the hellhounds wouldn't return for a full twenty-four hours after they descended into the fire. That bought Luke and Leo a bit of time.

Time enough for Leo to get back in Fate's good graces.

Time for Luke to try and figure out…just which enemy was gunning for the destruction of both Luke…and his brother.

Hellhounds. Fucking hellhounds.

Beasts that could never truly die.

Beasts that were going to be a serious pain in his ass.

***

Machines were beeping, the repetitive sounds filling the small hospital room. Dax was in the bed, a sheet pulled up over his chest. His eyes were closed, and his face was pale, but the terrible bruising that had marked him before was gone. His nose didn't even look broken.

Mora eased out a slow breath. She let her senses open wide, reaching out to test and see…*What are you, Dax? Are you still human?*

She hadn't made a sound, but his head suddenly turned toward her as if he'd sensed her presence. His eyes opened, and she found herself staring into a gaze that had turned bright, bright blue. An otherworldly blue.

Not human anymore. She'd wondered about that. Part of her vision had come true. She was afraid that Dax's human side had died.

She just wasn't sure *what* was left inside of him.

"Mora?" He growled her name. Even his voice was different. Rougher. Darker. "Why are you looking at me that way?"

She immediately schooled her features.

He lifted his hand. "Come closer."

She wasn't so sure that was the best idea. Not until she figured out what she was dealing with.

He sat up in the bed, frowning. "What's going on?"

She looked over her shoulder. The doctor hadn't followed her inside the room. The poor guy was probably in the hallway, having a breakdown. Mora cleared her throat. "How do you feel?"

"Pretty fantastic. And that's weird, right?"

"Right." She tried to smile. "Um, are you noticing anything different about yourself?"

"Different?"

Her hand waved vaguely in the air. "Oh, you know. Enhanced hearing. Super sense of smell."

His eyes widened.

She kept going. "The urge to bite me, drink all my blood, or maybe just rip me limb from limb?"

Now he was staring at her in shock.

"Is that a yes? Or a no?" Mora rocked back onto her heels. "It would help me enormously if you could answer my question, please."

"I don't want to bite you." He shoved aside the covers and rose. The guy was just wearing one of those paper hospital gowns, so he gave her a serious peep show. "And I don't want to rip you apart. You *saved* me. I want to repay you."

Okay, that was good. "So you feel...human?"

"Uh, I *am* human."

So said the man with the glowing blue eyes. Someone was going to be in for a hard new reality.

"What happened to Sammy and his goons?" Dax demanded.

"I have no idea." She'd never actually made it into the bar.

"They'll be coming after me again." His hands clenched. The tattoos on his arms appeared far more vivid than they had before. "They know I can take down their entire operation."

She needed to touch his hand. Needed to see what waited in the guy's future. Needed to see *what* he was. "You should call in your DEA buddies." She shuffled forward, making herself move. "They can help you out. You give them the intel you have on Sammy, and that will be one less problem for you."

He nodded grimly. "I need protection. I can't just stay here like a sitting duck."

She reached out, steeling herself, and wrapped her fingers around his upper arm. She hoped it looked as if she were giving him a supportive squeeze but really...

His future flashed before her eyes.

Fire. Screams. Pain.

"Mora?"

She blinked. And she let him go. "Don't w-want you to be a s-sitting duck." Mora nodded decisively. "You should go…call the other agents. Get a pick-up out of here."

"I'm not calling them—I can't wait for a ride that may take hours to get here. I feel fantastic, like I said. I'll steal some scrubs and head out on foot."

"I-I have a truck you can use." Not that it was her truck. "It's outside. It's a little tricky to get started." *I can help you hot-wire it.*

He pulled her close in a quick, hard hug. "I owe you so much, Mora. One day, I *will* find a way to pay you back."

No, you won't. Because you didn't escape death. You just delayed it for a while. She'd seen him burning. He'd just traded one brutal death scene for another. But she didn't say that. Instead, she squeezed him back and she could have sworn that she smelled ash in the air. "Of course, you'll pay me back. There will be plenty of time for that." And she didn't have tears in her eyes. Not when she hugged him.

Not when they snuck out of the hospital and he drove away in the truck.

And certainly not when she looked after him, wondering just how long he had left…until the fires consumed him.

CHAPTER ELEVEN

The taxi driver slowed near Mora's house. "Thanks for the lift," she told him. She shoved some cash his way.

"Miss...you sure you're okay?"

Mora knew he was asking because of all the blood that was still on her. When you picked up a woman from the hospital and she appeared to have been gutted because of the sheer amount of blood on her clothing, well, it was only normal for a person to worry. "Never better," she lied. Then she jumped out of the car and headed up her sidewalk.

He pulled away, the flash of his headlights momentarily illuminating her front porch.

And—

Someone's there. Someone's waiting.

She stopped.

The shadowy figure—the guy who'd been sitting, with his head bowed—on her doorstep— looked up at her. "You sure you're all right?"

Leo.

"I-it's not my blood." She was going to throw her clothes away. Mora took a few quick steps forward. And the stupid refrain—*He's come back. He's come back!*—filled her head. "It's Dax's blood. I found him after you pulled him out of Sammy's."

Leo rose. "After I—what?"

"You saved him." Her hands reached out to him. She wanted to hug him but...*I need to ditch the bloody clothes.* So she just stared up at him, feeling as if a weight had lifted from her heart. "It might not have done any good." *Might? Ha. It didn't.* "But you still tried to help him. Thank you. I owe you for that."

"Mora..."

"Come inside, okay? I just...I want to talk."

He nodded and relief filled her. Mora fumbled a bit and managed to unlock the door. She turned off her security system and then gestured toward the couch. "Sit for a few minutes, okay? I need to shower and change. I'll be right back."

She hurried toward the bathroom.

"Mora?"

She glanced back at him.

"Something has changed." His voice was soft, confused. "What happened?"

"You did. *You* changed."

"I'm not sure I understand."

"You told me that you were going to make things right for me, and then you left. I didn't know what you meant." *Be honest.* "No, I didn't believe you."

"Because you don't trust me. I understand. With everything that's happened—"

"But then you went and you saved Dax. You knew I wanted to change his fate, and you got him out of Sammy's Place."

Leo's face hardened. "Mora..."

"You saved him. By time I got to that club, Dax was in the bed of that truck, but he told me you were the one to rescue him. You...you went to get an angel, right?" She tucked a lock of her hair behind her ear. "You were probably trying to heal him, but it's okay. He, um, healed himself."

"What?"

"Whatever paranormal side he's been hiding—that side came to the forefront and saved him. Dax said he owed you a debt, but I told him I would repay it." She turned to fully face him, and her shoulders stiffened. "I'm letting the past go."

He shook his head. "You don't understand—"

"No, I do," she cut through his words. "I understand that I've held on to bitterness and anger and pain until I am just sick of it. It's eaten away at me, and I don't want that any longer. I don't want to live that way. You said—you said you had nothing to do with those men who attacked me."

"I fucking swear, I didn't."

She gave a quick, nervous nod. "I believe you. And I also know that I don't want to keep hating you."

His face tightened. She saw the pain in his stare. "Baby…"

"It's too hard to hate you." Her hand moved to press over her chest, right over her heart. "It's too hard in here." Because her heart had once only beat for him. "You saved Dax, and I'm paying his debt. I'm letting the hate go. I'm starting again with you. A long, long time has passed, and we're not the same people anymore. I'm not the same, and neither are you."

"I would give my life for you not to hurt again."

His life. She smiled at him and refused to let any tears fall. He was running on borrowed time right now, but she wasn't going to tell him that. She wasn't going to tell Leo that he had only days left. And that she couldn't keep hating him, not when he'd be gone soon. She wanted better memories of him.

Mora turned away from him and hurried into the bathroom. She shut the door with a soft click, and moments later, she was under the warm spray of the shower. She let her tears fall then. No one could see them, after all. They just mixed with the shower water on her face.

***

I didn't save Dax. What was Mora talking about?

He'd tried to tell her the truth. Tried to say that he hadn't seen Dax since they'd left the guy in the burned out parking lot of Resurrection. But then...

Then Mora had stared at him with her wide, beautiful eyes. She'd offered him a new chance.

Leo wasn't stupid enough to turn down that chance. He wanted to grab Mora and hold her tight, and *never* let her go. He wanted to give her anything—everything—in the entire world. He wanted to make her smile. He wanted to make her laugh. He wanted her happy.

And he was freaking lying to her.

Leo's shoulders hunched. Everyone had always been right about him. He was such a bastard.

He heard the soft click of the bathroom door opening behind him. Then her scent reached him, that sweet, flowery scent that he'd always liked. Her footsteps were swallowed by the thick carpet, but he knew she was coming closer. He could feel her.

That was the way it had always been between them. An awareness that was physical. When she was near, his body reacted. His muscles were already tensing. His cock was swelling. His heartbeat was racing faster. It was as if he were priming himself for her.

"There's something I want…" Her voice was husky. Seductive.

His eyes squeezed shut and his hands clenched into fists. *You should tell her the truth. Stop being an asshole. With her — stop.* But he heard himself say, "I'll give you anything." His words were rough. "What do you want?"

"I want you."

He whipped around to face her. She stood just a few feet away, her wet hair combed away from her face. A white towel was wrapped around her body, with a knot tucked between her high, firm breasts.

"I've always wanted you." She stared straight at him when she said those words.

He had to shake his head, hard, because Leo feared this was another dream. She'd said stuff like this to him before—in his dreams. And when he'd reached out to touch her, to take her, she'd vanished.

Her hands went to the top of the towel, and she pulled at the cotton fabric. The towel fell to the floor, pooling near her bare feet. His gaze immediately locked on her body. It had been so long since he'd seen her this way.

I only had dreams.

She was still perfect. Absolutely perfect. Her breasts were round and tipped with pretty pink nipples. Her stomach dipped in and her hips flared out, tempting him. Her sex...shit, it was bare. *That's new.*

He was pretty sure he was drooling. He'd always loved tasting her...right there. He remembered the way she'd liked it when he licked her clit. He'd loved it when her nails sank into his shoulders and her hips arched against him. Then when she'd moaned his name as she came for him, his control had always shattered.

"Leo?"

His gaze jerked up to her face.

Uncertainty darkened her gaze. "Don't you...still want me?"

Still? He walked toward her, far too aware that his steps were like those of a stalking predator who was closing in on his prey. He felt big and rough, while she was small and delicate. He wanted to grab her and hold on tight. But...

He was afraid his touch would break her.

No, I'll break her. I'm lying to her. I need to step away.

But her hand rose and pressed to his chest. At her touch, his heartbeat changed its rhythm, going even faster and harder, as it beat for her. "I will always want you."

She smiled at him. "Then I want you to fuck me. Tonight. I want to feel…the way only you have ever made me feel."

Maybe he wouldn't break her. But Leo was pretty sure the woman was going to break him. *Fuck me.* Once, she'd asked him to make love to her.

But she wasn't asking for love any longer. Just sex. Just pleasure.

She should have asked him for the whole world. He would have put it at her feet. He would deny Mora nothing.

"Leo?"

"You didn't want me close to you before." She'd spent years running but…

"Time is a fickle thing," she whispered back, licking her lips. "Sometimes, you think forever is waiting. Plenty of days for the world to change, but that isn't how things work." She rose onto her toes. "I'm not looking for any kind of forever. I'm looking for tonight. With you."

He bent his head. His lips pressed to hers, and Leo knew there would be no going back. Not that he wanted to go back. He just wanted to be with her. Did she have any clue how much she obsessed him? Day and night? Every single moment?

Her lips parted beneath his. His tongue swept into her mouth even as his hands flew to curl around her hips. Her *bare* hips. That pert ass. How he'd missed it.

His dick shoved against the front of his jeans. He wanted his clothes gone, and so, with barely a thought, they were. He and Mora were both naked, flesh against flesh. And he wanted this moment to last, wanted to savor her, but desire burned in his blood, and Leo knew his control wouldn't last long. At least, not the first time.

Maybe he'd do better on the second attempt.

He was planning for a busy night.

I'm going to stay with her. Won't leave her again. The hellhounds will have to go through me before they can hurt her.

He lifted Mora in his arms, and her legs wrapped around his hips, a move that put her sex right against his cock. She was wet for him. Already. Sweet cream.

He was pretty sure he was losing his mind.

Leo carried Mora into her bedroom. He put her on the bed and when she reached for him, he pushed her hands back. "Need…taste…" Absolutely guttural.

She gave him a fast, welcoming smile. "Please, go right ahead." Then she eased back onto the covers. She parted her legs for him.

He fell on her like a fucking starving man. His hands curled around her thighs, opening her even more as he positioned his body between her legs. Then his mouth was on her sex, licking and sucking and kissing, and her hands locked around his shoulders.

Mora's taste. Missed her taste.

Her nails bit into his shoulders.

Mora's passion. Missed her passion.

The thunder of his heartbeat filled his ears. His cock was heavy and swollen, and he wanted to sink balls deep into her. But...

Mora moaned. A sexy-as-sin sound and then, *"Leo!"*

She came against his mouth. Her body went bow tight as she lifted her hips up, pressing them hard against his mouth. He kept right on licking her. He loved the taste of her pleasure. Nothing was better.

He let her ride out her release. His head rose as he licked his lips, still tasting her. Mora's breath came fast and hard, and her nipples were tight peaks. He reached for her right nipple. Stroked it and plucked it.

She gave another moan.

His cock pushed at the entrance to her body. *Not a dream. She's real. She's mine.*

"Look at me," he ordered.

Her long lashes lifted. Her stare — so much gold there now — met his.

"You're mine," he told her. He needed her to understand. This wasn't just fucking.

Her lips parted.

He sank into her. Drove in on a long thrust and his control was gone. Leo caught her wrists and pinned them on either side of her head. He withdrew, then thrust into her, again and again. Her legs rose and circled his hips as she arched to meet him. Her passion had always been a perfect match for him.

Just as *she* was his perfect match.

Her body was tight and hot and so wet. His sanity was gone. Nothing could have stopped him right then. He had Mora. He had everything.

She came again. Her head tipped back against the pillows as she moaned his name. He took her left nipple, lashing it with his tongue, and then he erupted into her. Pumping and pumping, the release didn't seem to stop. Her sex squeezed him, contracting with her release, and Leo was pretty sure that his mind fucking exploded.

The thunder of his heartbeat, the smell of her skin…that was all he knew.

Leo held her tight and understood *she* was his fate.

***

Mora couldn't get her heart to slow down. It raced in her chest and her whole body seemed to shake with aftershocks of pleasure. She'd had plenty of lovers in her time. She enjoyed sex but...

When she was with Leo, it was different. So much more intense. Consuming her — body and soul.

He pressed a kiss to her temple as he pulled her close against him. His body was warm and strong, and she wanted to just stay there, wrapped in his arms, pretending that they were a normal couple.

Humans had a perfect life. Did they realize it? They could fall in love, get married, and have a family. They could be happy, never knowing about all of the monsters and the evil that lurked in the darkness.

She didn't have that luxury. She knew too well what waited.

But she wanted to pretend, for just a little while. What was the harm in pretending?

The monsters would be at her door soon enough. But for this moment...

Her eyes drifted closed.

I'll pretend.

She'd pretend that Leo loved her. That they had a future waiting.

It was such a pretty fantasy.

And as she drifted to sleep, Mora was sure the scent of ash followed her.

CHAPTER TWELVE

"You're needed."

Mora's eyes flew open and she gave a gasp—a gasp of absolute shock and fury because a strange man was at the foot of her bed. He was tall and golden—golden tan skin, blond hair, and even golden eyes.

His golden eyes were also dipping over her naked body.

Shit. What is happening here?

A low growl sounded beside her even as the bedcovers were suddenly flying up to cover Mora's body. "Get your fucking eyes off her!" Leo snarled.

Leo—still with her. Well, he *had* been in bed with her. But he was currently lunging up and going for the blond in a serious attack move. Only…the blond flew away.

Literally flew.

Because he has wings. Not the scaled dragon wings that Leo possessed. But soft wings. White wings. Angel wings?

Her heart thudded hard in her chest. She'd never come face-to-face with an angel before. But she was pretty sure she was staring at one right then.

The guy lowered his head to Leo. "Sorry, but I had to see you. There's trouble, and you're needed. Humans are under attack by a paranormal force just north of Vegas. Your brother is up to his old tricks again."

Leo's back was tense and his shoulders were stiff. "I'm dealing with an emergency right here, Ramiel. You'll have to take care of those humans yourself."

Ramiel? The name was oddly familiar, but Mora couldn't quite place it. She was *sure* she hadn't met his guy before.

He looked up and she saw the angry flash of his gaze. "Obviously, she's an emergency." Bitterness laced his voice. "Your priorities haven't been where they should be in a very long time."

And just like that, the guy had pushed Leo over the edge. Mora saw it happen—wings burst from Leo's back and he grabbed the angel, holding Ramiel by the neck and shoving him against the wall.

"Stop!" Mora yelled. She scrambled from the bed, wrapping a sheet around her body. "Don't— don't beat up an angel!" That seemed wrong.

Leo slowly turned his head and his gaze—bright with power and tainted by a slow rage—met hers. "You are my priority."

She swallowed.

"*You* are what matters. I will not leave you defenseless."

Okay, that was pretty intense. And it made her nervous. Mora held her sheet tighter. "Why do I need a guard? Is there some threat you haven't told me about?"

His claw-tipped fingers were still around Ramiel's throat. Leo's jaw hardened.

Oh, crap. There is a threat. "You said you killed the men who took me."

"I did…"

Ramiel was dead silent. Probably because he couldn't speak with Leo's hand around his throat.

"I did…" Leo muttered. "But they're coming back."

Coming back? Now her heart was pounding too fast. "Even most paranormals don't come back from the dead." Vamps could…but that required some serious special circumstances.

Leo slowly released Ramiel's neck. The angel made no move to slide away from the wall. He just stood there, watching Leo, his gaze hooded.

"I burned them to ash," Leo revealed quietly.

Ramiel licked his lips. His stare shifted from Leo to Mora, then back again. When he stared at her…

He hates me.

Mora took a step back, shocked to see such fury on an angel's face. But in the next instant, the rage was gone, and she almost wondered if she'd imagined it.

Almost.

"But apparently, that wasn't enough," Leo continued grimly. "Not when you're dealing with hellhounds."

"Let's go over that part again." She shook her head, certain she'd misunderstood. "Dealing with what now?"

"There *are* no hellhounds on earth," Ramiel snapped, speaking before Leo could. "They're just tales to frighten weak-minded paranormals."

Uh, oh.

Leo's head turned, a bit snake-like, toward the angel. "Do I look weak-minded to you, old *friend*?"

Ramiel swallowed. He gave a quick shake of his head. "Your brother…Luke is just tricking you. You know how he works. There are no hellhounds, and even if they were here, Luke couldn't control them. He couldn't—"

"He isn't controlling them." Leo blew out a rough breath. "Someone else is. The same someone who sent the bastards after Mora in the first place."

Her mouth was hanging open in shock. "There are *hellhounds* after me?" Dammit. Not good. Actually, very, very bad. Because she knew about the hounds, unfortunately. They could shift into the form of any beast... *Oh, crap. That's why they looked like angels at first...and then one of the bastards turned into a panther.*

They could die again and again, only to come back from the fire.

Leo said he burned them to ash, but that won't stop them. Hellhounds can never truly die. Not if the stories I've heard are true. She'd even deliberately sought out information on hellhounds because their power terrified her so much. And everything she'd learned — every whisper — had just made her more fearful.

She lurched forward and grabbed Leo, whirling him to face her. "Why didn't you tell me this sooner? If hellhounds are coming for me, you should have *told* me — "

"I was going to tell you." His gaze swept over her face. "I came back because I'm staying by your side. I will protect you, I swear. When the hounds come again, I'll stop them. You will never face them on your own again."

"Who is going to protect the humans?" Ramiel demanded. "They are your charges, not her! You're the Lord of the Light! You're supposed to

CYNTHIA EDEN 184

take care of humans and *good* paranormals. Fate isn't for you!"

Fate isn't for you. Mora flinched. So the guy knew who she was. Unfortunately, he was also spouting some hard truths. Her fingers slid away from Leo's arm. "You should go protect the humans. They're under your shield, right?" *I'm not.* "Human lives are so delicate. So easily lost."

Leo's eyes narrowed as he closed the small space between them, pulling her against his body. "You matter more than *any* human. More than *anyone* else. Understand that."

Her own eyes widened.

"I will never forsake you again. You will never know pain while I am near."

Her lower lip wanted to tremble. She pressed her lips together so he wouldn't see the telling movement.

"The hellhounds will come again," Leo stated flatly. "Luke told me they will be coming, and you will not be alone when they attack. I vow it."

Behind him, Ramiel let out a cry of disgust. "Then the humans die so your lover doesn't get a bruise on her flesh?"

A muscle jerked in Leo's jaw. "Tread carefully, Ramiel," he warned.

"*I've seen her future!* She can't die! We both know that!" Ramiel shouted back. "She can suffer. We all suffer. But Fate doesn't end. The humans will! We can help them! It's your *duty* to help them!"

I've seen her future. Was it possible? "H-how?" Mora asked and she pulled from Leo to stare at Ramiel. The stranger…the angel who'd broken into her home and slipped into her bedroom. The being who'd stared at her with hate in his eyes. "How can you possibly know what happens to me?"

Ramiel offered her a cold smile. "You think you're the only one who can see the future?" He laughed. "Tell her, Leo. Tell her just what *I* can do."

Leo gave an angry growl, but then he said, "Ramiel has visions. He can see what's coming."

Her stare slid back to Ramiel. He was smirking at her. "Thought you were the only one gifted this way?" Ramiel asked and there was a hard edge in his voice. "I'm a creature of the light. My visions aren't tainted."

Her hands fisted. *I don't like Ramiel.*

"I can change the darkness that comes. I *have* changed it for centuries." His golden eyes seemed to bore into her. "What about you? Do you change the darkness or do you just make it worse, *Fate?*"

Her chin notched up. "Leo, get your angel out of here."

Shock flashed on Ramiel's face. Then he shot toward her.

Bad mistake.

Before he could touch her, Leo grabbed the angel, once more locking his fingers around Ramiel's throat. "You forget your place," Leo snarled. He shoved Ramiel back.

Ramiel's wings spread wide behind him. He pointed at Leo. "And you forget *yours.* You've been under her spell for centuries. Always hunting her. Always lusting for her. And when I find you now, when humans are being attacked by your brother's forces, you're fucking her. You wear her scent like it's some kind of honor."

"Get the fuck out, Ram!"

"She's never been what you think. She's no all-seeing power. She's a demon. I've told you that before. *My* opposite. There are always opposites in this world. My visions help the humans. Hers do nothing but destroy. She isn't *fate.*" His lips twisted. "She's just another bad paranormal who should be locked away."

Leo drove his fist into Ramiel's jaw. Once, twice. Unprepared for the attack — *didn't your visions tell you that would be coming?* — Ramiel stumbled back. Leo's claws became longer, sharper, and he slashed out, cutting into Ramiel.

Angel feathers drifted to the floor.

"You turn on *me...*?" Shock was in Ramiel's voice.

"No one will hurt her." Leo put his body in front of Mora's. She was rooted to the spot, as shocked as Ramiel. *Leo was hurting an angel…for me?* "And you don't fucking insult her that way. Mora isn't dark. She. Is. Mine."

"The humans—"

"You help them. There's an army of angels who can aid the humans. My place is with Mora, and this is where I'll be."

The room was heating, the temperature literally rising as the tension in the air increased. She heard the blast of thunder in the distance.

This is so not good.

Ramiel gave a jerky nod of his head. And then he was flying up and away—flying—

"No!" Mora yelled. But it was too late. The guy had just flown through her roof, leaving a big, gaping hole in his wake. One final…*screw you*…to her. Why did everyone seem to always fly right through a roof? Could Leo and his group *not* use a door?

"You aren't dark."

Her breath heaved out as her head whipped back toward Leo. He was standing there, claws bursting from his fingertips, and his wings spread behind him. "The angel is wrong. You aren't evil."

But…but staring at him right then, seeing the bright red of his gaze, the claws, his fangs…

Are you, Leo?

He frowned at her. "Mora?" The red of his gaze dimmed, the normal golden color bleeding through once more. "Don't be afraid. No one will hurt you, I swear." His hand reached for her. She tensed, but the claws didn't touch her skin.

His claws had vanished in a blink, and his fingers slid over her cheek. "I will not leave you unprotected again."

Her breath was heaving. Her knees were locked so that she wouldn't fall.

"You're looking at me as if you've never seen me before," Leo murmured. "Mora, what's happening?"

Something very bad. "What about the humans?"

"You heard what I told Ramiel. The angels can protect them. I won't be taken from your side."

But his job was to protect humans. That was what the Lord of the Light was supposed to do. For him to turn away from that job...so easily... "I'll go with you," Mora blurted. "We'll stay together. We can figure this out."

A line appeared between his brows. "Mora?"

Time is running out. "We can't just stay in this house, not if the hellhounds are coming here. We can help the humans and buy ourselves more time in the process."

His hand slid down her cheek. "You're afraid."

Terrified. As much as she hated to do it, she knew she needed to talk with Ramiel again, too.

She needed to know about his visions. *That* was why his name had seemed familiar to her. There'd been whispers, long ago, of an angel who received divine visions. But those whispers had ended abruptly. So abruptly that she'd only gotten a name...*Ram.* Ramiel.

"You're afraid," Leo said again, his head cocking to the side. "Of me?"

"No." An instant denial. The truth was...*I'm afraid for you, Leo.* But she couldn't say that. Everything was so confused and messed up. She'd gone from having incredible sex with Leo, insane pleasure to...

Waking up with an angry angel at the foot of her bed.

"I want to help the humans." She made her voice firm. "Let's do it, together, okay?"

"I'll do anything you want." He caught her hand and brought it to his lips. He pressed a soft kiss to the back of her fingers. "Remember that."

***

Mora was changing. She'd stared at him with a gaze that had been heavy with fear and worry. And even though she'd denied it, Leo had known the truth.

Mora fears me.

He'd used his magic to repair her roof. It had only taken a few moments. And while she was in the bathroom, he slipped outside. He stared up at the sky, hearing the distant echo of thunder, always a sign that Ramiel was close. Leo tilted his head back and summoned the angel. *"Ramiel."* As one of the light paranormals, angels fell under Leo's dominion. They had to obey his commands.

Whether they liked it or not.

So he just waited and a few moments later, Ramiel shot out of the sky and landed right in front of Leo. The angel bowed — and his wings wrapped around his body before vanishing in the next moment. When Ramiel rose, he was dressed as a man, wearing a t-shirt and jeans, all signs of his wings gone.

You could have hidden the wings when you faced off against Mora. You kept them out deliberately, because you were trying to intimidate her. "We have a problem," Leo announced.

Ramiel's eyes widened. "What is it?"

Leo stalked forward. His hands wrapped around Ramiel's shoulders. "The problem is you, old friend." Ramiel had been at his side for centuries. He'd used the man's visions to help him many times. They'd saved countless humans. Stopped so much suffering but... "You're treading on thin ice."

He could feel the tension in Ramiel's body. "You summoned me so that you could berate me?" Ramiel snapped. "I was on my way to save the humans from a paranormal attack — an attack by *werewolves*. It's a job *you* should oversee yourself and — "

"Don't worry, Ram. I'm coming to help them."

Relief flashed on the angel's face. "Good. Luke has sent his beasts after the humans. I've seen what's coming. The wolves are going to rip those humans to shreds. The land will run with blood unless we kill those paranormals. We can stop them, though, together, the way we have so many times in the past. We can eliminate the werewolves before they take a single human life."

"We will protect the humans." His hold tightened on Ramiel. "And you will not say another fucking bad word about Mora."

The faint lines near Ramiel's eyes narrowed. "When will you get over her? She's a temptation, nothing more. Another trap sent by your brother. She's *dark*. She isn't yours. She belongs to *him*."

For a moment, Leo could hear nothing but the pounding of his own heartbeat. A slow, hard thud.

Ramiel exhaled roughly. "The world is full of opposites, you know that. You and Luke — you are perfect opposites. Good and bad. Like angels and demons. *I* have the same gift that your lover does. She isn't Fate. That's just what she wants the world to believe. What she wants *you* to believe. She's nothing but a demon, tricking you.

Feeding you lies so that you'll fall at her feet. When the final battle comes," Ramiel continued starkly, "she wants you weak. She wants Luke to win. That's what she has *always* wanted."

"No." He was battling rage. He could feel it firing in his gut.

"Are there really hellhounds hunting this earth?"

They weren't hunting, not yet… "Luke said they're coming back."

Ramiel swallowed. "Someone has to summon the hounds. I've heard the tales about them. They aren't just freed from the fire by their own will. Someone has to call them forth."

So he'd learned. "There's more. They used bullets on me—bullets had had been made from angel feathers."

Ramiel's gaze was stark. "They hurt…angels?"

"Looks that way. We *must* stop them."

Ramiel hesitated.

"What is it?"

"Are you so sure they're *hunting* her and not following her commands?"

"Ram…" Rage was nearly choking him. Ramiel had been at his side for centuries. But he wanted to use his claws and cut the man to pieces. All because of the bastard's words about Mora.

"I have seen her future," Ramiel continued quietly. "It's not what you think. You cannot trust her."

The door opened behind Leo. He heard the tread of Mora's footsteps and her soft gasp of surprise.

"Um, Leo? What's happening?" Mora asked. "The angel is back already?"

Leo stared into Ramiel's gaze. "Mora is coming with us to this fight, Ram. She'll be at my side. *Always.*" *And if you have a fucking problem with that...too bad.*

"This is a mistake," Ramiel gritted out. "Don't say I didn't warn you..."

Leo smiled. "You warned me." He leaned in close, keeping his voice low, just for Ramiel to hear. "I just don't care. I *won't* give her up again." He eased back.

Sadness flashed in Ramiel's eyes. "I see what she's done to you. I wish I could help you."

"Uh, hello?" Mora called out. "What's happening?"

"I don't need help." Leo freed Ramiel. *I just need her.* He turned his body slightly, offering his hand to Mora. She was dressed in jeans and a blue shirt, her hair tumbling over her shoulders and her eyes on him. She looked so beautiful. So innocent.

Was she really set to be his end?

She came forward and her soft hand slid against his. His fingers immediately curled around hers, holding her tight. She gave him a faint smile, and her eyes seemed to light up.

She'd told him that she'd let go of their past. That she didn't want to hurt any longer.

He lifted her into his arms. Ramiel had already taken to the sky. Leo let his wings slide out behind him. He'd follow Ramiel to the humans.

He'd end the threat of the dark paranormals and then…

Then I will face the hellhounds. I'll find a way to stop them. He wasn't going to lose her. He wasn't going to let Mora suffer.

If she was his end, he couldn't think of a better way to go.

CHAPTER THIRTEEN

Darkness still reigned when they touched down on the small road just north of Vegas. A thousand glittering stars filled the sky, and the desert seemed to stretch as far as the eye could see.

"The wolves have a base just around the bend." Ramiel pointed. "They pose as a motorcycle gang, even call themselves the Pack. Bold bastards."

Mora could hear the faint growl of motorcycle engines in the distance.

"Their leader is an alpha named Bruce. In my vision," Ramiel continued quietly, "I saw Bruce leading the others. Wolves are territorial beasts, and the Pack owns this area. No other wolves would hunt here without the Pack's permission."

"Is that why they attack the humans…" Mora blurted. "Because they're territorial?"

Ramiel's head turned toward her, an oddly snake-like move. "They attack because they're monsters. Because they're evil. And it's going to be a horrible, savage attack. The wolves will ravage their prey. The beasts will rip out the humans' throats. Slash open their bodies. In my vision, the blood is everywhere. Those who try to flee will be hunted down in the desert. I saw the wolves dragging the bodies for miles…"

She shivered. The air was so still around her, and Ramiel's voice had just been too creepy as he talked. And the things he said… Mora swallowed. "Why would Luke allow this? I thought…I thought there was a law, of sorts, in place. That he punished any paranormals who tried to step out of line—"

Ramiel laughed. "You see, Leo? She's still pretending she doesn't know what Luke is really like. When she's been on his side all along."

Her shoulders stiffened. "Angel, you're pissing me off." Then she marched toward him, her tennis shoes kicking up dust along the road. "You don't know me, and I don't know you."

"Oh, I know you…"

Two more angels appeared, seeming to fall right from the sky. One was a woman. The moonlight fell on her warm, dark brown skin. The other was a male. Tall, imposing, with skin a gold to match his hair. Their wings disappeared in a blink, and normal, human clothing covered their bodies.

"I know plenty about you," Ramiel continued in that creepy voice of his. "You're the one who obsessed Leo—"

"Stop," Leo barked. "We're not doing this shit again now."

Her chin couldn't notch higher into the air. Ramiel was looking at her as if she were a piece of trash that had stumbled into his path. The other two angels didn't have any expression on their faces.

"You think you know me so well," Mora said. She ignored Leo's order. After all, he didn't control her, and she was pretty sure the *stop* had been directed at Ramiel. "Isn't it only fair that I get to know you?"

Then before Ramiel could respond, Mora lunged forward. She put her hand on the angel's chest. *Touch.* It had always been something she feared, but she wanted to see this angel's future.

She wanted to see—

Leo…slashing Ramiel with claws. Cutting the wings from Ramiel's body. Ramiel screaming, begging for mercy—

"Mora!" Leo roared. He grabbed her and jerked her back against him, locking his arms around her body. And that was when she realized that she was shuddering. Her whole body was twitching as if she'd gotten some sort of electrical jolt.

Ramiel was staring at her with wide, shocked eyes. "What did you do?" His words whispered out.

Leo held her tighter. "Baby, why won't you stop shaking?"

She couldn't speak. Her teeth were chattering and she was afraid she'd bite her tongue any moment. The visions kept playing in her mind. *Leo, attacking Ramiel. Leo, roaring his rage. Leo, slashing…blood…so much blood.*

Leo put her on the ground.

"She seems to be having a seizure." It was the female angel who spoke. "Should I heal her?"

"*Don't touch her!*" Leo blasted. "Touching angels could be dangerous to her. Dammit, it sure as hell seems to have been dangerous." His hand slid over her cheek. "Mora, Mora, baby, look at me."

She was looking at him—and seeing him kill Ramiel. Over and over again.

"Mora, Mora, breathe with me. You're not breathing, baby, and I need you to breathe."

She wasn't breathing?

His eyes gleamed at her. The visions of blood and death slowly faded as she stared into his gaze.

"Breathe in," he said, his fingers so gentle against her cheek.

She eased in a breath for her starving lungs.

"Out," he told her.

The breath whispered past her lips.

"Again," he said, the thread of desperation in his voice reaching out to her. "Keep breathing.

You're going to be okay. *Keep breathing with me. In…"*

She breathed in with him.

"Out."

The breath left her.

Again and again, Mora focused on breathing with Leo. And soon the tremors stopped raking her body. Soon she was just lying there, staring up at him.

A wide smile slid across his face. "There you are."

I was always here.

He pulled her up and into his arms, his hold so tight it almost hurt. "Fucking scared me," he muttered as he pressed a kiss to her cheek. "No more touching angels for you."

Ramiel was the first angel she'd ever touched. Maybe she wasn't supposed to use her power on angels but…

Her head turned. Ramiel was glaring at her.

She lifted her head from Leo's shoulder and she mouthed the words. *I saw your fate.*

Ramiel paled.

So, yes, maybe she wasn't *supposed* to see an angel's future. But she *had* seen it. And it had been horrible.

The vision had just backed up what she'd feared. Leo was changing. With every moment that passed, he was becoming something far different than he'd been when she first met him.

Ramiel cleared his throat. "Are we going to stand around your *Fate* all night," he called, "or are we going to help the humans? Their time is running out."

Leo's jaw hardened. "Take the other angels and get near the humans. Stay there as a line of defense. Mora and I will go to the wolves."

Her heart was still beating far too fast in her chest.

"I think I should go with you," Ramiel argued. "Me and not her. What possible good will she do for you—"

"Angels always protect humans." Leo's voice was menacing. "You know that. Your job is to stay with them. Do your job."

"And you should do *yours*," Ramiel fired back with a gleaming glare. She hadn't thought angels were big on emotions, but this guy sure seemed to feel a whole lot. "Eliminate the dark things in this world."

His furious stare clearly said she was one of those dark things.

He hates me. So much.

"Tread carefully, Ram," Leo warned him. "Or you could find yourself eliminated."

And once more, the visions flashed before Mora's eyes. Leo's claws. Ramiel's blood. She wanted to scream…*Listen to him, Ramiel! You don't have much time left.*

But without another word, Ramiel took to the sky. The male angel followed him but the female…

She eased closer to Leo and Mora.

The angel's eyes swept over Mora. "Are you quite sure you're all right?" Her hand was in the air, as if she'd touch Mora. "I can…I can help."

Leo caught her hand before she could put her fingertips on Mora's skin. "No, Trina, she's fine. I have her."

"Of that, I have no doubt," Trina murmured. Her lips curled the faintest bit.

She was absolutely gorgeous. Her gaze was warm and dark, and when she looked at Mora, it was devoid of the hate that filled Ramiel's gaze.

"You have to excuse Ramiel," Trina said.

I do? Why?

"He's…had a lot of visions over the years. When you see so much pain and death, it can get to you. He wasn't supposed to feel all those emotions — that isn't an angel's lot — but they always hit him when the visions come." Then Trina's eyes widened. "Though, I suppose, you would understand that more than anyone else, wouldn't you? Just how painful it can be to see another's fate?"

"Yes," she rasped. *You see so much that it can drive you to the edge of sanity.*

"He's told me that…he's seen a lot of visions about you." Trina's gaze slid over Mora. "It's odd, though, you don't look as evil as he said."

A rough laugh broke from Mora. "Good to know."

Leo's shoulder brushed against her. "Mora isn't evil. She's *not* dark."

"Light paranormals, dark paranormals…good and bad…" Trina shook her head. "After all these centuries, I'm not so sure that it's one or the other." Her focus was on Leo. "Are *you*?"

For a moment, he didn't speak. Then, he finally said, "You should go help the others."

Trina nodded. Her hand had fallen back to her side. "Right." She turned away, but then paused, glancing over her shoulder. "You saw Ram's future, didn't you, Mora? I don't think…no one has ever seen an angel's future before. Wasn't sure anyone *could*. Ram can't, he—"

"I saw his fate." Her words came out sounding rusty. Her voice was oddly weak.

Trina's face slackened with surprise. And… her hand lifted once more, as if she'd touch Mora.

"No." Leo was solidly in front of her. He'd moved instantly. "You saw what happened when she touched him. She *isn't* going to be getting close to another angel anytime soon."

"Of…course." Trina's laugh was soft and musical. "Doesn't matter. I know my fate. It's to be an angel, to help others, and I have humans waiting on me right now." Without another word, she flew into the sky.

Mora was left alone with Leo.

He turned to face her. He reached out to touch her…

And Mora flinched back.

Leo stilled. "You're afraid of me?"

"No." *Yes.* "I didn't realize exactly what would hit me when I touched Ramiel. I was angry and I wasn't thinking clearly." She raked a shaking hand through her hair. "I have to work so hard to see your future. I thought…I thought I might get a few blurry images from Ramiel, but not much more. I just wanted to stop him. And I never thought—" Her words broke off.

Leo's body was stiff. "What did you see?"

If I tell him, will that change Ramiel's fate? Make it better or worse? Could it get worse? She swallowed. "You're changing, Leo."

"What?"

"Do you feel it, on the inside?" She wanted to put her hand over his heart, but fear was holding her back.

He took a step closer. "What I feel in me…I feel *you*, Mora. Beneath my skin. Like you're a part of me."

A howl split the night. Deep and echoing. Angry.

"Tell me what you saw," he urged her. "And then I have to go kick the asses of some wolves."

"I saw death." She saw it a lot. "I saw Ramiel dying."

His face hardened. "Someone killed an angel? Who would dare do something like that?"

The howl came again. Even louder. Even angrier. She swallowed twice and revealed, "You would, Leo. You would dare."

He backed up. "What?"

"You kill him. You slice away his wings. You destroy him in a river of blood." She swallowed once more and made sure that her spine was straight. "So I ask you again, do you feel yourself changing on the inside? Is something happening?"

Leo shook his head, a hard, jerky move. "You are wrong."

If only. "I have been wrong before." Her voice had turned soft. "I can see it now. But I wasn't the only one…"

His brows furrowed. "I'm *not* killing Ramiel. I might want to kick the guy's ass because of the way he talked to you but—"

Howls. Loud and wild.

"Screw it," Leo snarled. "One problem at a time. And right now, the wolves are problem one. I'm taking them out before they can go after the humans." He offered his hand to her. "I need you at my side, Mora. I have to keep you close. If the hellhounds appear, you will *not* be unprotected."

She stared at his hand.

"Touching me has never led to a vision before. Not without a blood offering and a mirror."

But everything is changing with you…

Her hand slowly rose—and settled over his. She tensed, but no visions hit her. There was nothing…just the darkness around them.

"Was that so hard?" Leo murmured.

"You have no idea."

He stared at her. "When we get to the wolves, when the blood starts flowing and when my fire comes at them, you stay behind me, understand?"

"Leo—"

"I need you safe, Mora. If I think you're in danger…" He rolled back his shoulders. "Just…let me protect you, okay?"

She hesitated a moment, staring hard at him. Then she gave a grim nod. "You're the one with the fire power." Literally, she'd seen fire shoot from his hands. But she wasn't going to promise to stand back helplessly. That wasn't her style.

***

"So what's their story?" Trina asked as her feet lightly touched down on the ground. She could see the light from the humans' fire. Nearby, there were about two dozen humans, camping out, laughing, pitching their tents for the night and thinking they were safe in the desert. *You aren't safe, not even close.* "Leo and Fate, how long have they been together?"

Ramiel's wings had vanished. He didn't reply to her question. The other angel—Merius—he was always the quiet one. She'd barely heard the guy speak a handful of words in the last decade. So she wasn't particularly surprised when he didn't talk. But Ram? The fellow usually wouldn't shut up.

"Uh, Ram?" Trina pressed as she crept closer to him. His eyes were on the humans. "Want to clue me in here?"

"I think she owns him. Body and soul."

Trina blinked. "Seriously?" It was hard for her to imagine Leo falling for anyone. The guy was often so…cold.

Like ice.

"Seriously." His voice was flat. "She's a threat to him. To us all."

Trina licked her lips. The humans couldn't see them. Humans could never see angels, well, not unless an angel *wanted* to be seen. But that was kind of against the rules. Leo's rules. "I think she saw your future."

He whirled toward her. "She was playing a mind game. That's what she does. She's dark. She manipulates humans and paranormals. She makes them think she knows their fates, but she doesn't. She's just jerking everyone around."

Her heart lurched. What could have been fear slid through her. Only—angels didn't generally experience fear. They didn't experience many emotions at all.

Ram seems to be feeling plenty, though. Anger is in his eyes. She'd seen anger often enough in the expressions of humans. She could easily recognize that emotion. "Do you think she was…jerking you around?"

"Doesn't matter." He squared his shoulders. "She won't be a problem for long."

That didn't sound good. "Ram?"

Merius stalked closer to them.

A howl split the night. Then another…

Trina shivered.

"We have to protect the humans," Ramiel said curtly. "Nothing else can matter." His gaze slid to Merius. "Agreed?"

Merius, still silent, nodded.

Ramiel's gaze turned to her. "Agreed?"

"O-of course." She knew her duty. "I'll always keep the humans safe."

Ramiel smiled at her. "I knew I could count on you."

CHAPTER FOURTEEN

The bar sat in the middle of nowhere—just right on that long, dusty road. Lights gleamed from inside the small building, and over two dozen motorcycles were parked along the place's perimeter. Music trickled from the windows, something rough and hard, and, behind Leo, Mora let out a little sigh. "Makes me miss my bar." Her voice was wistful. "Resurrection was a lot like this place."

"It wasn't a werewolf den."

"No…"

More howls reached him. The wolves were all inside—and from the sound of things, they were building themselves up to a fever pitch. "They're getting ready to attack." He took a few more steps toward the bar.

Then Mora's hand curled around his arm. "Wait!"

He glanced back at her.

"Just…what are you going to do? What's the plan?"

It was a simple, straight forward plan. "I'm going to eliminate the threat." Luke should have taken care of a wild pack of wolves. To let them go after humans—

Her face scrunched up a bit. "But there isn't a threat. Not yet. There are just…howls."

What? "You heard Ramiel. He has intel on these werewolves. They are going to attack the humans. His visions are never wrong."

She flinched. "But what? Mine are?"

Shit. "No, that's not what I—"

"Are you going to kill them all, just on Ramiel's word? Because I've got to tell you, I don't like that angel."

"You may not like him, but…angels don't lie. He's telling me exactly what he saw. I have to stop these wolves or they will torture and kill humans tonight." And as the Lord of the Light, the humans fell under his domain. He was supposed to—

"Are you going to burn them? Is that it? Send fire bursting from your fingertips and right at the bar, with them all trapped inside? Never giving them any chance?"

His back teeth clenched.

"Because that seems a little familiar to me. I mean, it wasn't so long ago that I was in my bar, minding my own business, when some fire happy jerk tried to end my life, too."

It was *not* the same. Was it? "Mora…"

"I want to give them a chance."

He shook his head.

"I want to give them a chance."

Her voice was even stronger the second time she made that statement. He could only stare at her in confusion. "A chance to do what? Attack humans? Attack *you?*"

"A chance to prove their intent. I want to see their fates for myself."

That hadn't been part of the deal. She'd agreed to stay behind him so—

Her eyes trapped him. "I've got you at my side. The big, bad Lord of the Light. If they attack, I have no doubt you can take them all down. That's your thing, right?" She put her hands on his chest and leaned up on her tip toes. "You go all beast mode and you take out the threats near you."

Yes, he did.

"I'm just saying…hold on. Let me see what's happening in that bar. Let me see—"

The scent of blood filled the air. He heard a scream. A roar. And the blood and screams and roars—they were coming from inside the bar.

Werewolves…*fucking wild animals.*

"Let me see," Mora whispered again. "Hold the fire, okay?"

Her eyes were so big and deep. And she was staring up at him with…what the hell? Hope? What did she hope he'd do?

Werewolves weren't his to protect. He could end them all and it wouldn't matter. No loss for him. Humans were his. Humans...*Her gaze is so damn deep.* "Fine," he snapped in frustration. "But if a wolf so much as growls in your direction, he's dead."

Her smile slid across her face. *So beautiful.* Then she was grabbing his hand and practically dragging him toward the ramshackle bar. But when they reached the door, he stopped and made sure she was safely shielded behind him.

Another roar echoed in the night.

Leo kicked in the wooden door. It flew back, banging against the wall. He stepped inside and the scent of blood was so much stronger. And he could see why — two werewolves were circling each other in the middle of the bar. All of the others were surrounding the two fighters, cheering and howling.

The two werewolves fighting had fully shifted. One was a long, sleek, brown wolf and the other was a gray wolf — a wolf that was on the floor, slipping in a pool of blood as the beast struggled to rise to his feet.

"You don't belong here." A big, burly guy with a mess of red hair stepped into Leo's path. "You both need to get the fuck out."

Leo smiled at him. "I belong everywhere."

The fellow locked his hand around Leo's shoulder.

Big mistake. "Listen up—"

"Are they fighting for alpha dominance?" Mora asked, breaking right through Leo's words.

The redhead's gaze swung to her. His stare narrowed, then swept over her. His eyes began to warm—

"Watch your damn self," Leo warned him. "She's with me."

"Her poor choice," the wolf shifter tossed back without any pause. *"Lord of the Light."*

Leo's eyes narrowed as he stared at the redheaded wolf.

The wolf smiled grimly. "I've met your brother," the wolf stated with a shrug of his tree-like shoulders. "A time or ten."

Ramiel had been right. Luke did set this pack to go after the humans—

"He would never show up holding the hand of any woman who wasn't his Mina." The wolf shifter stroked his chin. "The guy is lost in her."

Mina…that was Luke's mate. For the wolf to know her name…Leo studied the guy with new interest. "Who are you?"

The two wolves were fighting again. The gray wolf had managed to rise, but in the next instant, the brown wolf sliced his claws over the injured beast's belly. A pain-filled howl shook the bar. The scent of blood deepened.

Mora flinched.

"It *is* an alpha fight," the redhead answered Mora's question with a wave of his hand and another unconcerned shrug. "Looks like we'll be keeping our current boss. Pity you didn't arrive five minutes sooner, you could have got in the betting pool before it closed down. Smart money was always on Bruce. He's the baddest alpha I know."

Bruce. He had to be the brown wolf. The one who was using claws and teeth to destroy his opponent. As Leo watched, the gray wolf collapsed on the floor, apparently too tired or too weak to fight any longer. He actually appeared more red than gray because so much blood covered him.

"Old Bruce doesn't much like you or your kind," the redheaded wolf said as he crossed his arms over his chest. "So if you and your pretty lady don't want to find yourselves in the middle of a blood bath of your own, then you'd better—"

"*I'm betting on the gray wolf.*" Mora's voice rang out—high and strong, clear and feminine. Sexy as hell.

Every eye in the room swung toward her.

Leo tightened his hold on her hand. *Mora, baby, what in the hell are you doing?*

"The gray wolf is going to be the new alpha." A smile spread across her face.

Murmurs filled the room.

"Who is that crazy bitch?"

"Is that Luke? Fuck, what's the Lord of the Dark doing here?"

Ah, obviously, the other wolves weren't as familiar with Luke as their redheaded greeter was.

Mora's shouts had attracted the attention of the fighting, brown wolf—the one that had been called Bruce. He turned toward Mora and bared his blood-stained teeth at her.

The hell he did. So the guy didn't like being told he wasn't going to win the fight, so—

Bruce leapt into the air and charged straight at Mora. Leo let out a guttural roar and jumped in front of her, more than ready to rip that alpha apart. Claws sprang from Leo's fingertips and—

The gray wolf shot up from his prone position. As his opponent rushed by him, the gray wolf attacked. His claws ripped into Bruce's back and then his fangs tore into Bruce's throat. Bruce let out a choked, desperate cry.

Everyone in that bar froze.

And then Bruce…fell. His body slumped to the floor as the gray wolf finally let him go.

Silence.

The fur slowly melted from Bruce's body. A man's pale flesh was revealed. And so was the gaping hole where his throat should have been.

"Holy fuck!"

"We got a new alpha!"

"Did you see that shit? That sexy piece of ass called the winner! She must be a damn witch!"

Leo turned and eyed Mora. "Not a witch," he muttered. *Fate.*

Mora bit her lower lip. Her hands twisted in front of her. "Was that…my fault?"

Her fault? She'd distracted Bruce, given his opponent the perfect moment to strike and now…

"We have a new alpha!" It was the redhead's booming voice. He'd waded through the blood on the floor. The gray wolf was at his feet, slowly transforming. Bones popped and snapped, the fur vanished, and soon, a young male — with jet black hair and bright green eyes — was rising to his feet. "Alpha Patrick!"

Shouts filled the bar. Howls. Growls. Leo couldn't tell if he was watching a celebration or a coming battle.

But…

"Bring the woman to me." Patrick's voice was gravel rough. "I want her, now."

Just like that — all eyes were back on Leo…and Mora.

Oh, the hell, no.

A slow smile curved Leo's lips. His fangs were out and so were his claws. His whole body seemed to burn as he stared into Patrick's gaze. "She's mine."

Patrick took a step toward him. All of the wolves had gone dead silent.

"Leo, I think we all need to calm down," Mora whispered frantically. "Let's talk—"

"*Leo…*" Patrick repeated his name. Of course, the guy had heard Mora's whisper. Werewolves had fantastic enhanced hearing. "The Lord of the Light is *here*?" He rolled back his shoulders and laughed. "We don't bow to you. You made one big ass mistake walking into this bar…"

Leo glanced around the place. He counted at least twenty, maybe thirty shifters in his fast survey. He lifted both of his hands and fire began to dance over his palms. "You *will* be bowing." He could wipe them all out. And when he did, when he took out the werewolves, Luke would come for him.

War. The end. The battle to the death.

It was at hand.

Either Leo killed those werewolves—*and Luke comes for me…*

Or the werewolves went out and attacked the humans—*and I have no choice but to go after Luke in retaliation.*

Fucking hell. Fucking—

Mora stepped in front of Leo. "I'm Fate." She pointed at Patrick. "And I'm here for you."

***

"The werewolves haven't attacked." Trina's voice was soft. "And I can see the sun starting to rise."

Ramiel followed her gaze. Sure enough, he could see the streaks of red and gold sliding faintly across the sky. Night still reigned, for the moment.

"Does that mean that Leo stopped them?" Trina pushed.

Beside her, Merius was silent. But, like Trina, his gaze was on the rising sun.

"Or does it mean…" Her voice was even softer now. "That the werewolves are stopping *him?*"

"Leo's stronger than the wolves." Of that, Ramiel had no doubt. "He'll kill them all."

Trina's gaze swung to him. "And then what happens? Luke won't take kindly to his brother killing those under the Lord of the Dark's dominion."

Like he cared what the Lord of the Dark liked. "Everyone has to pick a side, sooner or later." He'd been waiting for this moment a very long time. He looked back over his shoulder, his gaze sweeping over the human camp. They slept, so easily. So deeply.

Safe…

Because angels are watching over you.

Humans were lucky. They had no idea what dangers really waited in the world.

A faint growl broke the silence of the coming dawn.

Trina tensed.

Merius spun, his gaze searching the darkness.

And then the attack came.

CHAPTER FIFTEEN

She could feel the flames behind her, but Mora didn't think for even a second that Leo would burn her. *He'd sure as hell better not.*

The new werewolf alpha was standing in front of her — completely naked, with claws springing from his fingertips and blood on his skin. His eyes were glowing and he —

"Thank you." Patrick inclined his head toward her. "I appreciate the help you gave me." A faint smile curled his lips. "Though I am sure I would have still defeated Bruce even without your rather timely…distraction."

Her breath was coming too hard and too fast, and her heart was about to leap right out of her chest. Both were unfortunate side effects of the fear that filled her. She tried to calm her nerves, but she was seriously stressed since she'd never been surrounded by a room full of werewolves before.

"Why did you distract him?" Patrick murmured.

She licked her lips. "Um, because I knew you were going to be alpha."

A strong hand curled over her shoulder. *Leo.*

"How did you know that?" Patrick asked as he cocked his head to the side and studied her.

"Damn naked werewolves," Leo groused. "I swear, I get tired of this crap." And clothes suddenly appeared on Patrick's body. In Mora's ear, Leo rasped, "I *don't* want a naked werewolf touching-close to you."

He was jealous? Right then? With everything else going on? That was almost cute. Or it was crazy. Crazy cute.

"I'm Fate," Mora announced, making sure that her voice carried. She wanted all of the wolves to hear what she had to say. "And I knew it was your destiny to rule this pack."

Patrick's gaze slid over her. "Bullshit."

"Watch your fucking tone with her," Leo snarled. "I can burn this whole place to the ground in seconds, and your pack will go down in flames."

Patrick tensed. Mora saw the nervous — and furious — glances that were being exchanged by the pack members.

She also saw Bruce being picked up. He was still alive. Healing, slowly. His head sagged forward, and his eyes were covered by his thick, long hair. Mora cleared her throat. "Can we go somewhere and…talk, privately, Patrick?"

But Patrick shook his head. "What you say to me, you say to my pack." His stare shifted to Leo. "And I'm dying to know why the Lord of the Light thinks he can come *here*."

"Because I can go anywhere," Leo threw right back. "Especially when you're planning to attack humans. To *kill* and destroy the peace." He stepped toward Patrick, standing toe-to-toe with the wolf. "Did my brother give that order? Did he *tell* you to attack? Or are you breaking his law, too?"

"What?" Patrick shook his head and appeared genuinely confused. "No, you've got it wrong. We aren't attacking any humans—"

And she saw it happen. Because Mora was staring at Bruce, still watching him, she saw the exact moment when he dropped his fake pose of being too weak to move...

His head whipped up. The hair flew away from his eyes and she saw the pure hate glittering in his stare. He rushed forward, his claws out, lunging to attack.

Oh, shit, he's coming for me!

Patrick whirled to grab Bruce, but...

Leo beat him.

Leo leapt forward and put his hand on Bruce's chest. Just his hand...and the ex-alpha ignited. Bruce was screaming and howling as he burned and in just a few seconds, ash was the only thing left of the guy. Ash that drifted to the floor…and then vanished.

Mora had forgotten to breathe during that fast attack. In the aftermath, she sucked in deep gulps of air.

Leo can incinerate someone with a touch? Since when?

"Any questions?" Leo drawled. "Or do you all get that I am not here to screw around?"

Patrick gaped at him.

"Want to be next?" Leo's body seemed to vibrate with power. "Or do you want to take Fate up on that private talk?"

Patrick swallowed and pointed to a door on the side of the bar. "Let's talk."

"Excellent choice," Leo announced.

Patrick turned and hurried toward that door. Mora followed him, with Leo on her heels and as they walked, the other wolf shifters slowly bowed their heads. Were they showing their submission…to their new alpha? Or…

She risked a fast glance over her shoulder. *To Leo?*

Patrick shoved open the door, and she followed him quickly, entering the small, tight confines of a back office. He turned to face her, crossing his arms over his chest, even as she heard the door click shut behind her. Mora glanced back at Leo. He'd closed that door and now he stood in front of it, his legs braced apart, and his hands loose at his sides.

"You're not really…her…are you?" Patrick asked as his gaze swept over her body. "I mean, that was just some BS line to impress the others out there, right?" And, before she could answer, he inclined his head. "You can speak freely in here. This place has special sound-proofing installed. Our, um, recently deceased pack member Bruce always wanted a room where he could talk without being overheard by the others."

Mora squared her shoulders. "I'm Fate. No BS involved."

Patrick's eyes widened. "Then you knew — just looking at me — that I would be the next alpha?"

Actually, no. "To know your fate, I'd need to touch you."

His brows flew up. "But, you said — "

"A word, a whisper…a look…that's how easy it is for me to change some things." This was a truth that she rarely shared, mostly because it was so dangerous. "I wanted you to win because we knew Bruce was going to lead the attack on the humans. I figured you were our best hope of avoiding that attack."

"He…he never mentioned an attack to me." Patrick's lips pressed together, then he said, "But Bruce was a secretive bastard. And a fucking twisted alpha. He got off on pain—giving it to his own kind…and, I've suspected, to humans, too. It was past time for him to be stopped. Someone had to step up." He nodded. "So I did."

She wanted to touch him. To see just what fate waited. Mora inched toward Patrick and her hand lifted.

But before her fingers could touch his arm, Leo was there. His hand caught hers. "Careful, baby, I don't trust this wolf."

"You don't trust any wolves," she retorted instantly. Her gaze dropped to Leo's hand. He was touching her so carefully, holding her so gently, but that same hand had incinerated a man moments before. She stared at his hand a moment longer and then her gaze lifted to his face.

What is your real fate, Leo? But, as always, she couldn't see what the future held for him. Not just from a touch. If she wanted another peek, she'd need his blood and she'd need to scry.

"I have nothing to hide," Patrick drawled, a faint Texas accent roughening his words. "Let Fate touch me. She can see for herself that I'm not planning to attack humans. And I won't let any of my pack members do it, either. They'll follow my orders. Luke has laws in place for a reason. We don't want a war with humans or with you, *Lord of the Light*."

Slowly, Leo let her go. She put her fingertips on Patrick's forearm and…

Patrick bows his head…to Leo. The wolves surround Leo, forming a tight circle. As one, they turn to face the threat.

"Don't stop until they're dead!" Leo shouted.

She jerked back her hand. Blinked.

"Did you see my future?" Patrick asked her.

Mora nodded.

"And am I attacking humans?"

She looked back at Leo. It had been Leo in her vision, not Luke. She knew him…always. "Patrick is on your side, Leo."

Leo frowned at her.

"He's not going to attack humans." *Not unless you order it.* "He will stand with you. You have nothing to fear from Patrick or his pack." She tucked a lock of hair behind her ear. "Ramiel was wrong or maybe…maybe things would have been different if Bruce lived. But he didn't. And the humans are safe. Their blood won't spill on the ground."

The tension slowly left Leo's shoulders.

But it didn't leave hers. "We should go meet the angels. Let them know the danger has passed."

"Angels?" Patrick repeated. "Serious fucking *angels?*"

Leo opened the door. He offered his hand to Mora, and she took it, wrapping her fingers around his. They walked out of that bar, and the werewolves didn't speak as she and Leo passed by them. The shifters barely seemed to move.

Mora and Leo were just about to exit the building when—

"Fate!" Patrick's shout.

She looked over her shoulder.

"I won't forget what you did! You need payback, remember I'm here."

She blinked in surprise. She didn't usually make deals with people. That was…Luke's thing. Leo's thing. But…a werewolf alpha owed her?

Interesting.

Leo pushed open the door and then they were outside. The sky was lit with red and gold streaks. Dawn had come. The darkness had passed. For now.

Leo pulled her into his arms and his wings swept out. As he flew them high into the sky, Mora glanced back down. The werewolves had followed them outside, and they were watching as Leo took her away.

"They aren't going to forget us anytime soon," she said even as the vision of those wolves—circling around Leo as if to protect him—filled her mind once more.

"Ramiel was wrong." Leo's voice was a deep rumble, one that she could almost feel sliding through her body. "I went there, intending to do anything necessary to stop their attack. I…I was going to kill them all." There was a hesitation in his voice that she'd never heard before.

Leo wasn't exactly the hesitating type.

The wind whipped her hair back and her arms tightened around him. "Do you…" Oh, jeez, how to ask this question? "Do you often kill with a touch?"

Silence. She saw his jaw harden. "I've killed many that way." His head turned. His gaze met hers. "You think I'm a monster." He was taking them back toward the ground.

She swallowed. Her mouth had gone absolutely dry. When he touched down on the earth, he kept holding her in his arms. "I've never called you a monster."

His wings vanished. "Calling someone a beast…and *thinking* it are two different things."

"Let me go. I can stand on my own now."

Slowly, he lowered her to the ground, but his hands stayed on her. He didn't let her go. "Do you think you fucked a monster, baby?"

Mora flinched, but her chin lifted. "No, I think I fucked a man. Because that's how I see you. I don't see the big, tough Lord of the Light. I don't even see the dragon that I know sleeps inside of you."

Most people didn't realize that was the nature of his beast…not until the fire came for them.

"I've *never* thought you were a monster," Mora continued as her stare held his. "But I can't control how you see yourself."

His eyelids lowered, concealing his gaze from her. "You saw what I did to the wolf, Bruce."

"Turned him straight to ash." Like she'd be forgetting that act anytime soon. "And I'm betting you can do that to anyone, can't you?"

His fingertips pressed a bit harder to her skin. "I would *never* do anything to hurt you. I need you to believe that. Our past—"

"I let it go," Mora cut in, heart racing. "You have to do the same, don't you see that? We have here and now, not the past."

"But what about the future? About what's coming?"

She didn't want to think about the future right then. She'd spent centuries worrying about the future. It would be nice to just live in the moment. But that was an impossibility for them. "I'll scry for you," she told him even though she'd vowed to do no such thing in the very recent past. "Once you and I are far away from here, I'll tell you exactly what waits. No conditions. No hesitations. I'll—"

He kissed her. It was a rough and demanding kiss, wild with hunger and a stark, almost savage need. Maybe she should have pulled back.

She didn't.

Her need for him was just as savage. Her lips opened. Her tongue met his. Greedy, frantic desire erupted within her and Mora pressed her body desperately to his. She'd gone so long without him in her life. She'd thought she was long over him.

But there were some things…some men…

That you just *didn't* get over.

"The only thing that waits in my future…" Leo breathed the words against her lips. "It's *you*. You're the only person that matters to me."

Instinctively, she shook her head, denying—

"You, Mora. I would rip this world apart for you. I would fucking live and die…for you."

She'd squeezed her eyes shut, but at his rough, utterly terrifying words, her lashes lifted. She found herself staring into his eyes, but it was a stare so different…bright, glowing. Shining with power and intent.

He meant what he was saying.

"I lost you…" He kissed her again. But softer, with more seduction, as if he were trying to woo her. "I lost you, and I swear, my whole life seemed to go dark."

A fist squeezed her heart…*No, no, it can't be… Because of me?*

"I need you, Mora. I want to fucking kiss every single inch of you. You gave me a taste before, but I need you again. I will *always* need you. Always crave you."

She was afraid that she'd always crave him, too.

The wind blew against them, sliding her hair over her cheek and…

He tensed. *"Blood."*

"What?"

"I smell blood on the wind." His head whipped toward the right and she saw his nostrils flare. "A whole lot of *blood.*"

"The humans?" Her heart nearly stopped. "I thought they were safe! The werewolves aren't attacking them—"

"Someone is attacking. They're *dying.*"

"We have to get to them!"

His wings were already out. She locked her arms around his neck and they burst up into the sky, and as they flew, the scent of blood reached her.

The scent of blood…

And the sound of screams.

CHAPTER SIXTEEN

"It's not the werewolves," Mora said, her voice tight and scared in Leo's ear. He hated her fear. As far as he was concerned, Mora should never know a moment's fear. "Someone else is attacking them."

Attacking them, killing them.

I sent the angels to watch over the humans. What happened to the angels? Why aren't they stopping the carnage?

Then he saw the first body. Ripped apart. Blood thick on the ground. A human...

Fury beat inside of him. "Stay with me. At my side." Each word was gritted out. He had to get down there. But Mora...

She cannot be hurt.

They touched the ground, and there were no more screams. Only silence. The wind whipping against him. And blood.

Tents had been torn to shreds. Bodies lay broken.

And...

Feathers drifted in the wind.

"Please…" Mora's voice was so small. "Tell me those aren't from an angel's wings."

He couldn't lie to her. He—

Mora bent before he could say a word, and she locked her fingers around a feather. A shudder went through her body as she knelt there, and then her head was snapping back. Her eyes turned absolutely black for a moment as she stared at him. "Merius…they took his wings…they're *killing* him." She pointed to the left, and Leo took off running. *With* Mora.

Merius…the silent angel. The one who always seemed so stoic, but Leo knew the truth about him. Merius was quiet because he had a weakness the others angels didn't. Merius felt *too much.* Angels were supposed to be immune to the emotions of humans, but Merius wasn't. He'd gotten a taste for emotions a long time ago, when he'd first met a little blonde vampire. One who hadn't realized she'd bitten an angel…

And turned his world upside down.

Leo ran to the left, but he kept Mora close, yanking her against him because he knew she didn't move at the same speed he did. He burst around two massive boulders and found Merius. The angel was lying face down on the bloody ground and his wings were gone…

Three wolves circled him.

Fully transformed wolves.

What in the hell? Patrick swore his pack wouldn't attack. They swore…

Leo lifted his hand and sent a blast of fire at the wolves. Two of them immediately leapt back, but the third…that hulking white beast tore into Merius's throat.

Mora slipped from Leo's grasp as he bounded toward the white wolf. He grabbed the bastard and yanked him back from Merius, sending a bolt of fire ripping across the wolf's body.

The white wolf howled and shuddered…

And then he turned to ash.

The ash rained down on Merius. A still, bloody, barely breathing Merius.

The other two wolves had raced away.

Leo put his hand on Merius's throat. An angel fell under his domain. He could heal Merius. He could…

Blood pumped between his fingers. The wound didn't close. Merius shuddered.

"Where are the others?" Mora cried. "Where's Trina? And Ramiel?"

Merius's lips parted, as if he'd speak, but nothing came out.

The bastard wolf ripped out his throat.

Leo pulled up more of his power, sending it all pouring right at Merius. Of *course,* he could heal the angel. He could heal any creature of the light.

A scream reached him. High, desperate, and then there was silence.

Leo's head snapped toward the sound. He found Mora staring with wide eyes. "I'll go," she yelled even as she whipped away from him. "I'll help—you save your angel!"

"No!" Leo bellowed after her. Mora was no match for werewolves. She—

"I can't die!" Mora yelled back at him. "I can hurt, but I can't die, so save him and get your ass after me!"

Fuck, *fuck*.

She was gone.

And Merius was still pumping out his blood. His wings had been slashed right from his body. He was at his absolute most vulnerable. He *needed* Leo's help.

But I can't help him. I can't heal him. He's dying right in front of me.

Why? How?

"I'm…sorry," Leo said, the words grinding from him.

Merius lifted his lashes. There was so much pain in his eyes. Pain…and what looked like fury. Betrayal?

"Merius…"

The life faded from the angel's gaze. Just…emptied.

"No." The ground trembled around Leo. "*No!*" His roar echoed like thunder as lightning split the overhead sky.

His hand was still on Merius's throat. Blood soaked his fingers. He'd given the angel all the power he had. Merius *should* have healed.

But something is wrong.

Leo jumped to his feet. "*Mora! Come back to me!*" His voice bellowed out as terror clawed at him. But she wasn't there. She'd gone to help another victim.

Claws burst from his fingertips. He felt his teeth lengthen, sharpen, and the white-hot fury of his rage burned inside as the beast he kept chained began to struggle for freedom.

***

Mora scrambled around the bodies. She tried not to look at them, tried not to see the men and women they'd been — before something had ripped them apart.

Patrick didn't lie to us. I saw his future. His werewolves haven't attacked.

Had Ramiel been wrong? Was there another pack in the area? Maybe rogues?

She stopped and spun around, searching desperately for Trina or Ramiel. There were no more screams and the scent of blood was coming from every direction. It was truly a blood bath. Truly hell and—

"*Help...*"

Mora raced toward that weak cry. She jumped over a tent in shambles, then saw a parking lot waiting about twenty paces away. A body was slumped on the pavement of the lot. A human who'd almost gotten to safety?

No, not a human.

As Mora ran closer to the victim, she saw the bloody wings. Wings that were still attached to—

"Trina!"

Trina turned toward her. The angel's hands were pressed to her stomach...to the terrible wounds that bled and bled. Mora's knees hit the pavement next to her as she reached for the angel. "It's okay. You're going to be all right. Leo is here. He's going to stop the werewolves." Mora's fingers brushed over Trina's.

And the images hit her.

Werewolves...stalking closer to Trina. Seeing the angel try to crawl away because she was so weak. Then the wolves form a tight circle. Growling and snapping, they come at the angel with their mouths open, only...

Their bodies are shifting. Transforming into something different. Not a wolf. Something—

Trina grabbed Mora's hand and held tight. "Not...wolf..."

The angel was echoing the vision Mora had just seen.

"H-hell…" Trina whimpered. "…hound…"

Oh, shit.

Then Mora heard the growl behind her. She whipped around and the vision she'd just seen…it was already becoming reality. Big, snarling wolves were coming out of the shadows. They were closing in on Trina.

And they're closing in on me. I didn't see myself in the vision…But they're here, and they're going to attack us both.

A big, tan wolf pawed at the ground, and as Mora stared at him, the beast seemed to grow even bigger. His teeth became even sharper.

"You're not a werewolf," Mora yelled. "It was a trick." All of it. "You're hellhounds!"

She could see it, in their eyes. In eyes that glowed with the fires of hell.

Leo had told her that the hounds would return.

And guess who is already back? Back…and they were coming for her.

"I know who you are," she spat at them. "I know *what* you are."

The wolf in the back of the group transformed. It wasn't the bone-popping, fur melting transformation of a werewolf. In a blink, the beast was gone and a man stood in his place.

A man she recognized.

He was tall, muscled, and wearing a go-to-hell grin. "Hello, Fate."

Mora sucked in a sharp breath. It was the same asshole who'd kidnapped her before. The bastard who'd held her in that basement—and…

I can see it now. The curve of his jaw. The hard edge of his nose. The sneer he wore…he was the same man who'd haunted her nightmares for so long. The same man who'd driven her to jump from her room in Greece because he'd been burning the place down around her.

Werewolves hadn't attacked the humans. Hellhounds had.

Hellhounds who were after her and Leo.

"Have we ever been properly introduced?" he asked with a slow smile. "I'm Reever."

Mora positioned her body in front of Trina. "Stay away from us!"

"But it's so much fun to take the wings from angels. They always think they're so fucking superior. Then you rip the wings away, and they have nothing." He laughed and the beast in front of Mora pawed at the ground. The third attacker was also still in wolf form, and he was starting to circle close. Soon the attack would come, *just like it did in my vision.*

"Did he leave you alone?" Reever shouted to her. "Leo deserted his favorite thing? Not very protective of him. Not very *caring.* But then, I've always maintained that Leo doesn't really give a shit for you. You're just a toy to amuse—"

"*Go back to hell,*" Mora screamed at him. It was bad enough he was about to attack. Did she have to listen to his BS, too?

Reever laughed—

And claws burst through the leader's chest. His mouth dropped open in shock as he stared down, because, obviously, he hadn't heard Leo's approach. If he had, then maybe the guy wouldn't have been such a boastful asshole. Blood began to drip from the hellhound leader's mouth and he tried to spin and attack Leo—

But Leo's fire took him. Reever was screaming as he burned and Mora had to look away from the terrible sight. She turned her stare away just as— *The two wolves attacked.* They came at Mora, and one locked its teeth around her arm. She yelled as she touched him, sinking her fingers deep in his fur.

Fire. Burning and burning and never stopping. Screams all around. Never ends. The gates will open...all will be free —

Leo yanked the wolf away from her. He tossed the beast into the air, and it slammed onto the top of a car. The beast didn't rise.

One wolf was left. A beast who swung his head between Leo and Mora. The beast began to inch back.

Leo lifted his hand. Fire danced over his fingertips. No, over his *claws*. "Hell is waiting on you. And I'm going to make sure you don't get a ticket back this time. You're staying down there. And you'll burn and burn. You'll pay for the humans you killed."

The beast transformed. He lifted his hands — pale hands. His hair was so blond it was almost white and his body was skeletally thin. "I was following orders! You can't punish me for doing what *you* wanted!"

Shock rolled through Mora. No, no, he was lying.

But the blond pointed to Mora. "Starting with her…I've always done what you wanted! Given the pain you ordered. Taken the lives you wanted claimed. You send us to the fire, but then you pull us back again and again, and we *always* follow your orders!"

Behind Mora, Trina was crying.

"He's lying, Mora," Leo snarled. "And it's the last mistake he's making."

Leo lunged, his hand outstretched, the fire streaking toward the blond, and Mora knew if the fire touched that hellhound, there would be no answers for her.

She leapt forward, moving as fast as possible, faster than most people realized that she *could* move. She felt the lick of flames along her back.

"*No!*" Leo roared.

She was in front of the fire. If he didn't pull it back — *can he even do that now?* — she knew it would pour over her body. But she'd heal.

She always healed. The scars were never on the outside, just the inside.

There were so many scars inside.

She reached out her hand and touched the hellhound.

At the same instant, she felt Leo's arms close around her body. He pulled her close, and her back pressed to his stomach. There was no fire. There was only...

Leo.

And the visions. Visions that flew through her head as she saw the hellhound's fate.

Leo's claws flash. The hellhound's head falls. The fire surrounds him again. He sinks down, down, and then he's waiting. Rising again because his master calls.

His master...

A flash of light came. Bright, blinding.

And then the wings were the only thing she could see. The hellhound master's wings.

"Mora!" Leo whipped her around to face him, and Mora blinked. The visions vanished and the scent of ash filled her nose.

Leo stared at her with a frantic gaze, his eyes sweeping over her face.

"It's okay," she whispered, "I'm—"

"Never step in front of my fire!" His roar was terrifying. His fury evident. *"Never!"* He held her so tightly she feared he might break her bones. "Mora, I was afraid I'd burn you. Your beautiful

skin…That I'd hurt you…" He shuddered against her.

She managed to turn her head to the right and look down. She saw the blond's head a few feet away. His head wasn't connected to his body. Immediately, her eyes squeezed shut.

That part of my vision has already come true.

"You can't risk yourself. You can't—"

"I saw who was controlling them. I saw who is going to summon the hellhounds back."

His hold eased on her. He pulled back, stared down at her, and swallowed. "Not…me."

"Of course, not you," she muttered and she shoved at him. She scrambled to Trina and put her hands on the angel's wounds. *Shouldn't she be healing?* Trina still had her wings, thank goodness, so she should heal. An angel's power was always tied to her wings.

Only she wasn't healing

Leo knelt next to Mora and immediately put his hands on the angel. Trina shuddered and her hand flew up. Her fingers linked with Mora's. "I don't…want to die."

"You're not dying!" Mora told her. And she held tight to the angel. "You're going to heal, okay? You'll be fine." She cut a quick glance at Leo. His hands were glowing as he touched Trina's wounds but… "Leo…" His name was a worried whisper. "What's happening?"

His head turned. His eyes met hers. "I don't know."

Mora kept her hold on Trina's hand, but she put her mouth to Leo's ear. "Why aren't you healing her?"

"*I can't!*"

There was such stark desperation and fear in his voice. Mora slipped back, staring at him, and she knew…"We need Luke."

Leo shook his head and his hands pressed harder to Trina. "He can't heal an angel. His power doesn't work on light paranormals." Strain showed on his face. "I couldn't save Merius, but I *will* save her. I swear, I will save her."

Mora tilted her head back and stared at the sky. "*Luke!*" She screamed for Leo's twin, knowing there was no choice, not if they wanted to save the angel.

But Luke didn't appear. He didn't come for her summons. She didn't even know if the guy could hear her cry. But there was one cry he'd never be able to ignore. "Call your brother," Mora told him.

Sweat slid down Leo's face. His focus seemed to be solely on Trina. "It's going to be okay. I'll save—"

"Call. Luke." Mora said, her voice choking because what was going to happen…she was afraid. "You can't save her. I've *seen* her dying, with you crouched over her just as you are."

He wasn't looking at Mora. So she grabbed him, and she shook him. *Hard.*

"Listen to me!" Mora knew she was yelling. "I've *seen* the angel die. Her blood is on your hands. You try to save her, and it doesn't work. I *saw* this. The image just came to me moments ago. You can keep trying, but it will do no good. If you want her to live, call your brother. Summon him, and do it right now."

His lips parted. "But Luke can't help angels."

Don't be too sure. "Neither can you," she told him, and when he flinched, she wondered if he already knew the truth. Had he suspected it, all along?

She hadn't known. She was fucking Fate, and the truth had been hidden from her. Concealed by all of life's little lies and tricks.

"Luke," Leo said, uttering his brother's name softly.

A streak of lightning slid across the sky.

"Luke," Leo said again as he kept his fingers over Trina's wounds. Her eyes had closed but ragged breaths still left her body. "*Luke!*" Leo roared as thunder boomed around them.

Mora kept her gaze on the dark sky. Powerful bursts of wind seemed to buffet them and then she saw the shadows up above.

Shadows...that could be wings. A long, snaking tail.

A burst of fire.

Luke had heard his brother. And he was coming to the scene.

Was he looking for that final battle? For the fight that had been prophesized so long before?

"Don't attack," Mora frantically ordered Leo. "We need his help. He is *not* the one who summoned the hellhounds. I told you, I saw their master when I touched—"

"Who is it?" Leo barked at her. "Who has been working against me? *Who hurt you? And Trina? Who killed Merius—*"

Luke touched the ground. He came down not as a beast, but as a man. Fully dressed in a fancy suit, but his eyes glowed with power.

"Who did it?" Leo demanded.

She licked her lips and knew the betrayal would hurt him. But then, betrayals always hurt, didn't they? Especially when you didn't see them coming. "Ramiel. Ramiel summoned the hellhounds. Ramiel watched while they attacked Merius and Trina."

With her words, Mora knew exactly what chain of events she was setting in motion. After all, she was Fate. She'd seen what waited for Ramiel. Seen him fighting with Leo. Seen Leo cutting the angel's wings away.

Now, well, now she knew why Leo would destroy the angel.

Because Ramiel has spent centuries trying to destroy Leo.

CHAPTER SEVENTEEN

"What in the hell is going on here?" Luke demanded as his hands fisted at his sides. "Who killed the humans? And, shit, is that an angel—"

Mora leapt to her feet.

Leo watched, his jaw locked and his hands still on Trina's terrible wounds, as Mora grabbed Luke's fisted hand and yanked him toward the angel.

"Yes, it's an angel," Mora fired back. "And hellhounds killed the humans. Now, save the other questions—because we need your help."

He pulled away from her. "What on earth makes you think I *help?*"

He wasn't going to help, Leo knew it. There was no reason for Luke to help a dying angel. Trina's eyes were closed. Tear tracks slid down her cheeks. "I'm sorry," he whispered. He'd failed her. He'd gone after the werewolves and left her with a traitor at her side.

Ramiel. I will find you. I will destroy you.

Trina's blood was on his hands—literally. So was the blood of the humans. Merius…

"Angels aren't bound to me," Luke continued, voice grudging. "Even if I were in the random mood to help—"

"Stop!" Mora's shout cut right through his words. "You think you can lie to me? I *see*. I know! I know what's happening, and I think you've known it, too, for a very long time." She stood toe-to-toe with him now. "I think you've known…ever since you met your mate. Ever since the Lord of the Dark fell for someone that was from the light."

Trina's body was shuddering. It was as if…as if the claws that had sliced her were coated in some kind of poison. *Were they? Her wounds won't close. She just keeps bleeding. And my power doesn't work on her.*

"My Mina isn't of the light, not anymore. Her *fate*," Luke emphasized with a sneer in his voice. "Changed."

"Yeah, I know," Mora threw right back at him. "Who the hell do you think changed that fate?"

Stunned silence came from Luke.

And Leo had to admit, Mora had just taken him by surprise, too.

"*I* am the one who put her in your path," Mora continued, her words tumbling out in rapid-fire succession. "I get that you think you're the big puppet master who makes deals and engineers the lives of everyone else, but I was playing this gig long before you walked the earth. *I* sent Mina to that low rent bar in the Keys. I'm the one who knew she needed protection, and what better protection could she get than from the so-called baddest of the bad?"

"You…no, that's not possible."

Leo pressed down harder on Trina's wounds. No matter how much power he sent flowing into her, she wasn't healing. And Luke was just standing back there, seemingly in shock because someone else had messed with his life.

How does it feel, brother?

"Mina has *never* mentioned you to me," Luke finally growled. "You're lying. Trying to trick me because you have *always* wanted Leo to come out on top—"

"Mina hasn't mentioned me because she doesn't know me by name." Mora's answer cut through his words like a knife. "Sometimes, all it takes is a whisper to change a person's whole life. Over five years ago, I whispered in her ear. I told her about you…and the magic you possessed in that damn ring you wear. The Eye of Hell. I sent her after you because I knew that you could change the end I saw for her."

"Wh-what end did you see for my Mina?"

Luke had actually just stumbled over his words. *Never happened before.*

"If I hadn't sent her to you, Minalynn James would have become a weapon. Used over and over by the government until there was nothing left of her. A trail of bodies would have been in her wake and eventually, her own blood would have soaked the ground. She would have been tortured, trapped, forced to become the monster she feared. *I* changed all of that. One whisper, that's all it took." Her breath heaved out. "So you *owe* me, Luke. And I'm calling in that debt. Put your hands on that angel and push every bit of your healing power into her."

"*It will do no good!*"

Something inside of Leo snapped at Luke's yell. "*Just fucking do it!*" Leo shouted back to his brother.

And…Luke did.

Luke put his hands on top of Leo's. A hot wave of energy blasted through Luke's fingers, over Leo's hands, and *into* Trina's wounds. She jerked at the contact and screamed, a high, keening cry as her eyelids flew open. Her eyes were wild and pain-filled. Her body heaved against them and then—

She stilled.

Luke's hands were still on top of Leo's.

Trina's eyes were open. Her breath slid weakly past her lips. "Thank…you."

Luke snatched his hands back. Slowly, Leo lifted his own fingers. Blood still covered him, but her wounds were gone. Closed completely.

Leo forced himself to smile down at Trina. "You're going to be all right."

She blinked. "Because you saved me." A faint smile started to curve her lips.

But Leo shook his head. Then he rose to his feet. Luke was pacing nearby, muttering about owing Fate, and Mora...

She was looking down at the ground.

Leo could smell the dead around them. So many bodies. Hurt. Lost. *Gone.* He lifted his hands and fire shot from his fingertips. The flames flew toward the human bodies, burning them, turning them to ash and clearing the scene. After all, he couldn't just leave the bodies out there. Cops would eventually come. If they found those mangled bodies, the gruesome discovery would just lead to questions. Questions that the paranormals didn't want to answer.

Trina rose to her feet. Her wings spread behind her, but she didn't take flight. She stood there, staring uncertainly at him.

"Ramiel..." Her soft voice barely carried over the crackle of his flames. "He...he just watched while those beasts attacked."

"They weren't wolves," Leo told her flatly. The flames had lit up the scene. "They were hellhounds."

"I-I...know," Trina gasped. "I saw..."

"They took the form of wolves because Ramiel wanted me to think the local pack had attacked." Leo turned his head toward his brother. "Attacked because of *your* command."

Luke swiped a hand over his face. "I haven't told *any* wolves to attack humans. And Ramiel? Shit, isn't that the tight-ass angel who spends so much time glaring at everyone? Judgmental SOB—"

"Ramiel betrayed me," Leo said and the pain of that truth tore at him.

Mora eased to his side. "He's telling the truth, Luke. I saw it all, in one of my visions. Ramiel was behind the attack. He was the one who has been summoning the hellhounds."

Now Luke stalked toward them. With a wave of his hand, he had the last of the flames sputtering out. The bodies were gone. "Why in the hell would an angel want to do this? If he sent the hounds, then that means he was the one behind the first attack on you, Mora, centuries ago. There's no reason why he would want—"

"Ramiel has visions," Mora informed him, her voice soft. "I think he had a vision that was clearer than mine. And he was trying to make everyone see what was so wrong."

A dull ringing sounded in Leo's ears. "We should get out of here." He pointed to Trina. "Get to safety. I'll find you later—just protect yourself, okay?"

She nodded and took to the sky.

The knot in his stomach grew tighter. He watched as she disappeared. He'd wanted her gone because…

I didn't want Trina to hear this part.

Mora's fingers curled around his.

"I couldn't heal her," Leo whispered. He had to swallow down the rock that had lodged in his throat. "And I couldn't save Merius."

Luke let out a frustrated growl. "Since when can't you save angels?"

Leo glanced at his brother. "Since when…*can* you?"

Luke blinked. "What?" Then he threw up his hands. "No, no way. *No.*"

Mora's hold tightened on Leo. "I need to scry again…scry for both of you, but I know things have changed. Your fates have changed."

"Not enough for me to heal an angel!" Luke blasted. "That's impossible. I rule the dark. I don't have any power over the light paranormals, I don't—"

"Yet you just saved an angel," Leo replied. There was no denial possible. "Want to try explaining that?"

Luke looked away from him. "Not like it's the first time we've used our powers together to help someone. Wasn't me. It was *us.*"

Leo wasn't so sure of that. "Luke—"

But Luke's wings flew out from his back. "If Ramiel was the one summoning the hellhounds,

I'll find him. I'll make sure he doesn't bring them back on this earth again—"

In a flash, Leo was at his side. His hand clamped around his brother's arm. "No, *I* will."

Luke stared at him. Their faces were the absolute same. Their eyes the same. Their power?

Different.

One was supposed to rule the light.

One was bound to the dark.

"You expect me to believe you'll kill one of your precious angels?" Doubt was heavy in Luke's voice.

"I'm not so sure they are mine."

Luke frowned at him. "If you don't control the angels any longer, then who—*what*—do you control?"

Once upon a time, twin boys were born. One was predicted to be a bearer of light, the destined ruler who would protect all humans. He would fly through the skies and guard from above. He would be on the side of good. The righteous.

The other twin…his fate was to be much darker. No goodness was seen in his future. Witches feared him on first sight. Seers turned away, shuddering at the visions they saw.

Because he was born for darkness. Every creature that hid in the night would bow to him. He would rule them. The world would fear him.

He would do very, very bad things.

Leo shut his eyes as he remembered the story of their past. "I think you know."

"Screw that." Luke ripped away from him. "Here's the deal, *brother*. If Ramiel summons the hounds, they'll rise again in twenty-four hours. That's how the spell works — *twenty-four hours*. You're on a ticking clock, got it?"

Leo's eyes opened.

The wind beat at Leo's body as Luke took flight.

And in seconds, Luke was gone. Ash drifted around Leo. He felt the light touch of Mora's fingers on his shoulder. "You understand what's happened, don't you?"

He put his hand to his chest. Inside, his beast was clawing and fighting to break free. "I understand that no matter what else fucking happens, you'll always be mine."

A tear slid down her cheek. "Leo…"

"Mine." Then he took her into his arms and flew them the hell away from there.

***

Leo took Mora away from the blood and ash. Away from the location of a savage truth he wasn't ready to face. He flew her back to Vegas, back past the busy streets and to the outskirts of Sin City.

Back to…

"Resurrection?" Mora gasped in his ear, her shock plain.

He lowered them down in front of her bar. A bar that was no longer burned to ash. A bar that wasn't wrecked.

A bar that was…almost perfect again.

"Turns out," Leo murmured as he kept a tight hold on her wrist, "it was a fitting name for this place."

Her jaw had dropped. She stared at the ramshackle building in wonder. "This matters, Leo, more than you even realize."

He stared at her. "I have a confession."

Her stunned eyes swung toward him.

"I didn't save Dax. He's not alive because of me. But I'm a selfish bastard, and when you looked at me like I was a hero, like I'd done the right thing and made you proud, I just went with it." He eased out a slow breath. He felt like some nervous kid.

She blinked. "What? But Dax said—"

"Yeah…" His thumb slid along her inner wrist. Her frantic pulse raced beneath his touch. "About that. I'm guessing he doesn't know I have a twin. Dax saw someone with my face and just assumed it was me."

She licked her lips—those delectable lips that had haunted him forever. "You're saying that Luke saved Dax."

"Becoming a habit, isn't it?" His thumb stilled. "He saves the day." Leo paused. "So what does that mean I do? Destroy it?"

She glanced away from him, her gaze sliding back to Resurrection. "You didn't destroy this place. You rebuilt it."

"Magic can fix *almost* anything. It was actually easy to repair this place. Getting the humans to forget they'd battled a four alarm fire here? That was the tricky part."

"Why?" She wasn't looking at him. "Why do this?"

"Because the place mattered to you. And I wanted to give you something because you matter to me."

She took one step toward the building. Another. Her hand slid free of his grip, but Leo just fell into step behind her. Vaguely, he had the thought that he might just follow her anywhere.

So how far fucking gone and obsessed was he?

Mora reached the main door. She tried to turn the handle, but it was locked. A wave of Leo's hand produced the key, and then they were inside.

"It's the same." She spun around in a circle, her gaze flying in every direction. "You fixed everything."

For you.

He waited until her stare came back to him. And when it did, tension swept between them. Less than five feet separated them, but he thought that was a good thing. He needed to be away from her for what would come next.

Behind her, he could see the big mirror that hung over the bar. His reflection was in that mirror, and he looked dark. Intense. Dangerous. He eased out a slow breath. "I can be more than a monster."

"I *never* said you were—"

"I know. I know what's coming." He kept his own voice low. Kept his control in place. It was a battle, though, because his beast was changing. "You think I can't feel it? Inside?"

She took one step toward him, but then stopped herself. "Leo…"

"I can't heal angels. I couldn't even convince the humans to forget the fire here…I had to call in some vamps to do the deed because they owed me a few favors." He laughed, and the sound was bitter. "I'm going to kill an angel. I want to hunt him right now and rip him apart. That's not something the Lord of the Light does." He forced his hands to unclench. "But Ramiel sealed his fate the instant he went after *you*."

She stared at him. Her eyes were so deep.

"We both know what I am. That old prophesy has followed me for my entire life." Leo couldn't look away from her. "The real question is…can you handle it? Can you handle *me*?" Even as he asked the question, he feared her answer. If she was afraid, if she wanted to leave him, could he stand back? Could he *let* her go?

"I can handle anything." She gave him a smile that broke his heart. "Haven't you heard? I'm Fate. Immortal. Everlasting." Mora closed the distance between them.

"You're Mora." *You're mine. I can't lose you. I will fight anyone and anything for you.* He pulled her against him. Their bodies brushed. His hand rose and curled under her chin as he tipped back her head. "This is it…the only chance I can give you."

"A chance to do what?"

He could stare into her eyes forever. "To run away from the big, bad beast."

Mora licked her lips. Then she rose onto her toes and pressed her silken lips against his. "You are bad."

His muscles locked down.

"And I know you carry a beast inside of you." She nipped his lower lip. "But I will never, ever run from you. Not again."

Then it was done. No going back. Not for either of them.

He took her mouth, kissing her with a rush of passion and driving need. Mora. His Mora. Not afraid of him. Even knowing the darkness that plagued him, his beast…

She still wanted him.

He could taste the desire in her kiss. Feel it in her touch. Her nails were raking down his arms. Her breasts — with her nipples tight — were pushing against his chest. Her mouth was greedy on his. So eager.

Desperate, just as he was.

He picked her up in his arms and carried her to the long, gleaming bar. He sat her on the edge, and her legs splayed open. He stepped between them, the position putting his cock right at the entrance of her body.

"Clothes are in the way," Mora gasped.

He waved his hand. Gave a stray thought with his magic…and their clothes were gone. She was naked before him. Her hands flew back and slapped down on the bar top as she arched against him. His cock was heavy and full, so ready to thrust deep into her.

But he didn't. Not yet.

Leo took her nipple into his mouth. Sucked. Licked. He used his teeth in the softest bite. She moaned and arched toward him. Mora was wet. Hot. The heat between her legs pressed against him. It would be so easy to sink into her.

Like sinking into heaven.

Better.

He kissed his way to her other breast. Licked and nipped and savored. He loved the moans she gave in the back of her throat and the way she whispered his name. As if he were the only man in the world who mattered to her. As if…

As if I were just a man.

His hand slid between her spread legs. He stroked her sex, bringing her need to a fever pitch. Leo felt as if he'd explode any moment, but he didn't want to let go. Not yet.

When you touched paradise, you didn't just let go.

You fucking savored it.

He thrust two fingers into Mora. She was so tight and hot that he thought he'd go out of his mind.

And he knew…

Must taste.

He bent before her. Pushed her thighs farther apart. Then Leo put his mouth on her. Her whole body jerked at the brush of his lips against her sweet sex, but Mora didn't pull away. She arched toward him. And he licked and sucked and worked her with his tongue and his fingers until she wasn't just whispering his name any longer.

She was screaming it.

Mora came against his mouth, and he loved the taste of her pleasure. He licked his lips, wanting every last drop of her, then he slowly rose. His dick was rock hard, his control shredded. She was the only thing he saw. The only thing that mattered in his world.

The obsession that had haunted him for centuries.

"Why do you always make me wait?" Her husky voice was the most sensual temptation.

"You'll never wait again." He drove into her. His hands grabbed the bar's edge, and he held on with an iron grip. The beast in him wanted to take and take and take, but Leo knew he couldn't.

Not from her.

He withdrew, then thrust deep, driving right against the edge of her clit and making her shiver against him. She was tight and wet from her release, and he knew she was sensitive. So making her come again for him...

Easy.

He thrust. Withdrew.

Her sex squeezed his length, and his eyes slammed shut, but even then, he could still see her. Every inch of perfection, his dream.

He drove into her again. She climaxed once more, gasping out his name.

This time, he was with her. His thrusts became harder, wilder, and then he was erupting inside of Mora. Sinking into her and never, ever wanting to let her go.

She was the one thing that made his world better. The one thing that he *needed.*

He kissed her neck. Took in her sensual scent.

As long as he had Mora, Leo had everything that he needed. Everything he wanted.

Without her…

His eyes opened. He pulled his hands away from the bar and his fingertips trailed gently down her arms. Her breath came in ragged pants — so did his. Her eyes still gleamed with pleasure, and as he stared at her, Mora smiled.

It was a smile that she gave to a man, not a beast.

I can't be without her.

His chest burned. There were so many things that he wanted to say to Mora. But…

His gaze fell to the bar and he saw the deep, claw marks that he'd left in the wood. He hadn't even realized that his claws had come out. Had his beast been that close to the surface? So close that he could have hurt Mora?

Stunned, Leo withdrew from her. He eased back, still staring down at the deep marks etched into the wood.

Her fingers trailed over those marks. She stayed up on the bar top, naked and sexy, and didn't seem to realize just how much danger she was truly in.

I'm the danger. His heart pounded faster. "I…I can fix that." *I can fix all of this. I can make everything right…*

Couldn't he?

But Mora shook her head and his chest burned even more. Burned as if fire were churning inside of him. "Mora…"

"I don't want it fixed." She looked up and a smile was on her face. *A smile?* "I want to be able to look at these marks and remember exactly how they happened. I want to remember that we were so wild for each other we didn't care about anything else."

His control had been too frayed. "I could have used my claws on you." He took another step away from her.

Her laughter followed him. "I don't think so."

He rubbed his chest. She was naked. He was naked. And, shit, he couldn't think when she just sat there, her breasts bare for him and her body tempting. He waved his hand and clothes appeared on him, then her.

Mora sighed. "Disappointing. I'd rather hoped we were just getting started."

She hoped —

"I could have used my claws on you!" Leo said again, voice ragged. "And you want my touch again? *Why?*"

Her gaze hardened. She jumped off the bar and landed on her feet. Then she stalked toward him. "You wouldn't use them on me."

Fuck, fuck.

She put her hand on his chest, resting her palm right over his heart. "I'm not afraid of you, Leo. I know exactly what you are." She rose onto her toes. She licked his jaw.

He shuddered.

His dick jerked. He'd just had her and already...*Want her again. Always want her.*

Her hand curled around his neck and she pulled him toward her. Their mouths were barely an inch apart. "Do you think I'm afraid?"

"Maybe you should be." He wanted her fucking mouth. He wanted her — again. *Always.*

"I'm not." Her right hand was around his neck and her left still rested against his heart. "Sometimes, I'm afraid *for* you, but I'm not afraid of you."

What?

"I also think," Mora continued, voice ever so careful, "that you're the one who is afraid. You know what's happening and you think — "

"That I'll lose myself? That I'll give in to the beast inside of me?" Yeah, he did know. Neither one of them had said the words at that carnage scene in the desert. They'd flown away from that terrible place, and then he'd fucked her. Why? Because to him, fucking her was more necessary than breathing.

"No more doubt." She bit his lip.

He growled.

"I think it's time for you to truly see." She glanced over her shoulder and peered at the mirror that hung over her bar. "I'll show you the future. Good. Bad. Everything in between."

"Yes..."

She licked his lower lip. "But first, I want something from you."

Anything.

"I want you to tell me how you feel. About me."

Like she didn't know. Like everyone didn't fucking know. "There's a reason Ramiel targeted you. Why he sent those hellhounds after *you*."

She stared into his eyes. Her scent was making him drunk. "He wanted to break you," she said and her lips twisted. "He should have known you were stronger than that." Mora pulled away from him. Turned to fully face the mirror. She looked up and her gaze met his in the glass. "I don't have enough of a hold to matter that much to you. You lived for centuries without me. I realize…I understand you're not tied to me, but I just wanted to know that I mattered, a little bit, and—"

He grabbed her. Grabbed her, spun her around, and pinned her against that damn bar. The same bar that he'd just fucked her on top of. Only…

It hadn't been just fucking.

He could feel power humming in the air around him. "You don't matter a little bit."

She flinched.

He kissed her. Drove his tongue deep and *took*. Then… "Baby, you matter more than the rest of the whole world. You *are* my world. I love you, and hurting you, fuck, yes, that is the way to break me."

"You...love me?"

"I've loved you for centuries, Mora. I've searched for you. Dreamed of you. And I swore, if I ever found you again, I wouldn't screw up another time. I'd hold you tight. I'd do anything necessary to make you happy." Because Leo had thought he *could* make her happy. Before his life had been changed...

He brushed a lock of her hair behind her ear. "I'm going to kill Ramiel."

She caught his hand. "You're not supposed to kill an angel."

He smiled at her. Then he lowered his head and put his mouth right next to her ear. This secret was theirs alone. "And I'm also supposed to be the good one, but we both know I'm not."

Not any longer.

Yes, he'd felt the change inside of himself. The growing anger. The hate. The twisting desire to destroy. A darkness, getting bigger and stronger with every moment that passed.

"It's what Ramiel wanted," Mora said and there was sadness in her words. "To push you over the edge."

He thought of the angel he'd mistakenly trusted. The angel who'd let his own kind suffer. The angel who'd made *Mora* suffer. "He's about to see what happens when I go over that edge."

And he's about to die.

He turned from her. It was time to cross the final line.

Good and evil…such a thin, damn line.

CHAPTER EIGHTEEN

"You don't…you don't have to take this path." The words slipped from Mora as her heart thundered in her chest.

Leo stilled and glanced back at her. His face was hard and angry, cut into grim lines of determination. It was hard to believe that the same man had just so tenderly said…

I love you.

She wanted the words again. Even more, she wanted to believe them. But she wouldn't allow herself that luxury, not yet. She tried to smile for him, to give him hope. "You don't have to kill Ramiel. Once you do, that's a step that can't be taken back." *A final nail in the coffin.* "You have a choice. You've always had a choice."

His eyes glittered at her. "*You* are my choice." His voice was low and rough. "And when someone hurts you, that person pays."

Ramiel would know that. He wanted to destroy every bit of goodness inside of Leo. He'd been working at him, chipping away for years— Mora could see that now. Ramiel wanted Leo out of the way, and he'd used her to accomplish his goals.

"I'll see you soon, love," Leo promised her. "As soon as I end an angel." He stalked for the door.

No, she wasn't going to be left behind. Mora bounded after him just as Leo stopped in front of the door. She reached out for him, thinking that maybe he'd changed his mind. There was still good in him, it was just down so deep—

"*Vampire.*" Leo spat. His eyes were on the door. Fury radiated from him as he grabbed that door and yanked it open.

She strained to see around him, but when she saw the man in the doorway, Mora became rooted to the spot.

She *couldn't* be looking at a vampire...maybe a ghost, yes, but no way was that guy a vamp. Was he?

"*Merius?*" Leo's voice was strangled.

The fellow she'd met—the *angel* she'd met just hours before—stood in the doorway, his broad shoulders filling the space. He was dressed in jeans and a t-shirt that was too tight. Rain had plastered his blond hair to his head. She hadn't even realized a downpour had erupted outside. She'd been too distracted by the things happening inside Resurrection.

"I woke up…" Merius's voice was halting. "There was only ash there. You were gone. Trina…gone. And I was…hungry."

She could see his fangs, peeking out behind his lips. Long and wickedly sharp, they were the unmistakable fangs of a vampire.

Merius raked a hand over his face. "I…almost attacked a human. What…what is wrong with me?"

Leo's hand locked around Merius's shoulder. "I should have fucking thought…remembered…I am so sorry, Merius."

Her palms were literally itching to touch the guy. She was desperate to see just how fate had played with this vamp, but it didn't seem like the right moment to burst forward and put her hand on him. Mora rocked back on her heels. "You should come inside."

Merius glanced at her. Hunger flashed on his face as his gaze dropped to her neck. Mora's hands flew up and covered her throat — and her rapidly beating pulse.

"Don't even think about it," Leo ordered him curtly, but he yanked Merius inside the bar.

Merius shook his head, sending droplets of water flying. "Feeding is all I can think about. The hunger is constant…It's driving me mad. It was…the first thing I felt when I woke up." His head sagged forward. "My wings are gone."

"Because Ramiel fucking *took* them from you."

At those low, snarled words, Merius's head snapped up. "What?"

Mora cleared her throat. They had a new vamp in front of them, one battling a severe case of bloodlust. Driving the guy into a killing frenzy didn't seem like the best plan to her. "You don't remember what happened?"

His thick brows lowered as Merius recalled, "I was attacked…from behind. Something— someone's claws sliced into my wings and I hit the ground. I…never saw who hit me." He shook his head. "Ramiel?" Even as he said the name, his face twisted with rage. His fangs seemed to grow even longer. Merius's face had hollowed, his cheek bones becoming more pronounced.

Since she'd lived for such a long time, Mora knew a few things about vampires.

First, the newly awakened—like Merius— were often the most dangerous. New vampires felt only hunger. They understood only bloodlust. When the bloodlust got bad enough, they'd attack anyone near them. *Everyone* near them.

Second, a vampire's rage was a decidedly deadly thing. Rage and bloodlust blended together, creating a perfect killing machine.

Third, no way on earth could an angel-turned-vampire beast be some weak paranormal.

Mora knew she had to be staring at a powerhouse.

"Doesn't make sense," she whispered.

Merius twitched.

"You would have needed to be bitten, at the very least, by a vamp." Actually, he would have needed a blood exchange. "You couldn't just lose your wings and then wake up as a vamp. It doesn't work that way."

Merius gave a bitter laugh. "She marked me long ago."

Mora slanted a worried glance at Leo, looking for some help. "*She?*"

Leo nodded grimly. "Merius was bitten by a vamp who broke every rule that I had in place. Angels were *never* supposed to be on the paranormal menu, but she found a way to get close to him. She seduced him."

Now that was interesting to know. "I didn't think angels were supposed to feel anything." *So how had he been seduced?*

"I always felt…" Merius growled, "I felt it when Josephine was close." His eyes were practically burning with bloodlust as he said the other woman's name.

"Okay." Mora cleared her throat. "But a bite doesn't just do it. You would have needed her blood—" She broke off as understanding hit. She snapped her fingers together. "Your Josephine must have found you, after Ramiel attacked. She saved you."

But Merius gave a bitter laugh. "Josie hates me. She would never do anything to save me."

Don't be so sure. "Sometimes, love and hate are closer than you realize." Helplessly, her gaze was drawn to Leo. She'd spent so much time cursing him. *Hating,* yes, she'd done that, too. And then he'd come back into her life.

Everything had changed.

Only not all of the change was for the better.

"Someone saved you," Leo told Merius after a long, hard stare. "Because I couldn't." He ran a hand over his jaw. "You're a newly turned vamp—you should have been pulled toward—"

"The Lord of the Dark," Merius finished grimly. He stared straight at Leo. "Yes, I know." His teeth snapped together. "The hunger...it's driving me *insane.*" He licked his lips. "I need *blood.*"

A newly turned vamp could be savage in his need. If he attacked a human...

"Help me," Merius pleaded with Leo. Then, *"Stop me."*

Leo locked his hand around Merius's shoulder. "You need blood? I know just where to get you some. One bastard is begging for a bite."

Merius gave a grim nod. As one, he and Leo moved toward the door.

She was rooted to the spot. A fallen angel turned vampire? And Leo—no, no, this was going to end very, very badly. "You can't just leave me here!"

But Leo didn't look back at her. "This is the safest place for you. I can't have you near Ramiel. I can't risk him hurting you." His shoulders rolled back. "All of the hellhounds were sent back to the fire. They won't be able to get back for a while—Luke told me it took twenty-four hours for them to rise after a summoning."

Her heart lurched. "You think Ramiel is going to summon them again?"

He opened the door. "He'll try. But I'm about to stop him."

"Leo…"

But he was gone. He'd grabbed Merius and they'd moved so fast—just vanishing. Mora ran outside, her gaze searching frantically for them, but they were nowhere in sight. She wrapped her hands around her body. "Dammit, Leo, you said you were going to stay with me!" Her words were shouted angrily into the storm cloud-filled sky. "You don't get to just fly away!"

"He thinks he's keeping you safe." The low, rumbling voice came from right behind her.

Mora spun around.

A man was standing near her bar's entrance, his shoulders pressed against the wall as he leaned there, studying her. The rain fell onto him.

A man with Leo's face. Leo's eyes. Leo's...power.

"Luke," she said his name like the accusation it was. "What in the hell are you doing here? And why didn't Leo sense you?"

"Because he was preoccupied with other things." He straightened away from the exterior wall and sauntered toward her. All slow and easy, as if he didn't have a care in the world.

Maybe he didn't.

She backed up a step.

He laughed at her retreat. "Come now, Fate. You know I'm not here to hurt you."

The tension didn't leave her body.

"No?" He quirked a brow. "Don't know that?" He extended his hand toward her, offering her his palm. "Then how about you just take a look and see for yourself?"

"I...you're like Leo. So powerful that I'll need more than a touch."

He laughed once more, but the sound was dark and a little threatening. "Of course, you do. Tell me, what do you need?"

Mora stared into his eyes. "I'm going to need you to bleed for me."

***

"Stay out of sight until I call you," Leo ordered Merius. The guy was looking bad. Like warmed over death. His fangs were out, his eyes lined with dark shadows, and his nails had turned into claws. Leo had thought that his fire had destroyed Merius's body. When he'd let his flames loose to clean that horrible scene in the desert, Merius should have turned to ash.

"Can't...last much...longer..." Merius panted.

Leo squeezed his shoulder. "You won't have to. When the blood starts flowing, you come running, got it?"

Merius nodded.

They were about fifty yards away from a small house, one that sat, huddled and alone, at the end of a deserted street. There were no other homes nearby, just that little house. Its yard was overgrown, and the paint was peeling away. The place appeared deserted, only...*It's not empty now.* Leo had tracked Ramiel's scent to that house. The angel was in there, hiding.

Or maybe summoning hellhounds to do his bidding.

Either way, things were about to end for Ramiel.

"He should never have hurt her," Leo said. "Come when you smell the blood."

"Leo?"

He ignored his friend's worried voice and started walking toward that house. Slowly.

Steadily. And with every step, his rage grew. The rain pelted down on him.

I can never forgive…because of Mora.

***

She used a knife to slice a small line across Luke's palm.

"Ouch," he said.

She glanced up at him, her body tensing.

Luke smiled. "Just kidding. It takes a whole lot more than that to hurt me." His gaze drifted around Resurrection. "I was sure I'd heard that this place had been torched recently."

She put down the knife and headed behind the bar. She grabbed for the mirror, trying to yank it down off the wall. "It was." The damn mirror was heavy. "Leo fixed it for me."

"Did he?" And Luke was behind her. He pulled that mirror down effortlessly and placed it on top of the bar, right near the claw marks that had been left on the side of the wood. "How very *good* of him."

She ignored the jibe. "Put your hand over the mirror."

He did. Drops of his blood fell onto the glass.

"This is the part where I'm supposed to reach for your hand." Her words came out a little too fast. "I'll see what's going to happen for you."

She didn't reach for his hand.

He waited. "I've always believed my brother had an unfair advantage. An advantage that he got by seducing you."

Mora took that hit and flinched. "You think he used me."

"Isn't that what *you* think?" His blood dripped onto the glass.

She swallowed and didn't answer his question.

"Did you really send my Mina to me?"

She was staring at the blood, not his face. "Yes."

"*Why?*"

Her lips trembled. "Because maybe…I thought he had an unfair advantage, too."

Luke laughed. "Part of you hated my brother, isn't that so?"

A bigger part of me still loved him. "And maybe…maybe I sent her to you because I thought you deserved…" Now her eyes lifted to pin his. "Something good."

His jaw hardened. "Take my hand, Mora. Let's both find out what's going to happen."

Her breath eased out slowly. Her hand rose, but she didn't touch his fingers. "Once, I looked for Leo, and I saw you killing him."

His hand fisted. "*What?*"

"I could see the battle between the two of you. Leo…he didn't fight back when you attacked him. He just stood there, and he took the blows. He took the attack, and then he was dead at your feet."

Her fingers hovered over his fist. She could feel warmth from his skin — they were that close. "He never wanted to lift his hand against you."

"*Why not?*" The words seemed torn from him.

She gave him a smile. "Because he was your big brother. Born two minutes before you. He thought he should always protect you. Always look out for you. And taking your life was the thing he swore to *never* do."

Luke shook his head. "No. No. Leo has been a cold bastard for centuries. He has *not* secretly been working to save me."

"You're right. He hasn't been working to save you."

He nodded and appeared relieved. "Exactly. He's —"

"He's been trying to find a way to save you both." Her attention turned back to his fist. "Let's see if he succeeded."

***

Leo kicked in the front door. It was wood — weak and flimsy — and when his boot-covered foot hit it, the door flew inward. He strode into the house, his nostrils flaring. "Ramiel!" He bellowed for the angel. "I know you're here!" He walked over an old, faded rug that was on the floor. Raindrops fell from his body.

Chairs were inside. A small table. The house looked normal. Books were even carefully arranged on a bookshelf. It looked—

"They're dead."

Ramiel walked from the hallway. He stood there, right next to the empty fireplace. "Trina and Merius…" His shoulders slumped. "They both died during the attack. The…the wolves got them."

The bastard dared to lie to him? "Look at me," Leo ordered, his voice colder than ice.

Ramiel's head whipped up. Grief was stamped on his face. "I saw them get attacked. The humans were screaming. I tried to save them. I tried to save them all." His mouth tightened. "But I barely escaped myself. Your brother's werewolves were vicious. They were destroying everyone and everything in their path."

Leo's jaw was locked tight. He advanced with heavy steps, moving to stand right in the middle of that woven rug. "Wolves didn't attack. Hellhounds did."

Shock flashed on Ramiel's face. "What?"

Leo's claws were out. And when he exhaled, smoke came from his lungs. His beast was far too close. "You stood at my side for centuries. And all along…you were betraying me."

Ramiel's lashes flickered. "I don't know what you mean." He walked toward Leo and then he knelt on the rug, lowering his head in a pose of subservience. "You are the Lord of the Light. You hold dominion over all the angels." His hands slid into the pockets of his jacket. "I serve you."

"You *lie* to me." His claws lifted. He wanted to drive them right into Ramiel. "Your visions? How many of them were tricks? How many—"

Ramiel glared at him. "I don't know what lies *she* has told you," he said as he knelt before Leo. "But I only deal with truth. I'm an angel. My visions are real. They don't come from the dark. They show me what should be."

Leo put his claws to Ramiel's throat. "Trina and Merius aren't dead."

For the first time, part of Ramiel's mask seemed to crack. "Wh-what?"

"I sent all of your hellhounds back to the fire. Trina survived. And Merius…" Leo smiled. "Let's just say he can't wait to see you again."

Ramiel's wings burst from his back. White angel wings—big and broad—and Ramiel surged to his feet. And as he did—he shoved a knife into Leo's stomach. He drove the blade deep and twisted it. Leo's blood poured from him, but his knees didn't so much as buckle.

He locked his hand under Ramiel's chin and lifted the angel up into the air. "You know it will take more than a knife to kill me…"

"Wasn't...trying to...kill..." Each word was gasped, probably because Leo was crushing the guy's wind pipe. "Just...need...blood..." And Ramiel smiled. Then he said... "Kill her. Rip her...apart."

"What the fuck are you talking about?"

A growl sounded then, from right behind Leo. He glanced over his shoulder and saw that Merius had come inside the house. His friend's face was carved into deep lines of madness...and bloodlust.

Come when you smell the blood. Shit.

"Merius..." Leo began. *I didn't mean my blood!*

But Merius lunged at him, and Leo felt the vamp's fangs at his throat.

***

"Don't."

That one word from Luke froze Mora. Her fingers were barely a breath from his.

He jerked his fist away from her. "Changed my mind," he said curtly. "Don't need you to see a damn thing for me." He whirled on his heel and marched away from her. "I make my own fate. Always have, always will."

Her heart drummed too fast in her chest. "You don't want to hurt him, either."

He stopped. His shoulders were tense. He was in front of the door, standing in almost the exact same way that Leo had just a while before. Their bodies were held in a similar posture. Even their voices held the same mix of anger and determination as Luke said, "I spent centuries believing a prophesy was going to tear my world apart."

It will.

"Now I just say…" He glanced back at her. "Screw the prophesy. I *know* what I will do when the final battle comes. I don't need you to see anything for me." Luke inclined his head. "But I do thank you for sending Mina my way. That's a kindness I will never forget."

Then he strode out of the bar. Mora stood there a minute, gulping in deep gasps of air. Had it been enough? What she'd said to Luke? What she'd done for him? Would it be enough to change the destiny she'd seen for the Lord of the Dark?

And for the Lord of the Light?

He left the door open when he exited. The scent of rain drifted inside. The softest whisper of the wind blew over her cheek. She backed up until her arm hit the bar, and then she turned, running her hand along the marks left by Leo's claws.

He'd said he loved me. She wanted to believe those words so badly, but believing him would mean trusting him again.

If he betrayed her, it would rip her apart.
Mora knew it. She also knew…

I don't have a choice.

The wind blew against her once more. And
this time, it brought another scent to her. A
familiar scent. Her eyes closed and she gave a
little laugh. "I guess it's just the day for
unexpected visitors, huh?"

Silence.

"You're probably wondering how in the hell
Resurrection is back, aren't you?" Once more, she
stroked over the marks in the wood. "That's a
funny story." *Not really.* "But since you're in the
supernatural world now, I think I can tell it to
you…" She turned to find herself staring into
Dax's eyes. "I figured I'd be seeing you, sooner or
later." She tried to smile. "You doing okay?"

The door was still open behind him. She
could see streaks of rain pounding down outside.
She looked at the rain, then at Dax.

He stared into her eyes. His face was a hard,
unyielding mask.

"That bad, huh?" Mora shook her head and
marched around the bar. "Tell you what…for old
time's sake, how about I give you a drink, on the
house? I think we could both use a drink." She
grabbed for the scotch. Leo had even restocked
her liquor. How thoughtful.

He did all of this to make me happy.

The door creaked as it was slowly closed. She filled one glass with the amber liquid. Then another. The mirror still lay over the bar top, but she ignored it. A blood-stained mirror.

She wrapped her fingers around her glass and lifted it in a little salute toward Dax. "Drink up." She drained her glass, barely feeling the burn as it went down.

He moved toward her—a weird, almost lumbering movement that brought him to the opposite side of her bar.

"You know, I hate to say this…" Her gaze trailed over him. His hair was disheveled, stubble lined his jaw, his clothes were torn…and the guy had claws sprouting from his fingertips. "But you look like hell."

His hand lifted and then his fist came down, shattering the mirror on the bar top.

Mora yelled and jerked back as the mirror splintered and glass went flying. "Dax! Dammit, stop!" A chunk of the glass had cut across her arm, making a deep slice. Her blood dripped onto the floor. "What are you doing?"

"Trying…to…stop." His voice was guttural. "I…can't…"

Her heart stuttered in her chest. "Dax?"

"R-run…"

She did. She leapt over that bar and she ran past him. She didn't know what was happening, didn't understand at all, but the door was near, she was almost outside and —

His hands closed around her from behind, and he yanked her against his body.

"S-sorry…" Dax whispered into his ear.

He was touching her, and the images of his future spun through Mora's mind.

CHAPTER NINETEEN

When Merius attacked Leo, Ramiel escaped.
He lunged out of Leo's grasp with a wild, savage
yell of triumph.

"Trust me, man. You don't want my blood.
It's poison." Before Merius could sink his fangs
into Leo's throat, Leo threw his friend across the
room, and Merius rammed into the fireplace.
Bricks fell onto the floor.

Immediately, Merius leapt to his feet, body
ready to attack again.

"*Stop!*" Leo bellowed at his friend.

Merius froze. He didn't so much as blink.

But Ramiel didn't stop. He was running out
the door. He cleared the cabin and the guy
immediately leapt into the air, taking flight.

Leo chased after him as his own wings burst
from his back. "*You can't get away, Ram!*" Outside
now, his knees bent as he prepared to surge
after—

"*Leo!*" Merius bellowed. "*Leo…come look!*"

What? No, he needed to chase Ramiel and
end the bastard. He needed—

"*Mora!*" Merius shouted. "*Leo…Mora!*"

In a flash, Leo was back inside the house. The woven rug was in a twisted heap around Merius's feet, and beneath it, Leo could see the spell that had been carved into the wood.

One glance and he recognized the same fucking spell that had been used to summon the hellhounds before, only this time…

His blood was in the middle of that spell.

So was a picture of Mora. A picture of her, standing behind her bar at Resurrection and smiling at a customer. The picture had been taped down right in the center of the spell. He ripped it up, frowning at the photo.

It was Mora…and…that asshole Dax? When had the picture even been taken?

Then Ramiel's words rang through his head. Words that hadn't made sense before, but right then—they did.

"*Wasn't trying to…kill…Just…need…blood…*" Ramiel had smiled at him and then said, "*Kill her. Rip her…apart.*"

Leo didn't waste another second. He ran out of that cabin and erupted into the air. He moved as fast as he could, his wings beating against the wind. That sonofabitch Ramiel had used Leo's blood in his spell. Probably to make it more powerful. And he'd put Mora in the middle of that spell so…what? So the hellhounds would go after her? So they'd know their target? So they'd—

Rip her…apart.

No fucking way. It wouldn't happen. It took twenty-four hours for those beasts to rise. Luke had said that. *Twenty-four hours.* Leo would make certain Mora was well-hidden before those beasts walked the earth again. He followed Ramiel's scent, hunting him down.

Ramiel thought he would distract Leo by throwing Mora at him, but Leo knew she was safe for the time being. *Twenty-four hours.* That meant Leo had time to hunt. It meant he could kill.

It meant…

You're done, Ramiel.

But as the miles disappeared around him, a new tension slid through his body. Because the area around him was familiar. Ramiel was taking him to the outskirts of Vegas.

To a bar that waited, smelling of ash but in perfect condition…with an empty parking lot.

Taking him to…Resurrection?

He landed on the ground and his wings vanished. Ramiel's scent was all over the place, but Leo didn't see the angel. If that traitor was inside…

Leo rushed into Resurrection—

And the sight before him made Leo freeze.

Mora stood with blood covering her body. Dax was near her, his claws out, and blood covered him, too. He looked bigger than before, stronger, and the guy's total focus was on Mora.

She held a broken chunk of glass in her right hand, her fingers tight around it as she lifted it toward Dax. "I don't…want to kill you."

Dax's body contorted. His hands slammed down on the floor and fur erupted over his body as his muscles bulged.

Fuck! "Mora!" Leo yelled. She hadn't seen him, not yet, but at his cry, her gaze swung toward him. For an instant, wild hope filled her stare.

And then the beast lunged at her.

No. Leo lifted his hand. Fire erupted from his fingertips. It flew right toward Dax's body.

"Stop, Leo! *Don't!*" Mora screamed. She leapt toward Dax's shifted body — and toward Leo's flames.

Horror rolled through him, and Leo tried to pull the fire back, but it was too late. "Mora!"

Dax shoved her out of the way. One of his big paws swiped over her stomach as he threw her back. Then the flames took him. He howled and — screamed. A man's scream. The fire consumed him in mere seconds.

And then there was only ash.

Leo raced across the room. Mora was on the floor, covered in so much blood…and her stomach, where the claws had sliced across her…

The cuts are so deep.

"Baby, it's going to be okay." He put his hand over those slashes.

"You can't heal me." Her voice was a rasp. "Not you, not Luke. I don't belong to either of you."

Lie. You are mine. Always.

"I'll…heal…on my own. T-takes time…"

Leo didn't want her suffering for even another second.

"I didn't want him…to die." A tear tracked down her cheek.

She was *killing* him. Leo lifted her into his arms, needing to get her out of there. He'd given her back Resurrection because he wanted the bar to make her happy. But now the place was covered in blood and ash and memories that she'd want to forget.

"I saw his death coming…I saw the fire that would take him. I saw him burning again and again…" Her head slumped against his shoulder as he carried her toward the door. "I wanted it to change."

They were outside. The rain had stopped, but puddles were on the ground. The scent of her blood filled his nose, driving up his rage and his fear. *Mora said she'll heal herself. That it takes time, but, dammit, she needs to heal — now!*

"I always want things to change, but sometimes, no matter what I do, they *can't* change." Her hand lifted and touched his cheek. "I'm so sorry."

She was apologizing to him? *To him*? "Baby, I shouldn't have left you. You were right. I was fucking driven by rage and —"

"It's about to get worse," Mora whispered. "I'm sorry. I — I'm going to leave you…for a little while…"

"What?" Frantic, his gaze locked on her face.

But her eyes had closed. Her skin was stark white, marked only by the splatters of blood on her body. Her lips were parted, but no breath stirred from her.

He strained, but Leo couldn't hear her heartbeat, not even with his supernatural hearing.

He couldn't hear it because Mora's heart didn't beat.

Mora wasn't taking a breath.

Mora was…dead?

His knees hit the pavement, splashing in the puddles, and he held her with an unbreakable grip. "*Mora?*"

She didn't stir, and terror tightened its icy hold on him. Her blood was on him. In his mind, he could see the claws ripping into her skin, again and again. Going so deep. But those claws had only swiped at her...*because Dax was trying to get her out of the way. So my fire wouldn't hurt her.*

Laughter reached his ears. Taunting. Smug.

Leo's head lifted, and he saw Ramiel walking toward him. "You're a dead man," Leo promised the angel.

Ramiel shrugged. "Wrong on both counts. I'm not a man. I'm an angel." His lips twisted into a smile. "And the only one who's dead...that would be the woman you hold in your arms."

"Fate *can't* die."

"Of course, she can. She's died plenty of times." Ramiel smiled at him. "Oh, wait, you haven't been there for those deaths, have you?"

Leo blinked at him, and he kept his tight hold on Mora.

Ramiel held up his index finger. "The first time she died, that was right after you left her back in dear old Greece. After I sent my hounds to get rid of her. I couldn't stand her false visions and promises. She died when she leapt from that tower and plummeted to the ground." He lifted a brow. "If you don't have wings, you really shouldn't try to fly."

A growl built in Leo's throat.

"Technically, though, I think it was the fall *and* the fire that killed her that time. I got the hounds to use fire on her right after she hit the ground."

In his mind, Leo could see Mora falling...

Ramiel lifted a second finger. "The second time she died, well, you were searching frantically for her. It was a painful sight to see — someone who is as powerful as you, brought so low. You were *desperate*. I found her, of course. In one of my visions. I saw her, and then I killed her."

When Leo eased out a breath, smoke appeared before him.

"I sent a band of villagers to turn on her," Ramiel confided in a too-loud whisper. "It wasn't a pretty death. I convinced them that she was a witch, and well, you know the best way to deal with a witch..." He smiled. "Burn, baby, burn."

Leo leapt to his feet, still holding Mora. "You sonofabitch!"

"Shall I tell you about the third time she died?" Ramiel cocked his head to the side. "You were so close to finding her. I couldn't let that happen. You two are *not* meant to be. You should see that. So the third time, I went for a more intimate kill. I whispered the right words into the ear of a human she trusted. Mora has always had a bit of a weakness for the mortals. She didn't see this betrayal coming, and the human slid a knife right into her heart."

The beast inside of Leo was roaring. And Mora still wasn't breathing.

"I think this is death number four for her." Ramiel dropped his hand. "Or maybe it's five. I can't really recall. She dies and she suffers…" His face hardened. "But the really annoying thing is that she *always* comes back."

Leo carefully put Mora down on the ground. "*Why?*"

"I have no idea," Ramiel replied with a frustrated sigh. "But I figure, I just have to keep trying. Eventually, I'll find the right way to kill her. The way that ensures she won't wake up to walk this earth again."

Leo turned to face the angel he'd considered a friend. Then he slowly began to stalk toward Ramiel. "*Why* have you hurt her?"

Ramiel's face tightened. "Isn't that obvious? To hurt you."

Leo kept closing in on his target. Ramiel wasn't retreating. He was standing there, begging for death. Jaw locked, Leo spat, "You attacked your own kind. You killed humans. You *summoned* hellhounds…and you targeted Mora all because you fucking hate me?" Angels weren't even supposed to feel emotions like hatred, they weren't—

"I don't hate you." Ramiel's voice was flat. "I just know…you aren't the right one."

Leo lunged forward, and when he did, he drove his claws right into Ramiel's chest. *Right at his heart.*

Ramiel grunted. "S-see…what I m-mean?" His wings flared behind him. "Y-you'd h-hurt…angel…"

"I'm going to do more than hurt you," Leo promised. His control was gone, absolutely shredded on the inside. "I'm going to make your life a fucking *hell*." He jerked his claws out of Ramiel's chest and then Leo's beast took over. Leo felt his body getting bigger and stronger. Ramiel was screaming, begging, but Leo didn't care.

He ripped into the angel's wings. His razor sharp claws tore them apart. Feathers fluttered to the ground — white feathers now stained with blood.

Ramiel was trying to fight but…

You aren't strong enough.

Leo swiped at Ramiel's chest again, and the angel screamed in agony. The sky darkened overhead. Thunder rumbled.

And Leo wanted more blood. He wanted this bastard to suffer. The things that Ramiel had done to Mora…*You hurt her. So I will destroy you. I won't stop. You will lose everything …and your agony will not end.*

His claws slashed at Ramiel. The angel fell to the ground, cowering, not even trying to fight back.

"*St-stop…*" Mora's voice. Mora's sweet, fucking perfect voice.

Immediately, Leo spun and ran to her. She was struggling to sit up, still too pale, but her eyes were open, she was breathing, *speaking,* and he could hear the steady beat of her heart. He grabbed Mora and pulled her up and into his arms, holding her tightly. Holding her as if he'd never let her go. As if…

"Leo…what have you done?" Mora gasped.

"Not enough." Not nearly enough. "But I'll finish him. I told you before…Ramiel will pay."

She pushed against him and stared into his eyes. There was grief on her face.

Ramiel's laughter reached him. Leo's shoulders stiffened. Why the hell would the guy be laughing? Ramiel had lost his wings. He was the Fallen now. Leo looked back at him.

Ramiel was still on the ground. His savaged wings and his feathers were all around him. "I knew…she was the key…just had to push you hard enough." He pointed at Leo. "I see you now. So does she. Everyone will see…"

"See you die?" Leo pushed Mora behind him. "Right. Because that's about to happen, it's—"

"*Lord of the Dark. I see you.*" Ramiel's smile split his face. "My visions weren't wrong…" Pain roughened each word as he shoved to his feet. "*She* was wrong…everyone else…wrong…You weren't meant to r-rule…angels…"

Leo looked down at his hands. Stained with blood. Tipped with claws. He felt the darkness inside of him, a hungry beast that wanted to destroy.

And behind him, he heard Mora's soft voice as she said, "Everyone assumed Luke was meant to lead the dark ones…"

No…

"But it was you, Leo," she told him, her voice so husky and weak. "All along…it was supposed to be you."

He shook his head but…

Ramiel was staring straight at him. "You know."

Leo took one step toward the Fallen. Another. "You think I didn't feel my own darkness?" He'd carried it all his life. But he'd kept it chained up, locked away deep inside. "Someone is supposed to rule the light. There has to be balance!"

"I *killed* those humans…I did it all…because you are *wrong,*" Ramiel cried. "I saw…in *my* visions…" His body shuddered. "What you will do…the vamps bowing to you…the werewolves circling you…*You, not your brother!* You fooled the others, but you didn't…fool me." He lifted his hands to the sky. "Now, they will all see…everyone will see you…for what you are…"

"They'll see you for what you are, too," Leo promised him savagely. "A bastard who got tainted by his own evil. An angel who *killed* — "

"Some had to die, for the righteous to reign." Ramiel stumbled, but managed to stay upright, barely. "You would have turned on the humans eventually. You have to be…stopped. The others will see…you'll be destroyed…"

"No, you will be." And he was done with the bastard's lies. With his tricks. In an instant, he was right in front of the angel. Leo pressed his hand to Ramiel's chest. Fire began to spread from Leo's fingertips.

"I'll die for my cause," Ramiel whispered. "The world has to see you…for what—"

"*Stop!*" Mora grabbed Leo, her hand tight on his arm. "You kill him…and Dax will stay in the fire." She gave a hard shake of her head. "That can't be Dax's end! I won't let it be!"

Leo let her pull him back. Because…it was her. Mora. The center of his fucking world. He would let her do anything…

She left me for a few moments. She was dead. And the world was dark. And I went mad. He knew it. The darkness in him had taken over, finally…when Mora was gone. When he knew she was gone.

And he thought of other times in his life…when the darkness he kept chained so tightly had broken free…when his control had slipped…when he'd put others in danger…

Were those all times that Ramiel had targeted Mora? Was he the one pushing me to the edge?

Mora was his weakness, Leo knew that.

She was also his greatest strength. So he let the fire hovering over his fingertips die away.

"Thank you," Mora murmured.

"I would give you the world." She needed to understand that. *But I will be killing this bastard. So get your information from him, fast.*

Mora squared her shoulders and faced the Fallen. "You've made my life hell."

"I'm only getting started…" Ramiel swore as blood trickled from his lips. Deep lines of strain and pain bracketed his mouth. His bloody feathers floated in the breeze. Without those feathers, he'd be battered by every emotion in the world.

Pain. I hope you like it, bastard.

"You used Dax," Mora accused. "You made him attack me."

Ramiel inclined his head. "Turned out…his father was one of my hellhounds. On a mission to stalk you…the guy took a side trip. Got Dax's mother pregnant. And just like that…for the first time in centuries, I had a…hellhound walking the earth."

"No, you had a human," Mora shot back. With each word, her voice seemed stronger. "Dax didn't become a hellhound until he died, and I know you engineered that, too, didn't you? The way you like to…whisper words to people."

Ramiel leaned forward. "Heard that part, did you? And here…I thought you were…dead to the—"

Her hand slapped against his chest and immediately, Mora started shuddering. Leo grabbed her, wanting to wrench her back because he knew she'd just gotten caught in a vision.

"No, have to…see…" Mora argued, fighting against Leo's hold. "Does Dax…come back?"

"Only if I call him," Ramiel snarled back. "Have I? Did…I?" Then he was laughing. "The others are coming…called them…already planned…so much. This time, they'll drag you back…too."

Enough.

Leo pulled Mora way from Ramiel. He stared into the eyes of the man he'd trusted.

Ramiel's chin was up. His shoulders back. And his wings were on the ground. "Can't kill her…but they…they can hold her there…It will work…the final push for you…when she's gone, your darkness will reign. You *can't* be controlled then."

Leo put his hand on Ramiel's shoulder. "This is for Merius. For Trina."

"With Mora gone, you'll destroy—*everyone.* *Everything.* I've seen it. Your brother will have no choice but to…stop you."

Leo ignored Ramiel's words. "It's for the humans you killed."

"Luke will win...even Mora knows that. And he will run the *Light*. The true one to rule—th-the angels will win then, the angels will—"

"You're not on the side of the angels. You're just on the side of death." His hold tightened on Ramiel. The fire raged and burned inside of Leo. "*Mostly...this end is for Mora. For what you did to her.*"

And the flames leapt out. They took Ramiel, burning him, destroying him in an instant until the only thing that remained was the dying echo of his scream.

Ash littered the ground.

Leo stood there, staring at the ash as it darkened the feathers that had fallen. He'd killed an angel.

"There is no going back from this." Mora's quiet voice had him stiffening. "You know that, Leo."

He knew. He turned. Caught her hand. Threaded his fingers with hers. "How long did you know?"

She was staring at the ground. "Know...that you weren't the one who was supposed to rule the angels? That you weren't the real Lord of the Light?"

He couldn't fucking wrap his mind fully around her words. He'd suspected that truth for a long time, had *felt* the darkness in himself, but… "The angels bowed to me. The shifters and the vamps — they followed Luke's commands."

"That's because you both have good and you both have darkness inside. For a time, the scales changed. They changed just enough for you to rule the light."

He caught her chin in his blood-stained hand and tipped up her head, making her stare into his eyes. "Then I lost you."

She wet her lips. "No, then you *met* me. Just meeting me…it changed you. I could see what was coming. But then when I left your life, the darkness took a deeper hold on you."

"I…tried to fight."

Mora nodded. What could have been sadness flashed on her face. "I know you did." She leaned forward and wrapped her arms around him. "And I tried to stay away, because I knew I would be the one who pushed you over the edge."

His arm curled around her waist. "You're the one who keeps me sane." It was more than that. "You're the one who makes me feel *whole*."

Her body was so warm and soft against him. And her voice was sad as she told him, "The hellhounds are going to come for me. Ramiel…I don't think he was lying. I couldn't *see* the beasts taking me when I touched him because I couldn't see past his own death. But he was a powerful angel, and if he has been controlling the beasts for centuries, then he could have figured out a way for them to take me. He probably would just need a few powerful components for his spell..."

Leo stiffened. "What's more powerful than my blood?"

Her head lifted. "I...I don't understand."

But Leo did. The bastard had used Leo's own blood in his final spell. "They won't take you." No matter what he had to do. No matter what deal he had to make. "I swear, Mora, I will fight for you."

"And I'll fight for you." Her lips curved but the shadows never left her eyes. "It's what I've been doing for centuries."

CHAPTER TWENTY

The island was nestled among the Florida Keys. A small slice of paradise, surrounded by crystal blue water. The waves crashed against the beach, and the scent of salt air filled Mora's nostrils as Leo lowered them toward the sand.

He'd flown her to the island — to Luke's private island. They'd moved so fast that she knew no human eyes had seen them. Even if the humans had caught a glimpse of Leo's wings, he would have been so far away from them, the mortals would have just dismissed him. Made up some excuse about him being a trick of the light.

Humans didn't want to see the supernatural world around them...so, they didn't.

And speaking of things people didn't want to see... Mora winced. "Your brother isn't going to be happy that you just dropped in on him."

Leo grunted. "Too damn bad. Luke can deal with me." He laced his fingers with hers and began heading up the beach.

They hadn't gone too far, though, when they heard the growl. *Growls.*

A big, black panther appeared in their path, its eyes glowing and fixed with deadly intent, and right behind him, coming up fast on the giant cat's six, was a snarling wolf.

"Relax." Leo squeezed her fingers. "These are Luke's shifters."

She knew that—she knew so much more than he realized. *Sorry, Leo, I have more secrets.*

"They're his inner circle, if you will. The cat is Julian Craig, and the pissed-off looking wolf is Rayce Lovel."

The wolf bared his fangs a bit more.

"If you want me to kick your asses," Leo announced clearly, "I will. But I am *not* leaving this island until I see my brother." He paused. "Didn't realize Luke was the type to hide behind his animals."

The panther leapt forward, claws coming to swipe, and Mora flinched because she remembered all too well what it felt like when her body was slashed open by—

"*Stop.*" A deep, rumbling voice. A voice very much like Leo's. Only…it wasn't. The voice belonged to Luke.

Luke Thorne. The man who'd been thought of as the Lord of the Dark for centuries.

The panther ignored Luke's command and hurtled right at Leo, but Leo just grabbed the beast and tossed him into the air. The panther let out a low, echoing roar, and he bounded back to his feet, immediately racing for Leo once more.

Before the panther could strike, Luke stepped into his path. He put his body right in front of Leo's. "Look, Julian, I get that you have a grudge against the guy." Now Luke was annoyed. "But I said *stop.*"

Leo laughed. The sound held no humor. "Sorry, brother, but that trick won't work any longer. You don't control him. You don't control any of the dark ones."

Luke peered back at him. "Bull."

Mora cleared her throat. "We…really need to talk."

Luke's gaze locked on her, and the guy looked extremely less than pleased. "You and I have already *talked.* Don't see how there is much more to say."

Leo moved protectively in front of her. "First, watch the damn tone with Mora. And second, we have *plenty* to say."

The panther immediately growled.

"Shut the hell up," Leo ordered him. "I don't have time for your shit, Julian. Mora is in danger, and she is the *only* thing that matters to me now."

The panther stopped growling.

Silence.

Mora peeked over Leo's broad shoulder. Luke's gaze had landed on the panther and his expression…*oh, boy.* "Figuring it out, huh?" Mora raised her voice so that she would seem more confident and not nearly as terrified as she felt. "Things have changed, and that's why we have to talk."

The panther transformed. The snapping of his bones made her wince and then the wolf started shifting, too—she looked away because she knew they'd both be totally naked when the change was finished.

The transformation was always brutal as the beast vanished and the man emerged. But then, shifters lived a very brutal life. A life in which they battled the savagery within every single day.

"Why can Leo control a panther?" Luke's voice held a definite edge.

She cleared her throat. "Probably for the same reason that you can heal an angel. Nothing in this world is constant. Everything changes. Sometimes, those changes come about slowly. Sometimes, they happen fast—*ah!*" Her words ended in a startled gasp because suddenly, Luke was just right there, at her side. He grabbed her wrist and yanked her toward him.

"*You* did this," Luke accused as a muscle jerked angrily in his jaw. "You played with our fucking lives!"

A low snarl vibrated in the air, a sound so distinct with fury and intent that Mora's mouth went dry. Her gaze slanted back toward Leo—a

Leo who had glowing eyes and rage etched on his face as he glared at his twin.

"Get your hand off her." Leo's voice was guttural.

Luke raised his brows. "You don't see it, do you? I thought you'd manipulated her years ago, but the truth is — *she's* the one who has been playing the games. She's been playing with our lives —"

Leo shoved his hand against Luke's chest and hurtled his brother in the air — a good ten feet.

The wolf and the panther were men now, and at Leo's attack, they both sprang toward him.

But Leo merely waved his hand at them. Clothes instantly covered their bodies…and they stilled. "I have no war with you," Leo told them flatly. Then he pointed at Luke. "And despite what you may believe, I want no battle with you, either."

Luke rose to his feet.

"Mora hasn't played either of us," Leo said, his voice loud and carrying in every direction.

Mora looked down at the ground, hoping she appeared suitably innocent. She needed Luke's help.

"You think I like this?" Leo snapped when Luke was silent. "You think I like knowing that my whole world has changed? A fucking angel was behind this mess — Ramiel did this. He's been working for years to break me. *He* said he had a vision that I wasn't the rightful ruler of the angels. He wanted to break my control, and he did it by going after the one person who mattered the most to me...Mora."

Luke laughed. "I'm supposed to buy that you love her? That you actually lowered your guard enough to let a weakness for another person slip in?"

Mora bit her lip, nervous now. *Total lie. I've been nervous all along.*

Leo strode toward his brother.

The two shifters were silently watching this scene unfold, but Mora noticed that both men had their hands fisted at their sides. *They're waiting for a chance to attack.*

"Didn't you?" Leo questioned when he was in front of Luke. "Didn't you lower your guard and let someone in close? Didn't you fall for your Mina? Wouldn't you do *anything* for her?"

"*Yes...*" Luke gritted out the one word.

"And if something happened to her...if someone hurt her...what would you do?"

Lightning flashed overhead. "Kill." Luke's immediate answer. "Destroy."

Leo nodded. "Ramiel went after Mora over and over again. He's *killed* her over the centuries. I could feel it. I knew she was hurting, but I couldn't find her. It drove me to the brink of sanity." He exhaled raggedly. "I killed Ramiel. He's gone, but the bastard had one last taunt for me. Before he died, Ramiel said that his hellhounds were coming back, and that he'd figured out a way for them to take Mora into the flames with them."

Surprise flashed on Luke's face. "Impossible. That's bull—"

"I wish it was bullshit, but it's the truth." Leo raked a hand through his hair. "And if I lose her…*if I lose her and I have control of the dark ones*…" He laughed, but the sound held a touch of madness. "What do you think will happen then?"

Destruction. War.

Luke would have to battle him. Luke would have to stop Leo.

Then…the end.

The wolf shifter—now a tall, handsome man with blond hair and gleaming, green eyes—shook his head. "I'm sorry, but could we all back up a bit. Did you just say *hellhound?* What the fuck is a hellhound?"

Mora nervously tucked a lock of hair behind her ear. "It's a powerful, very, very old shifter. They stay in the fires—"

"The fires of *hell?*" The panther cut in. He was in the form of a man, too. Broad-shouldered, square-jawed, with his dark hair falling over his high forehead.

"Yes." Mora straightened her spine. "They were sent there long ago because the hounds...they were the first shifters to walk the earth. They could become *any* beast. But their hunger for bloodlust grew too strong. So they were punished — sent to the fire. Only those beasts were so powerful that even the fires of hell couldn't kill them. Instead, the flames became just a prison. And the hellhounds stay in the fire, waiting to be summoned back here."

The panther — Julian Craig — widened his eyes. "How do you know that?"

Oh, well..."Let's just say that maybe I was around when all the madness first started." And she'd learned other details over the years.

The wolf — Rayce Lovel — took a step forward. "Are you really Fate?"

"I am." *And I know your fate, Rayce. I know all about you and the angel you love. Just as I know about Julian and the vampire he craves.*

Most people had no clue — they didn't understand how hard it was to keep up with all of the lives out there. To see the futures that could be...and to work to make sure that chaos didn't reign.

"I can't die," Mora continued doggedly. "At least, I can't *permanently* die." Her hand rose to touch her neck. "Though Ramiel has certainly tried his best to eliminate me. But since he realized I just keep rising, it seems he has come up with another way to get rid of me."

"The hellhounds," Julian supplied with a frown.

"Yes. *If* Ramiel truly found a way for them to drag me into their flames, I won't escape. I'll be gone." Her stare drifted toward Leo, and sorrow tightened her chest. "And then the war will come, just as it was predicted so long ago."

Luke's laughter was cold. "So I'm supposed to buy that you're the only thing keeping us all in check? That you're the reason my brother and I haven't torn each other apart long before now?"

"No." Her denial was immediate. "The reason you haven't fought before now…it's Leo. His control has held. But…" *But when I go, it will break.* Because she was his weakness. Just as he was hers.

"And what in the hell do you think I can do to help him?" Luke asked quietly, but, in the next moment, he was stiffening. He spun around and glared back up the twisting path that led to the main house on the island. "Mina, no! Love, don't come down here!"

"I won't hurt her," Leo groused. "You know that—"

And Mina was obviously not listening to her lover because her blonde head appeared. The breeze tossed her hair and her steps were certain as she hurried forward.

Luke swore and ran to meet her. He wrapped her in his arms and held her close.

Right against his heart.

Leo inclined his head. "Perhaps you *can* see how I feel, brother."

"I *feel* like you need an ass kicking, *brother*," Luke retorted, glaring with enough fire to melt snow.

Mora exhaled. "We are wasting time." She moved up the path a bit, needing Luke to let go of his anger and help them. But—

"*I know you.*" That was Mina's voice...the low, seductive voice of a siren. A siren's power was in her voice. She could compel anyone and anything to do her bidding. Well, mostly anyone.

Doesn't work on me. Won't work on Leo, either. Not since he's now pulling the strings of the dark creatures.

Mina lifted her hand and pointed at Mora. "You and I...we met in that old bar..."

"Resurrection," Mora murmured.

Mina smiled at her, a real, *warm* smile. "You told me about Luke. Said that he could help me. Could change my life." She laughed and the sound was musical. "It took me five years to find him, but I finally did...and you were right."

Mora shrugged.

Mina pulled from Luke. She hurried toward Mora and wrapped her in a tight hug. "*Thank you.*"

Inexplicably, Mora had to blink away tears. "It's kind of my thing. No big deal."

"It was to me," Mina whispered back.

A tear trickled down Mora's cheek. She hadn't been able to blink that one away. "Luke was your fate. I just pointed you in the right direction."

"Oh, hell." Now Luke's voice was loud — and very, very annoyed. He tugged Mina back into his arms and glared at Mora. "I owe you." Each word was tinged with distaste. "I *hate* owing anyone. You did this, didn't you, Mora? Played a fucking player."

Mora didn't let her expression alter. "I've just been trying to keep everyone alive. To balance the sides — good and evil, right and wrong. They shift, you know? Nothing stays the same, it never does."

Leo took her hand and curled it in his. "When the hounds come for Mora, I need you to stand with me, brother. I need your help, and I will pay *any* price. You want to rule the light and the dark? Fine, do it. I just need Mora."

Her head turned. She stared at him. He'd sacrifice so much for her?

Leo stared straight in her eyes. "I just need Mora."

And she needed him. *That* was the real reason she was on that little island right then. Not to save herself. None of the work she'd done had ever been about herself.

It was always you, Leo.

Luke swore—quite imaginatively and quite viciously. "Fine. Come inside and let's figure out what the hell we are going to do to save Fate."

CHAPTER TWENTY-ONE

"The hellhounds will find her," Leo concluded grimly. He hated saying those words, but he knew they were the truth. "Ramiel cast one more summoning spell for them before his death. And the bastard used my own blood to seal the spell."

Julian Craig's dark brows shot up. "How'd he get your blood?" The faintest British accent sharpened his words.

"I went to kill him, and he got in a lucky attack with his knife." Leo paced around the elaborately furnished room. They were inside Luke's mansion, and Leo's footsteps seemed to echo as he walked across the marble floor. "Ramiel knew that I'd figured out he was a traitor, and he wasn't going down without one final battle."

Rayce Lovel whistled. "So you're seriously telling us that you took out an angel? I thought they were the good guys."

Since Rayce was mated to an angel...or, a fallen angel, his opinion wasn't surprising. His Lila *was* good. But...

It was Mora who answered the wolf. "Ramiel wasn't good. Not anymore." Mora sat, with her spine ever-so-straight, on Luke's fancy settee. "His own bitterness had driven him past that point."

Luke downed a glass of whiskey. "Ramiel saw visions, right? Like you?"

Her lashes lowered. "Not quite like me, but, yes, he did. And he knew—"

"He knew Leo was supposed to rule the dark, and that I was the one bound with angels?" Luke's words were mocking.

Mora nodded. "Stop acting like you don't already know this." Her lush lips tightened. "We both know you've sensed it for some time now. Why else would you make all of your recent deals?" Her hand waved around the room. "You let your most trusted guard..." Now she was eyeing Rayce. "Even mate an angel."

"*Fallen* angel," Rayce corrected her as his eyes narrowed. "My Lila fell."

Mora's eyes closed. "Did she?" Her shoulders rolled back. "Maybe you shouldn't be so sure of that...like I said, things change."

"*What?*" Rayce bounded forward.

Even though Mora had just shocked him, Leo schooled his expression as he shoved his hand against the wolf shifter's chest. "One problem at a time, okay? The angel isn't here now so—"

The doors flew open and a female with long, red hair strolled inside, moving with a dancer's grace. "Actually, I am."

Leo's eyes squeezed shut. Everyone was coming to join their party.

"And I brought company," Lila added.

He already knew who the company in question would be. He could smell the vampire. Julian's mate…Rose. A former human who'd fought with all of her strength to stay with the man she loved.

Leo had even fought for Rose, too. Something about her had called to him. His breath blew out slowly as he opened his eyes. "You all don't need to be here. In fact, everyone but me, Luke, and Mora should leave. The rest of you should get as far away as you possibly can." He didn't want them to be collateral damage when the hellhounds came hunting.

Rose laughed and she hurried to Julian's side. "I'm not leaving him. Not now, not ever."

The angel took up a position near Rayce. "If Rayce is fighting, so am I." Lila's face was both serene and determined.

Leo growled and whirled to glare at Luke. "Tell them to get lost!"

"I don't control them any longer." Luke just shrugged. "I thought you did."

Asshole. "You can at least—"

"They're all here for a reason." Mora's voice was strong and when his gaze swung back to her, Leo saw that she'd jumped to her feet. "Don't you see? Good and evil, blending together. Because you can't have one without the other." She took a step toward him, her gaze intense. "Do you hear what I'm saying? *You can't have one...without the other.*"

"Fuck me," Luke suddenly drawled as he snapped his fingers together. "You set them all up, didn't you? Every single one of them. I thought I was making the deals, but you were behind the scenes, pulling the strings. *Fate.*" The one word sounded like a curse. But suddenly, he was in front of Rose and Julian. "What did you do here?" He touched Rose's shoulder.

Mora bit her lip.

"*What did you do, Fate?*" Luke demanded.

"Watch that tone..." Leo warned him again.

"Rose's brother was a twisted bastard who had to be stopped." Mora's voice came out quickly, the words almost tumbling over one another. "If left unchecked, he would have destroyed a significant portion of the paranormal population. So I...I gave Julian a push. In the right direction. Made sure he was in just the right spot to find the woman who would be the other half of his soul."

Leo saw that Julian's face had gone slack with shock.

But Mora wasn't done talking. "And I knew that once he met her, he would make any deal to assure she stayed in this world."

Julian paled. "She *died*. She was shot, bleeding out in front of me. I had to get Luke to transform her."

"That was her fate. She was always meant to be a vampire, not a human." Mora's attention cut to the angel and her werewolf. "And before you two ask, yes, I had something to do with both of you, as well."

Leo knew his mouth was hanging open. He'd always blamed himself for what had happened to Lila. He'd failed the angel, and guilt had been heavy on his shoulders. *I still carry it.*

"There was a race, right?" Mora questioned them. "To see who could find the fallen angel first. Would it be the powerful werewolf…or…" Now she looked at Leo and gave a little wince. "Or the so-called Lord of the Light?"

And he saw just what had happened, finally. "You slowed me down, Mora. When I was trying to find her so desperately to return her to heaven. You were in my path, and I didn't even know it."

She inclined her head. "Rayce needed the angel, and Lila needed him."

"Why?" Rayce demanded, his voice angry and tight. "Why move all the players like we're on a chess board?"

Mora was silent a moment. Her head bowed. Her shoulders slumped.

Leo wanted to take her into his arms and hold her against his heart. He—

Her head lifted. Her gaze was clear as she stared not at Rayce, but at Lila. "I had to change your fate, Lila, because when the battle is over— and the dust clears—you'll take the Lord of the Light to the angels. The others will listen to you because you are one of their own. You'll help to mend the pain there, you'll help them to see…that Luke isn't so bad after all."

Lila's mouth dropped. "They…they won't believe—"

"Luke saved you. You'll be the proof they need, standing right in front of them."

No one spoke. Leo couldn't look away from Mora.

Once more, her shoulders straightened. She gave a nod that was oddly regal. *Fate. I told her…she's a goddess.* "And that's why. That's why I did everything, even when I was supposed to hate Leo. So all the pieces could go together." She pointed at the vampire and her panther. "While Lila and her wolf see to the angels, you two will be at the side of the Lord of the Dark. You'll help him to keep the more dangerous paranormals in check. You'll guide him, you'll help him, and balance will be maintained."

Silence. The really uncomfortable kind.

"It gets so tiring," Mora blurted and Leo could tell by her expression that she wished she could take the words back. *Too late, baby.* "So tiring…always trying to make sure everyone is okay. Grabbing the little lines of a life and twisting them so that endings are different." She pushed back her hair. "And I never could see my own ending, but I knew it was coming." Her lips curved into a sad smile. "It's coming soon."

"It's *not* the end," Leo immediately denied. Didn't she get it? He wasn't going to let her go. He was ready to trade anything, *everything,* for her. She'd worked so fiercely arranging everyone else's life—couldn't she see that he'd do anything for *her* life? To keep her safe in this world?

"If it's not the end…" Luke drawled, sounding as if he were *bored* by the whole encounter. Such an ass. Leo knew boredom was the last thing his brother felt. "Then what's the plan? What's the big miracle that is going to save Fate?" He inclined his head toward Leo. "And us?"

Leo rolled back his shoulders and tried to block off his emotions. Mora's revelations had pretty much just knocked him on his ass. *All that time, she was working to protect everyone?*

"Leo?" Luke prompted. "What the hell is the battle plan?"

Focus. Protect Mora. Lock down your emotions. This was the part where things could get dicey. "We're going to lock her up."

From the corner of his eye, Leo saw Mora jerk. *"What?"*

But Leo focused on his twin. "Your prison can hold any paranormal, right? It's escape proof?" So the stories had always said.

Luke's jaw hardened. He sent a fast glare toward Lila. "It *was*, but then a certain angel escaped. However, I do believe I have things in order now."

"You'd *better* have them in order." Anger hardened each word. They couldn't afford any mistakes.

"Leo…" Mora grabbed his arm. "What are you doing? I thought we were going to get Luke to help defend—"

"He will defend you. He and I will both stand between you and the hounds. They *won't* take you." His words were a vow. A world without Mora? *No.* "But we don't know what sort of spell Ramiel worked before his death. For all we know, he set it so that the hounds will return again and again, until they get you."

Her lower lip trembled. "I…see."

"So we just make sure they don't get you, *and* we don't send them back."

She backed up. "The hounds have to go back to the flames. They're too dangerous to be loose in this world."

Luke gave a sharp bark of laughter. "Ah, my dear brother, now I see where you're going with this plan."

Beside him, his mate Mina gave a hum of frustration. "Well, I don't see…"

Luke's fingers trailed up her arm. "Leo wants me to keep the hounds in my prison, love. He wants to lure them in…with Fate as bait. And then Leo wants us to cage the beasts."

"Nice plan," Julian allowed with a nod. "If the beasts are caged, then they can't take your girl to hell."

Leo smiled, and he knew it was a cold and cruel sight. "Exactly. We lure the bastards into the prison, we seal them up, and they don't get out. Mora stays safe, and the world keeps right on turning."

Rayce's skin had gone a bit pale. "You're just going to keep them locked up…forever?"

Oh, right, Rayce had once spent a very, very long time in one of Luke's paranormal prison cells. "The prison cells were made for a reason. To hold back the beasts that were too dangerous for the world." A little known secret…he'd actually helped Luke to build those cells. "The hounds can't be free." Leo was determined to make this happen. "The plan can work, I know it.

We just have to make sure they go in the prison…if Mora is inside a cell, they'll rush straight to her. The trick is to get *her* out, and keep them inside."

"Before they rip her to shreds," Luke finished.

Mora swayed a little.

But… "Exactly," Leo told him. "That's what we have to do. We have to get Mora out before they can hurt her." His gaze swept the room. The "bad" paranormals—they were the ones on his side for the coming fight. Strange. "Are you all in?"

Julian and his Rose nodded.

"We're in," Lila agreed softly as her fingers locked with Rayce's.

Mina nodded. "In. Absolutely."

Luke just smiled. "Why the hell not? After all, what's the little matter of life and death between enemies?"

CHAPTER TWENTY-TWO

"I don't like this plan," Mora muttered. She sat on a narrow cot inside one of Luke's paranormal prison cells. Her hands were twisted in her lap, and her head was bent forward. Her hair hid her expression from him. "Being bait wasn't at the top of my to-do list."

Leo stepped inside the cell. The door was open behind him. No one else was in that area — the others were preparing for the fight that was coming. "I won't let the hounds touch you."

She still didn't look up. "The others — they all feel betrayed. They think I've been playing with them all. Toying with their lives. I could see it in their eyes."

He crossed the cell and stopped just a few inches from her. Her scent teased him, and Leo could feel the warmth from her body like a touch against his skin.

"Fate doesn't play," she whispered. "Fate isn't cruel. She isn't kind. She just *is*. Why don't people see that?"

"Mora…"

Her head tipped back. She stared up at him, her face very solemn. Her eyes were so big and deep. "My cousin, Sabrina…the muse—"

"Sabrina Lark." Yes, he knew all about Sabrina. Because of her, he'd found his way back to Mora.

"If things don't go well, if they don't go the way we hope, I need you to tell Sabrina…she was always like a sister to me. And I'll miss her, but I'm so glad she has a mate to stay at her side, to help her—"

Screw this. He caught her hands and pulled Mora up to her feet. "No."

"No?" Her brows shot up. "I need you to do this for me—I want her to know—"

"You're not giving me some I'm-gonna-die order, Mora. I won't deliver a message to your cousin because you'll be around to tell her yourself, got me?" And that icy fist pounding into his chest—it *wasn't* fear. He couldn't afford to feel fear. Mora was going to be fine. His plan would work.

Her gaze searched his.

"You will be here," he said flatly. "You can tell her yourself."

"I will be here," she repeated, her words husky.

"Damn straight."

Her lips lifted in the faintest smile. "Do you remember the first day we met? Probably not, I mean, it was centuries ago—"

"You wore white and you were standing at the foot of a volcano. One that was about to erupt. I thought you were absolutely mad because I didn't realize who you were, not at first. I raced to you because I wanted to keep you safe."

Her smile slipped.

"Your back was to me, but then you turned, and I saw your face. I stopped. I froze right then and there." And he'd known that everything was going to change for him. "That was the first time I saw you."

Her face had softened. Her hand lifted and touched his cheek. "You planned to use me."

I planned to love you. "I will not let you be hurt today."

Her fingertips felt like silk against him. "Once the hounds come in this cell, how will I get out?"

He'd worked this out. "I'll attack with the others. We'll distract the beasts, then knock them out. That's when you'll flee. Once you're clear—once we're *all* clear—we'll lock the cell door. They won't get out after that. You won't need to fear them ever again."

Her breath rushed out. She glanced around the cell. It was quite large and it snaked to the left and the right. "This is where they'll spend the rest of their lives?"

"It's better than the fires of hell."

She looked back at him. There was a strange wistfulness in her gaze. "We don't have much time left."

"Mora…"

"Will you make love to me, once more?"

His cock jerked. The damn thing was always eager for her. *Always.* But… "Here, baby? No, not in a cell, not you, not—"

She just nodded. "Here." She rose onto her toes. Her lips pressed to his. "In a cell. With me." She licked his lower lip. "I'm scared, Leo."

"No—"

"Yes. And I need you to distract me so that I won't be scared anymore." She nipped the lip she'd just licked. "I want these last moments to be so good. I want them to be filled with so much pleasure that I don't feel afraid any longer."

"There is nothing to fear."

She tipped back her head. "Of course, there is. Hellhounds are at the door—literally. And too much could go wrong. So I need this. I need *you,* okay?"

He could deny her nothing.

His mouth took hers. The kiss was deep and hard and hot. He pulled her closer against him, and her breasts pressed to his chest. He could feel the tightness of her nipples against him. He could smell the seductive scent of her arousal.

Just a kiss—and she wanted him, too. He liked to fool himself into believing that Mora had been made just for him.

He was pretty sure he lived just for her.

He tore his mouth from hers and began to kiss a path down her neck. He licked and sucked, and she gave a little moan as she rose onto her tip toes. "Leo…" She breathed his name in a husky voice that sounded like pure sex appeal. "Do that thing…where you make our clothes vanish…"

He did that thing. Their clothes vanished.

"We don't have much time." Her nails pressed into his shoulders. "I don't have much left…"

You have forever. I'll see to it.

"Right now, Leo. I need you *now*."

He lifted her up. Her back hit the bars as he trapped her between his body and the cell. Her legs wrapped around his waist. Her sex was open. Ready for him. He just had to drive inside of her—

"*No.*" His voice was guttural.

Mora stiffened in his arms. "Did you say…no?"

He pulled away from her. Mora's feet touched the stone floor. She trembled and pain flashed on her face. "You don't—"

"No room for fear, right?" That was what she wanted. "If that's the case, I need to give you enough pleasure to drive you right out of your mind."

"You do, Leo, you always *do*."

He dropped to his knees before her. "Let's make damn sure." His arms caught her waist again and he lifted her up. Her legs slid over his shoulders and she grabbed for the bars behind her head, stretching her body tight. She was in the perfect position, lickably close, and he put his mouth right on her.

"*Leo!*"

She wanted pleasure and no fear? He'd give her so much pleasure that she would go mad. He used his tongue on her, used his teeth in the most careful of bites. He licked and sucked, and he had her twisting and jerking feverishly against him. He didn't let up, if anything, Leo went harder at her. He worked her with his mouth until she let loose a wild, desperate scream.

He loved the way her pleasure tasted. She was still trembling against him when he rose and re-positioned her body. Her hands still gripped the bars. He wrapped her legs around his waist and then his hands covered hers as he drove into her. She was hot and wet, and he sank deep. She clenched her sex around his dick, and he was in paradise. He withdrew, only to plunge back even deeper. Harder. She arched against him, sending her hips surging up to meet his. His cock grew even bigger, even harder for her. His whole body tightened as he thrust wildly into her. He was too rough, this was the wrong place—

But to him, everything about Mora was right.

She came for him again, not screaming his name but whispering it, and he followed her into oblivion. The pleasure slammed into him and his body jerked and twisted. He caught her lips with his and kissed her—deep and hard, then slowly, carefully, tenderly. His heartbeat was a thunder that shook his chest and seemed to echo in his ears, but it slowly faded to a normal beat.

His head lifted. He stared into her eyes. "Still afraid?"

She smiled. "No."

He kissed her again, and then he slowly withdrew and eased her back onto her feet. A wave of his hand and they were both dressed. Her cheeks were still flushed and her eyes gleamed, but otherwise, they were both back to normal.

And not a moment too soon.

He caught the scent of the wolf and heard the thud of approaching footsteps.

"Company," Leo murmured.

Her hand immediately flew up to straighten her hair, but he caught her fingers in his. He brought her hand to his mouth and pressed a kiss to her knuckles. "You're perfect."

Her face softened.

"Hey, *asshole!*" The wolf shifter called out.

"You're perfect," Leo assured Mora, "but that guy is a jerk who is gonna push me too far..." He eased away from her.

The wolf shifter was near the cell's open door. "You have visitors, Leo," Rayce announced.

Leo's shoulders stiffened. "The hounds?"

"No, worse...a woman who said she's an angel and a guy I *know* has to be a vamp."

Trina and Merius. They'd tracked him? Unexpected.

Leo headed for the cell door. Mora followed behind him but... He turned. "You should stay here. The hounds could arrive any moment, and we need to make sure they come to this cell. They'll follow your scent. We can't afford any mistakes."

She held his gaze and smiled. "Right. No mistakes." The smile didn't reach her eyes.

He should say more. Tell her... "Everything is going to be all right."

"Of course." But her voice was so flat.

His insides twisted. "The plan *will* work."

"It's a great plan," Mora assured him. Again, though, her voice was...wrong.

He was missing something.

"Uh, dude, you coming out anytime soon?" Rayce pressed.

Shit. Leo whirled on his heel and marched from the cell.

"Leo!" Mora called.

He froze, then glanced over his shoulder. Mora had followed him, but stopped at the cell door. "I love you."

He lifted his hand and rubbed at his aching chest.

"It was nice, you know?" She gave him that half-smile again. The one that didn't reach her eyes. "To have a second chance with you. It was good." Her lips thinned. "*You* are good. No matter what anyone else ever tells you, just remember that, okay?"

He didn't want to leave her.

Rayce shifted a bit nervously. "Yeah, um, not to tell you your business or anything, Leo, but, that vamp looked as if he were about two seconds away from plunging his fangs into the nearest throat, so you might want to speed this little scene along."

Jaw locking, Leo headed away from the cell. Mora didn't call out to him again, but he found himself looking back, anyway. She'd returned to the cot. She sat there, her hands fisted in her lap, with her head bent forward. Her hair hid Mora's expression from him.

***

Leo strode through the corridor that led to the main house. After a few more twists and turns, he found Merius and Trina waiting for him — they stood right in the foyer, and they both looked uncomfortable as, well, all hell.

Trina was staring at Lila — Trina's eyes were huge and her lower lip trembled as she gazed at the woman who'd once been a fellow angel.

And Lila — Lila was looking anywhere but at Trina.

"I missed you," Trina suddenly blurted.

Lila's gaze rose to meet hers. Leo stilled. Once, he and Lila had been friends, and he'd hated seeing the angel fall. *It was my fault.* He'd wanted to move heaven and earth to give Lila her wings back but...

She wanted her werewolf more than she wanted her wings.

"I almost lost my wings," Trina continued, her voice husky. "I was under attack, and I thought I'd lose them for sure."

Lila edged closer to her.

"How do you live without yours?" Trina asked as tears gleamed in her eyes.

"It's easy," Lila said, her words soft and gentle. Lila had always been the gentle one. "I just found something that mattered more than them." She pulled Trina into a hug.

Merius watched them — and the guy's fangs were out. Rayce had been right about the fellow.

Merius seemed to be on the verge of lunging for the next available neck. Sighing, Leo marched forward and he clamped a hand around his friend's shoulder. "Tell me you're in control."

"I'm in control," Merius rumbled.

The words were a total lie and they both knew it.

"I can...I can help him." That was Rose...inching forward and nodding a bit. "I can teach him control." She bared her own fangs. "It's not easy, but you'll learn it."

How...odd. Leo's gaze swept the group. Dark and light paranormals were supposed to be natural enemies. Or maybe...perhaps they were just enemies because that was the way they *thought* things should be.

What if we're all wrong?

***

"What's the game?"

Mora didn't jump in surprise when the low question floated to her. After all, she'd heard the footsteps. And she'd known that Luke would be coming to pay her a visit.

He'd waited until Leo had left her, and then Luke had come sneaking in to see her. She almost smiled. If the situation wasn't so tragic, she would have. Instead, she was pretty much fighting just to keep her control in place.

"Mora..." Luke's voice held the note of command. "I know you're hiding secrets, and I don't like it when people hide things from me."

She lifted her head, then turned to gaze at him. The cell door was still open. He stood in the entranceway. He looked so very much like Leo.

"How's your sister?" Mora asked him.

His face immediately hardened.

"Sorry...forgot. Amber is supposed to be off-limits, huh? Good thing she has such a good protector to stand by her side." Her head tilted to the left as she studied him. "I mean, it's not every day that a Reaper will devote his life to protecting someone."

Luke grabbed the bar to his right. His hand clenched around the paranormally improved bar so tightly that his knuckles turned white. "I suppose you're going to say that you were behind that pairing, too?"

Mora rose to her feet. She wrapped her arms around her stomach. "My bad. Did you want to take credit for their alliance?"

A low snarl came from him.

She sighed. "Your beast is never far from the surface, is he?"

"I don't like being manipulated."

Weariness tugged at her. "No, you just like manipulating others. I have to confess, though, I truly could not have done all this without you.

Sometimes, I swear it was like we were partners. We both wanted the exact same thing…"

"And what is that *same thing?*"

She licked her lips. "For you *and* Leo to survive. For the balance to be maintained. For life to keep going."

He waited. She didn't say anything else.

Luke rolled his eyes. "Seriously, what the hell are you? A greeting card?"

"I'm Fate. And I know what's coming." She straightened her spine. "Some things can be altered. Some can't. Remember that. Remember…and help, if you can."

A deep line appeared between his eyes. "More secrets?"

"I love your brother."

Luke laughed. The sound seemed to echo around her. "That's no secret. You've been rooting for him all these centuries…"

"I wasn't supposed to meet him." Now she shared one of her secrets because it was time. "I wasn't supposed to stop by the foot of that volcano. I wasn't supposed to get close to him. When I did, I changed things. For him. For you. For…me."

"Mora?" For the first time, uncertainty hung in his voice. But then he stiffened and glanced over his shoulder.

She swallowed down her fear. "The hounds are at the door." If she tried hard enough, she could hear their howls. She knew he'd heard them, as well. "I think it's time to greet them."

CHAPTER TWENTY-THREE

Leo heard the howls. Deep, reverberating, unearthly. Leo turned to look at the front door, and he knew that the beasts had risen once more.

"Um...want to clue us in as to what's happening?" Trina asked as she rocked back and forth on her feet. "Merius and I tracked you here so that we could help, but we need to know—"

The explanation would have to be fast. The short version. "Hellhounds are about to burst through the door." Leo let his claws out. "Don't kill them. We're going to herd them back to the cells that Luke has in his place—fucking paranormal proof cells. We get them in there..."

Something heavy slammed into the front door.

"We *lock* them inside," Leo added as he bared his fangs.

The wood of the door began to splinter.

"And we fucking throw away the key," he finished.

The wood exploded inward as the hellhounds attacked.

***

Mora heard the screams — the howls of pain. She ran toward the cell —

But Luke slammed the door shut. "I don't think so."

She blinked. "What are you doing? The point is for the hounds to get *inside* to me."

"No, the point is to kill the fucking hounds *and* to keep you alive. I don't like this setup. It reeks of martyrdom, and I'm not in the mood for that shit."

"Luke!"

He turned on his heel. "Now, excuse me, but I have some hounds to stop, and if those bastard beasts so much as *breathe* on my Mina, they're toast."

"No! Luke, *no!*"

He wasn't listening to her. He'd left, rushing away. And she knew he was going to shift into the form of a dragon. He'd change and he'd use his fire to send the hounds back to hell...

But they'll come back. They'll keep coming back until they get what they want.

She yanked against the bars, pulling with all of her might. *Paranormal proof, dammit!* Not that she had super strength.

Her nostrils flared. She'd just caught the scent of ash...and brimstone. And the scent was coming —

From behind me.

Mora whirled around.

Dax stood there. *In the cell.* The same Dax she'd killed. The same Dax she'd sent to hell. He gave her a sad smile. "Hello, Mora."

Her lip trembled. "Dax…"

He lifted his hand toward her. "I'm afraid that I've come for you."

***

It was working. They were leading the hounds toward the cell, putting up a token fight so the bastards wouldn't be suspicious, but it was *working* and soon—

"Get out of the way." A savage bellow of command.

Leo looked up—and saw that Luke had shifted. His twin had let out his true beast, and the giant, hulking dragon was opening his mouth.

The hellhounds were in his path—and everyone else backed the hell away.

"No!" Leo yelled. *"Don't!"*

But the dragon opened his mouth. The flames flew out—and they went straight toward the hounds.

***

"I'm sorry, Dax," Mora said softly. He wasn't attacking her. He was just standing there, looking so sad and solemn, and her heart broke for him. "I tried to change your—"

"Fate?" Dax finished with a weary shake of his head.

Her heart jerked in her chest. The howls had stopped.

"They'll be back," Dax told her grimly. "Ramiel fixed things…they'll just keep coming back, and they don't even have to wait twenty-four hours now." His words were low. "He took Leo's blood and used it in his spell. I learned…I learned everything while I was down there. They don't want to hunt you. They just want to be left alone. But they can't stop. *You're* the fire in their blood now. They have to come after you." He looked around the cell. "I was supposed to sneak in here and take you while they distracted the others."

"I think the others are dead." Her lips felt numb. Cold slid over her body.

"Didn't you hear me?" Anger roughened his voice, breaking past the sadness. "They'll be back. Any second. They'll just appear—"

Her gaze flew around, frantic—

"Right here," Dax finished.

And sure enough, they were suddenly in the cell with her. Not *outside* of that paranormal proof cell, but right in there, with her.

How? How had they all gotten past the bars?

They were the men who'd hurt her so long ago…they were the men who'd kidnapped her recently.

They were the men who'd come to take her away.

"Distraction," Dax said again. "The hellhounds *wanted* the others to think they'd won. That way, no one would be back here, waiting to protect you."

"H-how did you know I was in the cell?" *How did you get past the locked cell door?*

"We can see everything when we're down there. See the whole fucking world," Dax whispered, "but we only feel the fire."

Tears pricked her eyes. So she'd still see the world when she was down in the flames. She'd still see Leo. That was good to know.

"How can you get past the bars?" Leo's great plan never would have worked, not if they could get in and out of the paranormal proof cells—

"Hellhounds aren't like the others." It was the redhead who spoke. Reever. "Only the fire contains us. Nothing else." There was no rage on his face as he stared at her. He was just…waiting.

Waiting for the end? "I've…lied," Mora confessed.

The men around her had formed a circle. Men, not beasts. Not right then.

"I said that I couldn't see my own fate," she murmured. Mora shook her head. "That was the lie. I've always known fire waited for me." That was why she'd been so terrified the first time Reever and his men had come for her. She'd thought her time was up then.

It hadn't been. She'd had a few more centuries waiting for her.

But not any longer.

"It will hurt," Dax warned her.

"I expected nothing less." She'd try not to scream, but she'd never liked pain very much.

***

The dragon vanished. Luke stood in his place—dressed in one of his damn fancy suits and with a smirk on his face. Luke tugged on his sleeve and lifted one pompous brow. "One problem eliminated…for now."

Enraged, Leo leapt at his brother. He drove his fist at Luke's jaw. Luke's head whipped back, and Leo took aim again.

But Luke caught his fist. "That's one hell of a way to say thank you."

"I had a plan! We were going to lock them in the cell! Now we don't know when they'll come back!" Leo jerked his hand free. "You screwed it all up."

Luke's face tightened. "I *helped*. I took a stand. It will be twenty-four hours before they come back. That gives us time to come up with a *better* plan because in case you missed it, I'm not ruling the dark any longer. *You are.* And you don't know a damn thing about running the prison on this island. It's not *safe* to keep the hellhounds here. We need something better. We need—"

A scream. High, pain-filled. Desperate.

Mora's scream.

Leo's eyes widened in horror, and then he was shoving past Luke, shoving past Luke's friends and the allies that had gathered now that the flames were gone. He ran past the vampires, the shifters, the angel—

He thundered through the old tunnel that led to the cells. He burst into the secure area—what *should* have been secure—and his heart stopped.

A circle of familiar figures were in that cell. He recognized the redheaded bastard on sight. *Reever. How many times do you have to die?*

And...Dax was there, too. Dax had his hand on Mora's shoulder.

Mora was in the middle of that group.

He grabbed for the cell door. The fucking thing was locked!

"I'm sorry," Mora cried out. "It just hurt so much, I didn't mean to scream—"

Didn't mean to fucking scream? She'd been attacked, she should damn well have screamed.

She should have screamed when she first saw those bastards.

Luke leapt forward and unlocked the door.

Leo lurched inside. The plan he'd originally had to trap the beasts could work. The hellhounds were back—he didn't understand *how* they'd gotten back so soon—but they were in the cell, just as he'd wanted. Now he had to get Mora out, and he could seal them inside.

"Don't watch, Leo!" Mora shouted.

What?

The men moved closer to her. They all put their hands on her—some on her shoulders. Some on her back.

"Get away from her!" Leo bellowed.

He could hear snarls and growls behind him. The others had chased him and Luke back to the cell. They'd help him. They'd all fight.

He lifted his hand, intending to rip right through that circle of men.

Then the flames erupted. Bright and hot, blinding with their intensity. He tried to reach through that fire. He just had to grab Mora—

The flames vanished. Mora vanished. Leo stood there a moment, stunned and lost as his gaze flew around the cell. There were black char marks on the floor. Nothing else.

"Mora?" He whispered her name at first. He spun around, desperate. *"Mora?"* She wasn't there. She wasn't fucking *there.*

She wasn't anywhere. Not in his world. He could feel her absence already, like a great, yawning hole inside of him. His body began to shake. His claws sharpened even more. His fangs were bursting out of his mouth. His wings had shot from his back. The beast was taking over. It was desperate, in agony, broken without his mate. "Mora?"

"*Leo.*" It was his brother's voice. His brother who now stood before him with a face that was tense and a gaze that was sorrowful. "I...didn't know. Didn't suspect..."

Leo shoved his claws into Luke's chest. "You did this."

He and Luke were the only ones in that cell. The others were outside, watching, waiting, on the other side of the bars.

"*You* sent your fire at them...and it didn't stop them. It just distracted us all while they came for her." Each word was savage, because Leo was more beast than man. "I...lost her. Because of you." *Gone, gone. Mora's gone. I can feel...emptiness. She's...*

Luke didn't fight. He just looked down at the claws in his chest and the blood that had soaked his fancy suit. "Is this supposed to be the part where I fight you?"

Leo needed Luke to fight him. He needed something to stop the pain he felt. Because that yawning hole inside? The one that told him Mora was gone? Now it *hurt*. Agony poured through him. Knives seemed to rip him apart. "*Fight me.*" That was what everyone had always wanted. A brawl to the death.

Mora isn't on earth. The world went darker. I felt it when she left. Because she'd taken his soul with her. The pain was excruciating.

The hounds took Mora away.

Leo raked his claws down Luke's chest.

More blood flowed.

Luke still didn't fight back.

"*Fight me!*" Leo bellowed.

But Luke held his ground. "Why? Do you think it will bring her back?"

Leo stumbled away from his brother. His gaze swept around, and he could see all of the others still standing just beyond the bars. He choked out a breath, and smoke drifted in front of him.

Mora. Gone.

Julian and his vampire were watching Leo — and pity filled their eyes. A tear had slid down Lila's cheek, and her beast wrapped his arm around her. Trina and Merius just stared with stunned, wild gazes. Luke's mate was there, too...Mina stood beyond the open door and her face was so pale and sad.

Why does Luke get a mate...when I have lost mine? Mora is gone...Mora is burning... "I said she'd be safe..."

Luke was still right there. Not attacking. Not…

He's blocking my path. He thinks I'm going to break loose and attack all of the others here. Leo could see it, in the battle ready tension that coated Luke's body. In the way his twin kept glancing nervously over his shoulder…

At his mate.

"I said she'd be safe," Leo whispered again. The rage built inside of him. Rage and pain twisted in a fire-soaked fury, until he could feel his very skin start to shred as his beast took over.

Luke won't fight me.

And Leo had never wanted to kill his brother…

He'd gone to Mora in the beginning, to try and change fate.

Fate. She was my fate. She was mine.

He'd hunted her down to Resurrection…he'd built that bar back for her…

Because Leo had wanted to give her the world.

He dropped to his knees. His hands slapped against the stone floor, right over the charred black stains that were all that remained of Mora. *"Get…out…"* He was losing himself. The pain and fury were too great. But this line…this line…*I will not cross.* His head jerked back. He glared at his twin. *"Get out…"* *While you can.*

While my control holds. Before I give in to the darkness and kill you.

Luke backed away. He kept his gaze on Leo as he walked — backwards — through the cell door. As soon as he was clear, Luke swung that door shut. The clang of metal was loud.

Too loud.

Mora?

The beast erupted. The man's pain was too much. The dragon sprang to life and the beast opened his mouth to let his fire reign.

"Get the fuck out of here!" Luke yelled. *"Everyone — now!"*

CHAPTER TWENTY-FOUR

Luke Thorne was used to getting what he wanted. He was used to ruling over the paranormals in his world — and he was used to the sweet rush that came from being the toughest badass in the room.

What he wasn't used to...what he damn well didn't like...*pain.*

Luke strode through the old tunnel that connected his home to the paranormal prison. He'd been warden at that prison for longer than he liked to remember. The worst of the worst were housed in those cells. The beasts who were beyond control. The predators who would attack humans if they were ever freed.

His steps echoed as he approached the cell on the right.

Now my brother is in the prison.

A week had passed since Mora had vanished. A week since rage and pain had broken Leo.

Luke had gone to that cell every single day, hoping to see a change. But every single day, his brother's fire had greeted him. Madness. Luke knew what stared back at him when he gazed into the dragon's eyes. Mora had known what would happen to Leo without her. She'd worked so hard to make sure that he would survive...

She even played me.

More than he'd realized.

But as he approached the cell today, the dragon wasn't there. Leo was back in the body of a man. He gripped the bars tightly with his hands, and his head leaned forward, resting against them.

Luke stopped, stunned...and hopeful. "Brother?"

Leo didn't move. "I still can't feel her."

Luke crept closer.

"When she was close...I swear, I could *feel* her before I saw her. Like a touch on my skin. Now...she's just...gone, and I'm empty inside."

The cell door was still shut. Luke walked to it, but he didn't open that cell. After all, he didn't want to kill his brother. And if Leo tried to come out of that cell, if the rage still ruled him...

"There...has to be more." Leo's voice was desperate. "It can't...it can't just end like this. I have to...Mora can't stay in the fire."

Luke glanced around the cell. He'd been here, talking with Mora, trying to figure her out...and that seemed like a lifetime ago. "She loved you."

Leo's shoulders stiffened. "*You aren't helping.*"

Luke's eyes narrowed. "Actually, I think I am." And he walked around the cell, moving until he was next to the bars that Leo gripped so firmly. "You're alive. I'm alive. I'd say Mora's plan worked, as far as that is concerned."

Leo slowly lifted his head. His face was ashen. His eyes lined with dark circles. He wore his grief like a shroud.

"I was a player…" Luke murmured, thinking this through, "and she played me. Mora…she even said…she couldn't have done it without me. That it was almost like we were partners."

Leo just stared at him with dead eyes.

Luke licked his lower lip. It was the first time Leo had been rational, and he needed his brother to stay that way so they could figure this shit out. "She said we both wanted the same thing."

"What…was that…?"

"For you and me to survive." Luke gave a rough laugh. "Sure, there are bars between us, but at the darkest moment of your damn life, you didn't kill me."

Leo lowered his lashes. "Never wanted to kill you…"

"Yes, I get that now…certainly explains a bit of your asshole-ness."

Leo's hold on the bars tightened.

Luke rolled back his shoulders. "She told me she knew what was coming..." Fuck, he was terrible at offering comfort. He was screwing this up and probably about to drive his brother straight into another dragon shift.

Leo's face became absolutely...blank. "*Lie.*"

"No, it's the truth. Mora knew what was coming. She told me, right in this room. And if she knew, then you have to see how this isn't anyone's fault, right? It was just—shit, I don't want to sound like the greeting card I accused her of being, but...meant to be."

Leo's hand flew through the bars and fisted in the front of Luke's suit. "You *lie*. Mora could never see her own fate. She told me..."

He looked down at his brother's hand, then back at Leo's ravaged face. "Maybe she didn't want you to know." Luke tried to make his voice gentle, a nearly impossible task. He wasn't exactly a gentle guy. "Because she knew there were some things that couldn't be changed. Maybe she lied to you so that she could spare you."

"This *isn't* fucking sparing me...I'm in *agony. I need her. She's in the fire. She's —* "

"Cordelia!" Luke called, cutting through Leo's rasping words. "It's safe for you to come in now."

Silence and then...the softest tap of footsteps. A few moments later...

"Ah, there she is." Luke smiled at his guest. "My favorite witch."

Cordelia stood uncertainly, holding a scrying mirror in her hands. She was a beautiful woman, bewitchingly so with long, dark hair and warm brown skin. As far as witches were concerned, she was powerful beyond belief. Though now Luke did have to wonder...

Did Mora play with Cordelia's fate, too?

"This is it," Cordelia announced, a sharp edge in her voice. "After this, we are *done*, Luke, you got me? No more deals. And no more frantic phone calls from you. My husband is tired of your crazy ass calling me in the middle of the night. You do it again, and he'll come after you."

Cordelia was married to a human, so Luke wasn't particularly concerned about the threat of an attack from him. But... "See something that helps my brother, and I won't be calling you again."

She cast a nervous glance toward Leo. "He looks...bad."

"You have no idea," Luke murmured. "Just...scry fast, will you?" *Because I'm not sure how long Leo's control will last.*

"I could use some of his blood...and yours." She didn't sound happy.

Not like he was in the mood to give it up, but...Luke's claws flew out. He sliced open Leo's hand, cutting his brother fast through the bars.

The blood sprayed, and Luke caught a few drops in his palm. He strode toward the witch and smeared that blood across her mirror. Then he used his claws on his own hand.

Cordelia didn't look down at the mirror. "I'm not Fate, you know." Her voice was shivery. Nervous. "I can't get the types of visions that she does."

Luke understood that. "What I need you to do…" Leo was still dead silent. Luke risked a glance at him and saw that Leo's wings were coming out. Shit. "I need you to focus on Mora. On Leo. See if there is something we all missed. She planned *everything*…so my money is betting on the fact that she had to plan for you, too. She had to know I'd use you." *It's like we were partners…*Once more, he heard Mora's words in his mind. "Hell, I even think she was counting on it."

"What if I can't help?" Cordelia still didn't look into the mirror. "Is he going to attack?"

"I won't let you get hurt." He was standing between Cordelia and Leo for a reason. "But if you could speed things along, it would *really* help."

Her gaze dropped to the glass.

"*This won't work!*" Leo bellowed. His voice was distorting. "*Mora is burning…We have —* "

"Resurrection," Cordelia whispered. Her head tilted up. Her eyes had gone jet black with power. *"Resurrection. He gave her...Resurrection."*

Luke wasn't following along. He threw a fast glance over his shoulder. "Leo, what the hell is she talking about?"

Leo blinked. His face was savage. "Mora's bar...in Nevada. It's called...Resurrection."

"That's good to know." Luke rolled his eyes. Hardly helpful intel. A damn bar—

"I...rebuilt it for her. After a fire. And she told me...said it mattered. More than I realized."

"Glad you rebuilt the bar." Luke exhaled on a frustrated breath. *I need fucking more.*

The blackness of power slid from Cordelia's eyes. "Did I...help?"

No. You—

"Resurrection!" Leo shouted.

Luke winced. "Yeah, bro, you said that before. The witch said it before, too—" But when he focused on Leo's face again...

Leo was smiling. It was the smile of a madman. "Don't you see? I can bring her back. I was so stupid...blind with pain...*I can bring her back.*"

Then he leapt away from the cell bars. He went to the middle of the room and stared down at the black char marks.

Probably not a good thing to be focusing on...

"I think you should go now, Cordelia," Luke advised. "Like *now*." Because Leo's claws were out. He was slashing his own arms and blood was flying.

Cordelia didn't have to be told again. She ran toward the tunnel.

"Leo, what are you doing?" Luke demanded. He thought he sounded relatively calm. Or not. Maybe he was shouting.

Leo didn't look up from the char marks. "My blood worked before. It was how Ramiel — the fucking bastard — used his spell. And I...I remember the pattern on the ground..."

Leo's blood dropped all over the stones. As Luke watched, Leo immediately fell and began using that blood to write symbols on the stone.

He is too far gone. "Brother, I'm sorry..."

Leo's head whipped up. "Don't be sorry...*fucking help me!* If Mora knew...if you aren't lying...then she was trying to tell me...in a thousand different ways...*Resurrection!* Didn't you just hear your own damn witch? *Resurrection!*"

And Luke hesitated. Mora *had* been good at altering lives...Could she really have found a way to cheat her own...fate?

"I'll get one of the hounds to bring her back!" Leo thundered. "I *have* to find a way. The spell will work. Mora will come back — I'll make a deal, I'll do *anything* — "

"Bloody fucking hell," Luke swore as understanding sank in, and he used one of Julian's absolute favorite expressions. "A deal with a hellhound…"

Then he was stalking toward the cell door. He barely hesitated as he opened it…*Leo won't attack. And he needs me.*

He strode into the cell and made his way to Leo's side. Then, sighing, Luke let his own claws out once more as he sliced his wrist so that his blood would join Leo's. "It's not your blood that we need for this spell."

Leo looked up at him. There was hope in Leo's stare. *And he's looking at me…the way he did when we were kids…when he was the brother — older by two minutes — who always thought we could do anything together.*

Locking his jaw, Luke said, "*I'm* the one who saved the hellhound's life — Dax, remember? I'm the one who helped him, and I'm the one he owes. So we need my blood for this to work."

Impossible, of course…Mora couldn't have planned for either him or Leo to save the hellhound that day, could she? *Yes…yes, she did.* And if she'd planned for that, then she would have known that the hound would owe his savior. And the way to pay back that debt?

Luke closed his eyes and summoned his power. "*Dax…I'm calling in my debt. You hear me, hound? Bring back Fate. Bring her…now.*"

CHAPTER TWENTY-FIVE

He could smell brimstone and smoke, but Leo was worried those acrid scents just came from his own beast. His heart beat like a freaking drum in his chest, and hope clawed at him. Desperate, wild hope.

Could Mora truly have seen all this coming? Could she have been pushing them all, trying to change the fate of everyone?

Come back to me. Come back.

"It's not working," Luke snapped. Frustration grated in his voice. "Dammit, I was so sure...I'm...*sorry.*" He started to back away.

Leo grabbed his brother's hand. Their blood fell together. "We stand together." They'd always been stronger together. "Dax, you bastard!" Leo roared as he threw back his head. "You owe a debt! Bring her *back!*"

Fire erupted—just shot straight up from the stones at their feet. Leo didn't stumble back. He didn't even feel the burn against his skin. The fire blazed and crackled and then...

The hellhound was there. Dax. The guy looked a little worse for wear…and he was holding Mora in his arms. Her hands were looped around Dax's neck. Soot covered her face and limbs. And she slowly turned so that her eyes met Leo's.

"*Resurrection,*" she whispered. Smoke drifted from her clothes—and from Dax's.

Hell, *yes.* He snatched her from the hellhound's grasp. Leo yanked her against his chest and held her so tight that he was probably hurting her. She was pressed against him, her body warm and soft and real, and his life wasn't chaos. He could think and feel and everything he felt—

"*Don't send me back.*"

Leo lifted his head. Over her shoulder, he saw that Dax was swaying.

"*I'll…I'll make any deal,*" Dax gasped. "*Just…don't send me back…*"

Dax's desperate stare was on Leo.

"Don't send him back," Mora whispered, her voice barely a rasp. "Please, Leo, don't…*please…*"

His gaze shifted back to her. "You never have to beg me for anything." He pressed a kiss to her lips. *She's real. And I will never let her go again.* "The deal…" Now his voice was as much of a rasp as hers had been. "The deal is that you'll protect Fate. *Always.* If she ever leaves this world…" Once more, he glanced at Dax. "Then you bring her back to me."

Dax nodded. "Agreed."

Fuck, yes.

Leo squeezed Mora even tighter. Held her even closer. She'd slipped from his world and everything…*everything* had gone dark for him.

It wasn't dark any longer.

He kissed her again. She met him eagerly, rising onto her toes and putting her soft hands on his cheeks. She opened her mouth, and he just wanted to feast. He wanted—

"So, yeah, this is great…" Luke drawled. "But you two kids seriously need to get a damn room."

Dazed, Leo lifted his head.

"But how about you start by at least getting out of the cell," Luke said with a wave of his hand.

Leo stumbled out, pulling Mora with him. Luke followed and Dax rushed forward—

But Luke slammed the cell door shut, blocking the hound. "Not so fast, hound. I'm not sure I trust you." His body was tense. "And you'll find that I added a few upgrades since your last little visit. As soon as I find a flaw in my security system, I eliminate that flaw. Once you're in the cage…now the *only* way out for a hellhound is through this door."

Fear flashed on Dax's face. "*Not another cage…Don't keep me locked up!*"

Mora's body stiffened.

Leo spoke before she could. "I trust him." He would give that hellhound *anything*. Leo knew just how much he owed Dax. "He brought Mora to me."

Luke spun to face him. "Yeah, um, did you miss the whole story about how hellhounds had to be sent to the fire because they get so crazed? That they just want to *destroy?* That they—"

"He's only half-hellhound," Mora announced quickly. "So his control will stay in place." A pause. "I know his fate. I've seen it."

Luke's gaze dropped to her face. He studied her a moment, then he slowly opened the cell door. A faint smile curved Luke's lips as he mused, "You planned every move, didn't you?"

"You can only plan so much," she replied, and there were echoes of weariness and pain in her voice. "Only *do* so much…without completely destroying lives."

Leo turned Mora toward him. His hands slid over her back. He couldn't stop touching her. "Why didn't you just *tell* me to resurrect you? Why not say the hounds were going to take you? Why not just tell—"

"If I'd told you. then you never would have acted on your own. You *never* would have changed." She pointed at Luke. "*He* never would have changed. People make choices. You both had choices to make. Just as I did. I put the dominos in place, but even I didn't know where they'd fall, not in the end."

Dax had walked out of the cell. He stood there, his body shuddering and smoke still rising from his clothes. "What...happens now?"

Mora's hand was on Leo's chest. She smiled up at him. "Leo takes his new place of power. He rules the Dark. The bad things aren't going to know what hit them."

"What about me?" Luke demanded. "What in the hell am I supposed to do now?"

She didn't look at him. "I think you know."

He swore.

"But then, I think you've always known." Her head turned. "Thanks, partner. I truly couldn't have done it without you."

And Luke inclined his head as a faint smile teased his lips. "Damn straight."

***

They were on a mountaintop—snow was falling lightly and the rest of the world seemed to be a million miles away. After she'd come back, Leo had asked Mora where she'd wanted to go.

Her answer had been immediate. *Someplace cold.*

So he'd taken her to this slice of paradise. She thought they might be in Switzerland, but…she wasn't sure.

She just watched the snow fall and thought about how truly lucky she was.

The door opened behind her. Mora's eyes closed. Her body tensed. His scent came to her. Masculine and sexy. Enveloping. Then she felt his warmth. Reaching out to her even though he was still steps away. She yearned. She ached.

So when he finally did touch her, just his touch alone brought her pleasure. Because it was…his touch was like coming home.

"Will you tell me what it was like?"

Her eyes were still closed. "You don't need to know, Leo." Because it would just be something he used to torture himself. There had been fire and pain, and Mora knew she'd never forget that terrible nightmare.

And I wasn't about to let Dax go back to the flames.

"I want to know. I want to know everything about you, Mora."

She opened her eyes. The snow was so beautiful as it fell. She shivered.

"It's cold. We should go inside," he said immediately. "I don't want you to get sick."

Mora laughed. "I've never been sick." She turned in his arms. "You don't have to worry about that."

His face was solemn. The lines around his mouth seemed deeper than before. "I worry—I will always worry about you. I never want you to hurt, Mora. If something happened, if I lost you again…"

She swallowed. "Do you want me to scry and see what our future holds?"

"You *are* my future."

"And you're mine." She knew this with certainty. He'd been her future for a long time, but to ensure that future…so much had needed to be done. "I love you."

He lowered his head. His lips took hers. "I love you."

Tears pricked her eyes, but she didn't let them fall. *Wouldn't* let them fall. "I knew you'd get past the darkness. If you had the right people around you…you'd get past it when it took over." The first true taste of darkness was always the most dangerous. "And once you had the darkness under control, then you'd be able to think clearly again. You'd find a way…" Her words trailed off.

"A way back to you."

"I knew you'd find a way for *me* to get back to you." She nipped his lower lip. "Now that you're ruling the Bad Things, you're going to need me at your side. You never know what might come your way."

His gaze drifted over her face. "What about the prophecy?" Leo asked gruffly. "Luke and I — the big final battle — "

"Some prophecies aren't literal. In a sense, you did die, Leo. The man you'd been is gone. You rule the dark now. And Luke? He's different, too." She hoped the world was ready for that difference. "You're both safe. Balance is here, and that's what matters."

Some of the tension left his face.

Her smile stretched a bit. "You know what I've always wanted?"

"Tell me. It's yours."

"To make love in the snow. To feel the snow against my skin…and you inside of me."

She could feel the change in his body. A very distinct change.

She leaned up closer to him. "Do that thing…" Mora invited. "Where you make our clothes vanish…"

His hand waved. Their clothes were gone. He lifted her up, holding her easily and she wrapped her legs around his hips. He carried her out into the snow. Its cold touch was like heaven against her skin.

I'll always remember the fire, but I'll also never forget the touch of snow and Leo's kiss.

His mouth was on hers. Kissing. Licking. Her breasts were tight and aching. His cock pushed at the apex of her thighs. She arched a bit, rubbing her sex over his hard length, not taking him inside, not yet, but enjoying the friction of his body.

She enjoyed so much about him.

He kissed a path down her neck, stopping in all of the spots she liked the best and holding her easily with his amazing strength. When the snowflakes touched her skin, he just kissed them away. Licked them away.

And then she was ready for him because she couldn't wait longer. His cock slid inside, lodging deep as the passion burned between them. He lifted her up and down, and her nails raked over his shoulders. The pleasure was building fast and she needed to slow it down because this moment mattered — she wanted it to last —

But the climax hit her. A wild burst of pleasure that had her crying his name even as she felt him inside of her, exploding and coming as he held her in an unbreakable grip.

Mora rode out the pleasure with him, blind for a time to everything around her, and when her eyes opened again...

They were in the snow.

Leo was on his back, with her cradled above him. He was still inside of her, and she knew they'd be making love again.

So they did. Only this time, she was in control. When his hands reached for her, she pushed them back down. She slid them over the snow and she rode him, rising and falling slowly, taking her time, drawing out the pleasure because she wanted it to last and last and last…

They climaxed together. A wave so hot she was surprised it didn't melt all of that wonderful snow. Soft snowflakes still fell down on her, dusting over her skin as Mora's breath heaved in and out, and her heart slowed back to its normal rhythm. She stretched on top of him, and her hands pressed to his chest as she stared down at him.

Then she laughed.

A bemused expression crossed his handsome face. "Mora?"

"Not sure how we did it…but you look like an angel." The marks around his body…a perfect snow angel. She could see his wings so clearly in the snow.

"I'm far from an angel." A wicked light made his eyes shine. "I think that deal belongs more to my brother now."

Yes, she supposed he was right.

Then Leo was surging up, holding her easily and her laughter came again as he carried her back into the cabin. There was no more need for worry or fear. She had her fate…he was holding her in his hands.

"I love you," Leo whispered.

And even in the cold, his words made her warm.

***

Luke Thorne had been called many things in his very, very long life. Evil. Bad. *The Devil himself…*

But now, it would seem he had a new title.

"Are you sure about this?" The question came from his delectable Mina. Her beautiful face was adorably worried as she bit her lower lip. "There are *angels* here."

He pressed a tender kiss to her cheek. "I know, love, that's the fun part."

A line of angels waited in front of him. All of the good paranormals would be coming to pay him a visit, coming to check out the new Lord of the Light.

It was fucking fantastic.

He might be ruling the Light, but he still had plenty of bad things up his sleeve. *Oh, Mora, you think I didn't know what you were doing? You were absolutely right. We were partners. I wanted Leo to live, too. And I also wanted to see…*

If it would be fun to raise a little hell in heaven.

"Showtime," Luke whispered.

A nearby angel flinched.

Luke smiled, but he knew his grin held a wicked edge.

Some habits were just hard to break.

###

A NOTE FROM THE AUTHOR

Thank you so much for taking the time to read TEMPTED BY FATE! I've had way too much fun writing about the Bad Things. Luke and Leo were such opposites when I started the series, and getting the chance to switch up the brothers— well, I hope readers liked that twist! And as far as the Bad Things are concerned...this isn't the end. I'm going to let readers help me decide which characters should get a future book or novella. Maybe there's a hellhound who should have a story...or a witch...or an angel-turned-vamp. Head over to my FB page and let me know your thoughts.

And don't forget, if you'd like to stay updated

If you'd like to stay updated on my releases and sales, please join my newsletter list www.cynthiaeden.com/newsletter. You can also check out my Facebook page www.facebook.com/cynthiaedenfanpage. I love to post giveaways over at Facebook!

Again, thank you for reading TEMPTED BY FATE.

Best,
Cynthia Eden
www.cynthiaeden.com

ABOUT THE AUTHOR

Award-winning author Cynthia Eden writes dark tales of paranormal romance and romantic suspense. She is a *New York Times, USA Today, Digital Book World,* and *IndieReader* best-seller. Cynthia is also a three-time finalist for the RITA® award. Since she began writing full-time in 2005, Cynthia has written over fifty novels and novellas.

Cynthia is a southern girl who loves horror movies, chocolate, and happy endings. More information about Cynthia and her books may be found at: http://www.cynthiaeden.com or on her Facebook page at: http://facebook.com/cynthiaedenfanpage. Cynthia is also on Twitter at http://twitter.com/cynthiaeden.

HER WORKS

Free Reads

Purgatory Series
- The Wolf Within (Purgatory, Book 1)

Mine Series
- Mine To Take (Mine, Book 1)

Bound Series
- Bound By Blood (Bound Book 1)

Other Paranormal
- A Bit of Bite

Boxed Sets

Blood and Moonlight Series
- Blood and Moonlight (The Complete Series)

Dark Obsession Series
- Only For Me (Dark Obsession, Books 1 to 4)

Purgatory Series
- The Beasts Inside (Purgatory, Books 1 to 4)

Mine Series
- Mine Series Box Set Volume 1 (Mine, Books 1-3)
- Mine Series Box Set Volume 2 (Mine, Books 4-6)

Bound Series
- Forever Bound (Bound, Books 1 to 4)

Romantic Suspense

Killer Instinct
- The Gathering Dusk (Killer Instinct, Prequel)
- After The Dark (Killer Instinct, Book 1)
- Before The Dawn (Killer Instinct, Book 2) - Available 07/25/2017

LOST Series
- Broken (LOST, Book 1)
- Twisted (LOST, Book 2)
- Shattered (LOST, Book 3)
- Torn (LOST, Book 4)
- Taken (LOST, Book 5)
- Wrecked (LOST, Book 6) - Available 05/30/2017

Dark Obsession Series

- Watch Me (Dark Obsession, Book 1)
- Want Me (Dark Obsession, Book 2)
- Need Me (Dark Obsession, Book 3)
- Beware Of Me (Dark Obsession, Book 4)
- Only For Me (Dark Obsession, Books 1 to 4)

Mine Series
- Mine To Take (Mine, Book 1)
- Mine To Keep (Mine, Book 2)
- Mine To Hold (Mine, Book 3)
- Mine To Crave (Mine, Book 4)
- Mine To Have (Mine, Book 5)
- Mine To Protect (Mine, Book 6)
- Mine Series Box Set Volume 1 (Mine, Books 1-3)
- Mine Series Box Set Volume 2 (Mine, Books 4-6)

Montlake - For Me Series
- Die For Me (For Me, Book 1)
- Fear For Me (For Me, Book 2)
- Scream For Me (For Me, Book 3)

Harlequin Intrigue - The Battling McGuire Boys
- Confessions (Battling McGuire Boys…Book 1)
- Secrets (Battling McGuire Boys…Book 2)
- Suspicions (Battling McGuire Boys…Book 3)

- Reckonings (Battling McGuire Boys...Book 4)
- Deceptions (Battling McGuire Boys...Book 5)
- Allegiances (Battling McGuire Boys...Book 6)

Harlequin Intrigue - Shadow Agents Series
- Alpha One (Shadow Agents, Book 1)
- Guardian Ranger (Shadow Agents, Book 2)
- Sharpshooter (Shadow Agents, Book 3)
- Glitter And Gunfire (Shadow Agents, Book 4)
- Undercover Captor (Shadow Agents, Book 5)
- The Girl Next Door (Shadow Agents, Book 6)
- Evidence of Passion (Shadow Agents, Book 7)
- Way of the Shadows (Shadow Agents, Book 8)

Deadly Series
- Deadly Fear (Book One of the Deadly Series)
- Deadly Heat (Book Two of the Deadly Series)
- Deadly Lies (Book Three of the Deadly Series)

Contemporary Anthologies
- First Taste of Darkness
- Sinful Secrets

Other Romantic Suspense
- Until Death
- Femme Fatale
- Christmas With A Spy

Other Romantic Suspense
- Abduction
- Hunted - Available 06/20/2017

Paranormal Romance

Bad Things
- The Devil In Disguise (Bad Things, Book 1)
- On The Prowl (Bad Things, Book 2)
- Undead Or Alive (Bad Things, Book 3)
- Broken Angel (Bad Things, Book 4)
- Heart Of Stone (Bad Things, Book 5)
- Tempted By Fate (Bad Things, Book 6) - Available 04/25/2017

Blood and Moonlight Series
- Bite The Dust (Blood and Moonlight, Book 1)
- Better Off Undead (Blood and Moonlight, Book 2)
- Bitter Blood (Blood and Moonlight, Book 3)

- Blood and Moonlight (The Complete Series)

Purgatory Series
- The Wolf Within (Purgatory, Book 1)
- Marked By The Vampire (Purgatory, Book 2)
- Charming The Beast (Purgatory, Book 3)
- Deal with the Devil (Purgatory, Book 4)
- The Beasts Inside (Purgatory, Books 1 to 4)

Bound Series
- Bound By Blood (Bound Book 1)
- Bound In Darkness (Bound Book 2)
- Bound In Sin (Bound Book 3)
- Bound By The Night (Bound Book 4)
- Forever Bound (Bound, Books 1 to 4)
- Bound in Death (Bound Book 5)

Night Watch Series
- Eternal Hunter (Night Watch Book 1)
- I'll Be Slaying You (Night Watch Book 2)
- Eternal Flame (Night Watch Book 3)

Phoenix Fire Series
- Burn For Me (Phoenix Fire, Book 1)
- Once Bitten, Twice Burned (Phoenix Fire, Book 2)
- Playing With Fire (Phoenix Fire, Book 3)

The Fallen Series

- Angel of Darkness (The Fallen Book 1)
- Angel Betrayed (The Fallen Book 2)
- Angel In Chains (The Fallen Book 3)
- Avenging Angel (The Fallen Book 4)
  Midnight Trilogy
- Hotter After Midnight (Book One in the Midnight Trilogy)
- Midnight Sins (Book Two in the Midnight Trilogy)
- Midnight's Master (Book Three in the Midnight Trilogy)

Paranormal Anthologies
- A Vampire's Christmas Carol

Loved By Gods Series
- Bleed For Me

ImaJinn
- The Vampire's Kiss
- The Wizard's Spell

Other Paranormal
- Immortal Danger
- Never Cry Wolf
- A Bit of Bite

Young Adult Paranormal

Other Young Adult Paranormal

- The Better To Bite (A Young Adult Paranormal Romance)

Anthologies

Contemporary Anthologies
- "All I Want for Christmas" in The Naughty List

Paranormal Anthologies
- "New Year's Bites" in A Red Hot New Year
- "Wicked Ways" in When He Was Bad
- "Spellbound" in Everlasting Bad Boys
- "In the Dark" in Belong to the Night
- Howl For It

Holidays

Contemporary Anthologies
- "All I Want for Christmas" in The Naughty List

Paranormal Anthologies
- A Vampire's Christmas Carol

Other Romantic Suspense
- Christmas With A Spy

78864927R00212

Made in the USA
Columbia, SC
14 October 2017